Twilight of the Gods

a Novel

Andrea
I hope you like my novel.

by Robert C. Covel

The one and the Many!
Robert C. Covel
29 November 2018
Music, Myth, and Magic!

Vabella Publishing
P.O. Box 1052
Carrollton, Georgia 30112
www.vabella.com

©Copyright 2018 Robert C. Covel

All rights reserved. No part of the book may be reproduced or utilized in any form or by any means without permission in writing from the author. All requests should be addressed to the publisher.

13-digit ISBN 978-1-942766-54-4

Library of Congress Control Number 2018909294

10 9 8 7 6 5 4 3 2 1

*To my wife Deloris Covel
the Many and the One*

Chapter One

As the limo sailed down darkened streets, Kris stole a glance at his companions. Sophia sat back, relaxed, champagne glass balanced in her hand. On her left wrist she wore a hammered silver bracelet with an image of an owl engraved. The slit in her skirt revealed her shapely white leg just above the knee. Barney sipped from his glass, poured more of the sparkling liquid, straightened his purple bowtie, and took another drink.

Kris slumped deep into the leather seat, fingering the burled wood of the bar nestled between the seats. He breathed in the luxurious bouquet of the leather mixed with Sophia's perfume and closed his eyes. Intoxicated with the fragrance, as well as the chilled champagne, he savored the deliciously decadent feeling. He was uncertain, he admitted to himself now, and a bit afraid of what awaited. Without thinking, he took a swallow of champagne, feeling the bubbles in his mouth as they tickled his face. He pressed his hand to his nose and resisted the impulse to sneeze. The alcohol took effect and he found himself relaxing.

The car drifted to a stop. He twisted his head left and right. His eyes widened. Where were they? It was hard to see through the tinted privacy windows. The door opened, and in the lamp light he could make out the driver, dressed in formal livery.

Kris stared. *Shades of Fitzgerald! Is this the Gatsby mansion? Did I have too much champagne? Unbelievable. I don't know why I'm surprised--everything else this evening is unbelievable. Maybe I really am having a psychotic episode. Like John Nash in that movie.*

Sophia held out her hand to him. "Would you escort me, Kris? I can't wait for you to meet our friends. We're going to have a great time." She turned to the well-dressed young man beside her, "Aren't we, Barney?"

Barney winked and smiled, a glint in his eyes like the bubbles in the champagne flutes.

They ascended the broad marble steps and approached the entrance as elegantly carved white doors opened. Two servants dressed in white jackets stood just inside.

The white-gloved attendant nearest them stepped forward and stood erect. "Welcome. Good to see you, Miss Sophia. Mr. Barney." Seeing Kris, he noted, "Your new friend?"

"Yes, this is Kris Singer."

"Indeed, a pleasure to meet you." He turned to Sophia. "We will announce him."

As they entered, one of the servants at the top of the stairs addressed the crowd,

"Miss Sophia and Mr. Barney. And their friend Mr. Kris Singer."

Kris surveyed the large ballroom floor. Several hundred guests appraised them as they entered. Everyone in the crowd was elegantly and expensively attired. A scene straight out of Hollywood.

Sophia acknowledged people as they descended the steps. "Lovely evening isn't it?" She quipped to the adoring crowd before turning to Kris. "Come, let's get some champagne before you meet the host."

As if by magic, a formally dressed waiter appeared, offering them champagne. Sophia tossed one-line compliments like flower petals as she passed by. "Nice tie. Love that dress! Great to see you!"

Then, taking Kris by the arm she tugged at his arm, guiding him away. "Psst... He's over there by the grand piano."

The crowd parted before them as if on an inaudible command.

A few feet away, they halted in front of a distinguished couple. *Beautiful people, Hollywood celebrities*, Kris decided. Intimidating a little maybe. He felt out of his depth.

"Kris, allow me to introduce Peter and his lovely wife June." She leaned toward Kris, putting her hand on his forearm, "Meet Kris Singer."

Kris sucked in his breath, amazed. Before them towered the host, at least six feet four, his bronzed face revealed dazzling white teeth. Gold specks glittered in his brown eyes. His broad shoulders and Herculean build intimidated Kris. His wife, as stunning as Sophia, though more regal, hung on his arm. Blond hair, twisted in ringlets, tumbled over her white shoulders. She smiled slightly, extending a jeweled hand, as if expecting Kris to kiss it.

"Mr. Singer. We're pleased you could attend our little gathering. Sophia has told us a good bit about you."

"I'm happy to be here." He surveyed the priceless antiques, statues and oil paintings. "Your house is beautiful. Almost overwhelming."

Peter smiled modestly, "We like it. It's a good place to have friends over." He fingered a gold fountain pen as he spoke, rolling the gleaming tube between his thumb and index finger. As the pen flashed the light from the chandelier, Kris watched, mesmerized.

A young woman in a silver satin dress swished by, throwing a smile in their direction. Kris watched as their host's eyes followed her every movement. His wife frowned, lips compressed. She glared at her husband, her expression a sudden thunderstorm on a summer day.

Peter took notice, suddenly attentive. "Please take our new friend to meet some of the others."

Sophia took Kris by the arm and escorted him across the floor. As they made their way across the room, they stopped at small groups. Every time, she spoke his name and then pointed at each person in the group, mentioning names. Kris's head was spinning. He felt on display.

She seems to know everyone in the room. I sure hope there's not going to be a quiz. And I feel this way on two glasses of champagne?

As they reached the far side of the ballroom, they came to a long row of tables, decked with a starched damask white tablecloth, massive centerpieces of orchids spilled out of cut-glass crystal vases. Silver platters of food stretched into the distance. Large crystal bowls of caviar and mountains of shrimp had been carefully placed to tempt the guests. Sliced meats of every kind were displayed artfully on golden chargers. On each table waited savory stews and casseroles. On one table Kris spied a crystal bowl of ambrosia, the fruit and coconut blend, a favorite from his childhood. *Finally something I recognize in this feast.* Platters of exotic fruit, including dragon fruit, slices of papaya and mango, and other tropical delicacies were chilled and waiting. Some were dishes that Kris could not identify, but they teased his nostrils, enticed his taste buds, seduced his senses. In short, he thought an Epicurean orgy. Who ate like this?

"I hope you're hungry," Sophia said, handing him a porcelain plate and a gold fork and knife.

"Here, allow me to serve you," she offered politely, "Have some of this and, oh yes, a little of that too. And you simply must try this," she tempted. His plate filled as Sophia added morsels from the trays and bowls.

When Sophia had finished, his plate was piled with enough food to feed a family of six.

Sophia chose a table secluded near a towering palm, and the three of them set their plates down. More champagne appeared.

Kris tasted each bite of food, savoring the unusual fare. *After this evening, the most elegant food I have ever tasted will taste like unsalted grits, like thin gruel. Where do they find food like this? And really, who ARE these people?*

Sophia leaned over and whispered in his ear. "Kris. Peter has all of this imported by contacts all over the world. As you can see he prides himself on serving elegant cuisine."

"I'll say." Kris commented, "I have never seen most of this food. This reminds me of something out of Cinderella. Or maybe the feast in the Odyssey."

Sophia smiled softly. Beguiled and a little unsettled, he realized that he could fall into those grey eyes of hers.

The delicate mixture of flavors overwhelmed his palate, the blend of sweet and savory, of tart and tangy, left Kris satiated as he swallowed each bite. Music swirled like a cloud of harmonies from the harps, flutes, delicate percussion instruments, and stringed instruments. The compositions drifted across the room like incense. He could almost smell the fragrance of the notes.

Sophia touched his arm. "Listen, we'd better go now. I know Peter wants to talk to you, and it's important. He'll be waiting for us."

Kris was more than a little spooked, he realized. *Now is when it gets scary. The fairy tale becomes Stephen King. Cinderella becomes The Shining.*

Barney joined them as they strolled down a long hall lined with murals of pastoral scenes. Kris was a little distracted by the elegant beauty of the woven artistry.

They stopped at the end of the hallway before massive mahogany doors, carved with images from Greek pastoral scenes. Two imposing guards held the door for them, bowing slightly as they passed through. The doors as the slammed shut behind them.

Chandeliers of untold value illuminated the walls covered with gold fabric. They crossed the marble floor and approached Peter and June who sat awaiting them. Seated on thrones, Peter loomed large, though not threatening. June sat erect, imperious, smiling at them as they approached.

"Well, Mr. Singer. We hope you have enjoyed our little soiree. Was the food to your liking?"

Kris mumbled, unable to speak.

Peter laughed. "Good. We do want our guests to have an experience to remember. What else is life for if not to be memorable? Don't you agree?"

"Yes. I do. And this has been a night I'll never forget." He smiled, his lips compressed.

"I hoped that it would be. We wanted you to come here so we could chat. When Sophia told us about you, we knew that we needed to meet you. To talk."

Kris's head began to spin.

"Please, sit." Chairs appeared behind them.

"What do you want to talk about?" Kris asked, not knowing if he wanted to hear the answer. He sat forward on the edge of his chair.

"Well, Mr. Singer. It is a little complicated. First of all, we are not who you think we are."

Kris felt the hair raise on the back of his neck. *Oh my god. They're spies. Or the mafia, or some weird cult. Now what?*

Sensing his anxiety, his host assured him, "It's ok. You have nothing to fear." He hesitated, giving Kris time to relax. "As a matter of fact, *you* are not who you appear to be. That's why we needed to meet."

Kris glanced at Sophia. She smiled, reassuring. Peter's eyes were serious.

"I beg your pardon." Kris paused, not sure how to respond.

"I don't understand. What do you mean I'm not who I appear to be? Are you saying that I don't even know who I am, let alone who you are?"

Kris cut his eyes over at Sophia. She touched his arm, but he pulled away.

"Let me try to explain. Sophia says you read a lot of mythology, books about the gods and their interactions with humans. Like you see in works such as *The Iliad* and *The Odyssey*."

"Yes, I do," Kris responded carefully, not knowing where the conversation was headed.

"And you have always assumed that those stories were made up. Fiction. Just myths."

"That's true." Kris admitted.

Peter tilted his head, watching the expression on the young man's face. "Let me ask you something. What if those stories aren't fiction? What if they are indeed based on fact?"

Kris stammered, "Well, I know that there are people who believe that the Iliad is based on a real event, a real war. And of course, they have found what they think are the remains of Troy."

"Yes. But what about the gods?"

"That's the myth part--the made-up part," Kris concluded.

"Well, wait, Think about this for a minute. What if it's not made up?"

"You're implying that it's real? How can that be?" Kris frowned.

Peter continued, "Think about it, what if those stories were true? The gods actually existed. And what if they interacted with the people?" They all stared at Kris, heads tilted and eyebrows raised.

"Uh. I don't, I mean." He searched for words, stunned by the questions.

The thought flashed through his brain. *It couldn't possibly be true. But what if it could be? What the hell are they talking about? Am I having some kind of a schizophrenic break?*

Peter watched him. "Ok, Kris. Let me just explain. I know it's hard to believe. As I said at the beginning, we are not as we appear to be. Have you ever seen those 'magic eye' pictures?"

"Yes, of course," Kris admitted.

"Our reality, your reality, is like those books."

"Or like The Matrix?"

"You mean from the movie? Yes, I have seen that," Peter said after thinking a moment.

Kris found himself getting defensive. "Are you trying to tell me that I can't see the world as it really is?"

Peter's brow wrinkled. He admitted, gently, "Partially. Most people are exactly as you think they are in ordinary reality. But have you ever felt that some people were somehow different? Some people, like us, really are unique."

"So there are others?" Kris asked in disbelief.

"Yes. Exactly."

"How do I know you're telling the truth?" Kris hesitated. The last thing he wanted was to be rude to his generous host. "Please excuse me, but this sounds like a huge practical joke."

Peter leaned forward. "That response is entirely rational. You want proof."

"Yes, I guess I do. But how can you prove what you are saying is true?"

"You just have to trust me. Us," Peter said earnestly.

Kris's throat tightened, his face flushed warm. His felt his heart fluttering. What were they about to tell him?

"You can trust us, Kris." She reassured him. "We would never hurt you."

Kris felt a wave of panic. Sophia's eyebrows raised.

"I'm sorry, Sophia. I can't do this. I just can't."

She touched his forearm. "What's wrong?"

"I have learned that when someone says 'Trust me' they probably can't be trusted. This just seems too out there, too unbelievable. I think I just want to go, if you don't mind."

Peter observed Kris quietly, his lips tightened as Kris glanced in his direction.

"I know this is a great deal to accept initially, Kris. Perhaps we can meet again later when you have had time to adjust."

Sophia arose. "I'll have the car brought around. Do you want me to ride home with you?"

Kris shook his head. "I'd rather be alone, if you don't mind."

As everyone stood, Kris said, "Thank you for inviting me this evening. This really has been an unbelievable party. I hope you don't think I'm being rude."

"Not at all," June said. She smiled and touched his shoulder. "We hope to see you again soon."

Sophia walked Kris back to where the limousine awaited.

The driver opened the door, and Kris slid across the seat. Sophia leaned over and peered at Kris.

"I'll call you in a day or two. Think over what we said tonight. It really is important, probably more than you know. And we would not hurt you."

"Ok, call me if you want. But I'm not promising anything." The limousine pulled away, and Kris glanced back at Sophia as she stood before the monumental villa like Cinderella awaiting her coach.

Chapter Two

Kris opened a beer and sat in his study. His mind whirled as he thought of the evening, the images a cyclone of luxurious food, spectacular architecture and designs, and unimaginable people. He felt like Alice in Wonderland, or Dorothy as she first encountered the Land of Oz.

He took a swallow and closed his eyes. He finished the beer as he remembered the events, especially the conversation at the end. Sophia still enchanted him, her beauty and her elegance like no other woman he had ever met. And the others, Peter and June, like royalty out of a story book. Even before they started talking about fairy tales and mythology!

Kris went to the kitchen and tossed the beer bottle. He put a couple of ice cubes in a glass and poured a couple of fingers of scotch and swirled the amber liquid, the ice clinking against the glass. He returned to his chair and savored the taste.

"Nothing like a little Celtic amber to get in touch with reality." He smiled and swirled the liquid, holding the glass to the light to the scotch and the ice dancing. As he took a sip, he thought of his mother. She loved to dance, and he thought of her swirling skirts as she danced sometimes in the barn, unaware that he was watching. She sang to the cows as they chewed the hay.

"Here's to you, Mom. I wish I could talk to you right now. You knew about how to approach weird circumstances, unusual people. And of course you were a little unique yourself. What would you tell me about all of this?"

He took another swallow of the smoky smooth drink. His mother's smile, enigmatic as the Cheshire Cat, flashed before him.

"I remember you used to say 'Son, people are all unique, some of them more different than you can know. You just have to accept them. And if you listen to them, if you are willing to take a chance sometimes, you may find that the world is complex. You may remember this one day when it will make sense to you'."

Kris laughed out loud. He could hear his mother's lilting laughter, as light as the tinkle of the ice in the glass.

Mom, you were amazing. Even if I didn't always understand you or appreciate you. He took another sip and sat back in the chair, his eyes closed and his mind quiet. He did not hear the ice clink in the glass as it melted. His dreams were filled with his mother dancing, half Cinderella and half wild princess in colorful skirts dancing to flute music.

Sophia called the next afternoon.

"Kris, how are you?"

He could hear the concern in her voice, the question more than just a casual comment.

"Hi, Sophia. I'm ok, I guess. I'm sorry if I was rude last night."

"No. It's fine. Peter and June expected you to be skeptical at least. We know that it sounds crazy."

"It does. I appreciated their hospitality. And of course the party really was like something out of a fairy tale."

"I know that Peter and June will be happy that you enjoyed the party. They do know how to put on an epic event."

Kris sat quietly. He felt Sophia's expectant silence on the other end.

"Have you thought about what they said?" Her tone was uncertain, concerned. Her question hung between them as he considered his response.

After a moment, he responded. "Well, I have. Actually, I have thought of nothing else since last night."

"And?"

"And—I'm not sure. It still sounds crazy. Like some drug-induced hallucination."

"That is not a surprising reaction at first. Are you willing to meet again, to hear more?"

"I may be. I was thinking of my mother last night and some of the things she told me about unique people and about taking risks. I think she would want me to take a chance. At least just to listen."

"I'm glad you listened to your mother. Would you like to meet with Peter and June again, maybe for lunch tomorrow?"

"I can do that. I'll try not to act like a jerk this time!"

"They do not feel that way, Kris. They really liked you. They felt a little bad that you were overwhelmed."

Kris laughed. "Maybe we can all just start over then."

"Good. I'll pick you up tomorrow about noon if that works for you."

"Great. See you then."

As he hung up, Kris stared at the ceiling.

"Well, Mom. I hope you are happy. Please make this not be a bad decision."

Chapter Three

When Kris was in high school, he helped his mother with the chores around the farm. Before he left for school in the morning, he followed his mother from the house to the barn to help with the morning milking. On fall mornings, he enjoyed the brisk cool air as the sun was rising, the grass sparkling as the first light touched it. His mother walked ahead, her long skirt touching the tops of the rubber boots she wore to the barn. Her dark hair, plaited in a long pig tail, swayed across the faded red flannel shirt as she walked. Kris hurried behind her purposeful stride as they approached the barn, the smell of hay, cow manure, and the maternal bovine smell of the cows swirling around them from the opening door.

As they entered the barn, the cows in their stanchions regarded them with large placid eyes. Steam swirled from their pink noses, their jaws chewing. Kris scratched the first one on her white forehead.

His mother pointed to the cow at the far end. "You go ahead and get started on Lakshmi down there, and I'll begin with Radha. We'll meet in the middle."

"Ok, Mom." He walked down the line of faces, patting each one until he reached the last cow. He scratched her nose and then patted her on the side as he moved to the rear, bucket in one hand and stool in the other. He sat beside the cow and placed the bucket under her udders. As he touched her she moved slightly.

"I know, Lakshmi. Cold fingers. Sorry, girl." He blew on his hands to warm them and then began the milking. Holding two teats, he pulled down, squeezing, and the streams of white milk hit the bottom of the bucket, making alternating splashes on the stainless steel.

As Kris milked the cow, he heard his low voice singing in a language that he did not know, but which he assumed to be Hindi. Her eyes closed and a slight smile on her lips, she leaned against the cow, her hands moving in rhythm to the song. She always sang as she milked, and she sometimes even danced from one cow to the next.

Kris leaned his cheek on the cow's warm side as he settled into the rhythm of alternating tugs. The bucket filled, and the cow stood patiently as he finished.

As Kris moved to the second cow, Sita, he saw that his mother had already started her second, Parvati. She sang a new song, but she worked efficiently, filling her bucket, her strong hands urging the warm milk from the udders.

They finished all six cows, Kris milking two while his mother did the other four.

As his mother finished the last, she stood with her hands on her lower back and leaned her shoulders back, her eyes closed.

"This gets to my back sometimes on these cold mornings. At least we're done for this morning. You best get in and get ready for school. I ought to get started processing this milk. I need to make butter today." She smiled in his direction.

"Ok, Mom. I have a math test this morning, so I can't be late."

He trudged up to the house, kicked off his boots at the door, and dressed for school.

The bus pulled into the drive shortly after Kris walked out. He jumped in and went to the back. Mike, who lived the next farm over, gave him a high five as he walked down the aisle.

"Get the cows milked?"

"Yep. Just like every morning. Now to face equations."

When they pulled up at the small school, Kris trudged to his locker and removed his math book and notebook. As he closed the locker door, a girl in a red gingham dress, her dark hair in a pony tail, opened the locker door next to his.

"Hi, Jill. Ready for the test?"

She turned to him and grimaced. "Don't know. I hate equations. Numbers are bad enough, but putting letters as variables is just wrong."

"I agree. Whoever invented algebra shoulda been shot."

"See you after homeroom." She hurried down the hall, and Kris watched her skirt swaying as she turned the corner.

Kris glanced at his math book during the pledge and the morning announcements, glancing at Mr. Kisko, his homeroom teacher, who had a strict rule about paying attention to those important homeroom activities. The bell rang, and Kris hurried through the door into the throng of adolescents in the noisy, crowded hall.

As Kris entered his math class, Johnny McCaskill stood in his way, his hands shoved in the pockets of his orange and black letter jacket.

"Saw you talking to Jill this morning, cow boy. You think about her while you're milking those heifers?" He extended his big hands, making alternating squeezing gestures. He grinned.

"Shove it," Kris muttered and pushed by to his seat at the back of the room. He knew that if he made an issue of the comment, he would be in trouble at school and at home. He opened his math book and glanced at it, hoping to refocus before Mr. Brown handed out the test. Kris stared at the test and sighed, shaking his head.

The rest of the day was easier. English class, as always, brightened Kris's day. Mrs. Staley talked about Shakespearean sonnets and their rhythms and rhyme schemes, her energetic explanations giving Kris a moment of pleasure as he took notes. American History class interested him, despite the endless litany of names and dates. Kris enjoyed thinking about the personalities of the founding fathers and the other people whose lives filled the events in the text.

Lunchtime gave Kris a welcome respite from the classes. The lunchroom ladies filled the plastic trays with the usual array of overcooked vegetables, an entrée that most just called "mystery meat," and a scoop of fruit cocktail. Kris grabbed a carton of milk and headed to a table where Mike and two others were already eating.

Mike glanced up, chewing on his roll in a way that reminded Kris of the cows.

"Well, how was the math test?"

"I passed. But some of the stuff wasn't even familiar. How can that happen?"

A blond boy with a few red blotches on his cheeks mumbled as he chewed, "It's like they make this stuff up just for the test."

"I know, John. But I got through it. Then I had another run in with that jerk McCaskill."

"He thinks he's so hot. Football captain, Mr. Quarterback. Go, Bears!"

Mike shook his head. "He's going to Pitt on a scholarship though."

Kris shrugged. "That doesn't make him a decent human being. I'd like to hit him, but I know what'd happen. He'd pulverize me, I'd get suspended. Then I'd have to explain my black eye to my mother."

They gobbled the rest of lunch and then ran to afternoon classes. Then Kris went home to do afternoon chores, cleaning the stalls, feeding the cows, and getting ready for the morning milking. When he got back to the house, his mother was cooking dinner.

"Chores done?" She stirred the steaming pan of vegetables.

"Yes, Ma'am. All done."

"Good. Go wash your hands, while I put dinner on the table."

They sat at the small wooden table in the kitchen, and his mother served the vegetables, the pinto beans, and the homemade bread. She filled their glasses with milk from the gallon jar, shaking it to mix the yellow cream that floated on the surface.

Kris drank the milk, thinking how unusual it tasted, so different from the milk that he had at lunch.

"How was your test?"

"Not bad. I passed, but I couldn't say beyond that." He glanced at his mother, her head over her plate as she chewed. He could see a little gray in her hair, especially at the part.

"That's good. You need to get good grades. College is coming up, and you want to be ready."

Kris's face was serious. "Mom, how are you going to manage this place without me?"

"You know that Joe and Mary are going to step up and do more. I'll manage."

"You always say that," Kris said

"Well, I will manage. Don't worry, son."

He dropped the subject and finished his meal. After helping with dishes, Kris sat down to the table to begin his homework. A page of math questions, a chapter of history with questions, and Act II of Shakespeare's *Macbeth* to read. He would read before he went to sleep. Reading always gave him an outlet, an escape from ordinary reality.

Chapter Four

Kris was still thinking about his past and his mother the next afternoon as walked into The Clock of Fives, an upscale downtown bar that he had occasionally passed but never entered. He walked through the double doors with their cut glass windows and glanced around. The booths along the walls were luxurious, with dark green leather upholstery on the seats and starched white tablecloths on the tables. The tables and chairs in the middle of the room matched. Large plants stood in gleaming planters around the room. Each table held a vase with fresh cut flowers, the kind of place he always thought of as a fern bar, where mid-level executives gathered in the afternoon to plan their financial coups.

"I'm sure they have an extensive martini menu and all top-shelf liquor," Kris muttered.

He noticed Sophia beckoning him from the door of one of the back rooms. He followed her and saw Peter, June, and Barney. Both men wore navy blazers and dress shirts with the collars open. Peter and Barney rose and extended their hands, as June gave a small regal nod.

Peter gestured to a chair. "Please sit. We're so glad you agreed to meet with us again."

"I'm glad you asked me. I feel a little bad about the way I left the party. I was a little overwhelmed."

"Peter wafted his hand and shook his head. "Not a problem. We knew it was a lot to take in all at once. We probably should have taken it a little slower at the beginning."

Kris agreed. "I hope my manners will be better today."

June touched his hand, a reassuring smile on her face.

The waiter appeared.

"Kris, do you like martinis?" Peter asked.

"I do, on occasion."

"Good. Please allow me to order. Dominique, we want the Five O'Clock Special. Doubles, with a twist."

"Very good, monsieur Peter. I will bring them right out."

"Kris, I believe these may be the best martinis in the world."

"I trust your judgment and taste, Peter."

"Kris, speaking of trust, do you mind if we continue our conversation from the other evening?"

Kris scanned their faces. Sophia had a serious expression, but June and Barney smiled expectantly.

"I think I'm ready to hear the rest of what you were saying before I freaked out the other night."

"Good." Peter paused. He reached into his shirt pocket and removed his gold fountain pen. He twirled it as he talked. Kris watched the light gleam on the gold. It was almost hypnotic.

The waiter appeared with a tray of martinis. The glasses were the largest that Kris had ever seen, like finger bowls with twist of lemon on the side.

Peter placed his pen on the table and lifted his glass. "This moment deserves a toast. To long life and fulfillment." He toasted.

Kris took a sip. The chilled liquid had an unexpected taste, not just raw liquor, but more subtle flavors and fragrances, perhaps a citrus bouquet, like oranges or tangerines. He closed his eyes as he swallowed, not just a drink but spirits.

"Well, Kris, do you approve?" Sophia's expression was amused.

Kris answered. "Definitely. This redefines the term 'martini'."

Peter took another sip and placed his glass in front of him and picked up the fountain pen.

"Kris, I want to continue where we left off. As I recall, I had just told you that some people are rare. I was about to give you some proof."

"And then I went off the deep end."

They all smiled.

"We understood. If you trust us, I wanted to give you that proof today. *Do you trust us?*"

Kris responded, "I guess so. I was thinking about my mother last night. She was an adventurous sort, a free spirit whom I never really understood. But I think she would say, 'Go for it, Kris.'"

"Kris. Your mother was exactly right," Sophia said. "People who never take chances, who never go for it, never live. They just exist in a half dream until they die. And that's not a life."

17

"You're right. I'm ready for the next step." Kris could feel his heart and he exhaled deeply. He took a sip of his drink, the citrusy taste settling him.

Peter placed the pen back on the table. Kris watched his hand. Kris felt like a gunfighter waiting to draw.

Peter reached inside the breast pocket of his blazer jacket and produced a small bottle with a silver stopper in it. He held it up to the light, and Kris caught the refracted light in a rainbow pattern on the wall. The others glanced at the vial as well. The tableau before him reminded Kris of a ritual in a Renaissance painting.

Peter extended the container. Kris reached for it, noticing his hand trembling. He breathed before he took it, settling his nerves.

"This will give you a temporary ability to see what I'm talking about."

This is crazy. Right out of Alice in Wonderland. A bottle that says Drink me? Carlos Castaneda. The red pill from The Matrix. Hallucinogenic drugs. Peyote. LSD.

Peter assured him. "The effects only last fifteen minutes. It's perfectly safe and has no side effects."

"It is safe, Kris." Sophia assured, staring deep into his eyes.

"Ok. But if anything happens to me, get in touch with my daughter, please."

"All right. But nothing is going to happen, I give you my word. Remember what your mother said."

Kris grasped the bottle and lifted the stopper. He sniffed. The fragrance was exotic, like spices from Scheherazade's Thousand and One Nights.

Kris paused, examining at the bottle. "As Morpheus says, down the rabbit hole."

"Long life," said Peter.

Kris tilted his head back, put the bottle to his lips, hesitated an instant, then drank. Somehow, the taste was like the martini, a fruit flavor like nothing he had ever tasted. For a moment he felt like Eve in the Garden.

At first, nothing happened. Like heat waves across the desert, the articles in the room blurred before his eyes. Thoughts flew through his brain. *Am I dying? Passing out? Going on a bad trip? This was such a bad idea.*

Then the room re-appeared. But it was not the same room. The décor was brighter, more elaborate. Majestic beyond words. He stared straight at Sophia. But she was not Sophia.

An imposing woman in a blinding white toga stood before him, gray eyes like lightning. She flashed her eyes at him. Kris took a step backward, witnessing the full effect of her dangerous beauty. On her left arm, where there had been a bracelet, was a magnificent shield. Kris knew instantly who she was. Who she had to be.

"Oh my god. You're . . .."

"Yes, I am."

Then reality struck him. "Athena! But--"

Kris then glanced at Barney, now dressed in a purple toga, grapes adorning the neck and sleeves. A crown of grape leaves circled his brow. Instead of a martini glass, he held aloft a chalice of red wine and grinned.

"Bacchus?"

Barney continued to sip from the golden chalice he held lightly, tipping head back to drink.

Peter and June, both clad in togas, reclined on royal thrones, stunning in their regal authority. Peter's physical presence, at once relaxed and menacing, stunned Kris. On Peter's leonine head rested a laurel crown. In his right hand instead of a fountain pen, he clutched a lightning bolt. Kris turned to stare at June, unabashed, enthralled by the splendid sight before him. His gaze swept over her, from her dainty feet, clad in golden sandals, to her gold tiara studded with diamonds which sparkled like stars in a midnight sky.

"So, you are….??" Kris stammered.

"Jupiter and Juno, or, if you please, Zeus and Hera."

Kris knew his mouth hung open, but he was too stunned to close it.

"Our names, or actually our aliases if you will, reflect who we are. Peter for Jupiter, and June for Juno."

Kris sized up Sophia/Athena before finally saying. "Of course. Sophia, the Greek word for wisdom!" He scanned their faces in disbelief. "But I don't understand. How can this be?"

Sophia assured him, "We'll explain all of it later. I think you have had enough for one day. The effects of your drink should be starting to fade."

The room returned to its drab reality. And before Kris stood the mortal forms of Peter, June, Sophia, and Barney.

Sophia touched his forearm gently. "We needed to reveal all of this to you. Now that you have seen it, you need to let it sink in. Then we'll explain the details to you. It is a great deal to accept all at once."

"When?" Kris asked, adding, "I mean, when are you going to explain everything?"

"We'll see you in a couple of days. At that time, we can tell you everything in full. And if you are still interested, we'll take the next step."

Kris made no effort to disguise his excitement. "I can't wait to hear the rest. I feel like the entire universe just changed. It has shifted ninety degrees, perpendicular to everything I've ever known."

Hesitating slightly, Sophia leaned in to Kris, whispering. "I would advise you to keep what has happened tonight to yourself. It would be a mistake to talk about this to anyone."

Kris laughed nervously, "Oh, don't worry. I won't. I'd be locked up and be wearing a straitjacket."

Sophia put her hand on his shoulder. "We should probably go, Kris. You'll be very sleepy in a few minutes."

The next morning, when the sun broke through his window blinds, Kris sat bolt upright, stunned and wide awake. Surprised to find himself in his own bed. He brushed his hand against his face, as if to check that he was really who he thought he was. He shook his head vigorously, shaking the cobwebs out of his mind.

Was that some kind of bizarre dream? None of that could have happened. The mansion, that incredible banquet. And those people? They were normal, and then the next moment they transfigured. Was any of that real? Or a hallucination?

He threw off the covers and staggered across to the dresser. He leaned close toward the mirror. He tilted his face left and right, stroking the stubble on his cheek. He flashed a weak smile at his reflection as if to reassure himself. Yes, he decided, the face staring back at him appeared to be normal. He flopped down on the bed, thinking, replaying the night. He fell backward onto his pillow and pulled the sheet up to his chin. In a matter of minutes, he was sound asleep.

He awoke again as the sun was setting. He opened one eye, unsure of his surroundings. Or even what time of day it was. The lengthening shadows on the far wall told him that he had slept most of the day. As he replayed the previous night's events in his mind's eye, he knew that, outrageous as it seemed, it was all real. It had actually happened.

Chapter Five

Starving, he tumbled out of bed and headed for the kitchen. After surveying the food in his fridge, he decided to make dinner. When he had finished, he laid his dinner plate on the table, taking stock of his efforts. A chip on the edge of his plate, rumpled table cloth, a napkin with a grease spot on it, a wilted plant on the window sill. He frowned. These things had never bothered him before. In truth, he had not even noticed before today.

The taste of the food from the party, plus the martini from the previous evening still on his mind, Kris eyed the fare before him. Vegetarian chili, stir-fried vegetables and cut fruit. The meal on his plate now was bland, nearly tasteless by contrast. It filled him and satisfied his hunger, but it did not satisfy his taste for delicious food. He realized that life would never be the same. He sighed pushing the thought back in his mind. After he finished eating, he called his daughter, Starr. He had not talked to her since the party.

She answered and got right down to the crux of the matter. "Well, Dad, tell me everything. How was the party? I've been waiting to hear from you!"

"It was great. Good food, nice music. A lot of interesting people."

"You had fun? How was your date? Did you enjoy the time with her?"

Kris admitted, "I did. We had a pleasant evening together."

"But no sparks?"

"No. Just a pleasant evening."

"How boring!" You need some excitement in your life."

Kris laughed to himself. Little did she know.

As Kris talked, he knew that Starr wanted more detail. He was not about to tell her the truth. The only alternative was to make it seem a little boring. She was unsatisfied, wanting the juicy details of his night on the town. She just could not know what really happened. And he still was not sure of what had actually occurred himself.

He went back to bed early and slept soundly, the phone awakening him at nine the next morning.

The voice at the other end of the line sounded familiar. Since the voice was real, Kris reasoned with himself that meant the person he'd met the night before was real.

He held the phone closer. "Peter," he said, a little incredulous. "I'm sorry. Would you repeat what you just said?"

"Yes. Would you be available for lunch today at 1:00?"

"Of course," Kris fumbled, trying to sound normal. "Where do you want to meet? Oh, and how should I dress?"

"Casual. Slacks and shirt. I'll have a car pick you up. I know it's a little soon after what you experienced yesterday, but it is important. We're eating at a little Italian restaurant not too far from you. My friend owns it."

"Great. I'll watch for the car. See you in a bit."

He glanced at his watch. Better hurry. He ate a bowl of cereal and two cups of strong coffee. He felt almost functional. Casual dress, huh? What did he have that was clean? And ironed? He plundered through his closet, digging for a pair of chinos and a pullover.

"Maybe that is casual and not just sloppy," he said as he regarded his reflection in the mirror.

Hedging his bets, he decided it would be smart to call Starr and tell her that he was having lunch with some people he'd met at the party. He called and left a message on her answering machine that he was going to lunch with some of the people he had met at the party. He felt unreasonably paranoid.

If something happens, I want her to know some of the details. In case the police need the information. If I'm this paranoid, why am I going? Curiosity trumps paranoia, I guess.

As planned, on the dot of one a Mercedes pulled in front of the house. Kris recognized the driver from the night of the party.

"Hello. Good afternoon," Kris said hesitating. All this was new to him. But he could get used to this special treatment. The driver smiled and doffed his cap as he opened the door. Kris entered.

The restaurant was on a side street. Kris had never seen that street before or the restaurant.

Kris entered the restaurant and stumbled, his eyes adjusting to the dim light. As they adjusted, he glanced around. The walls were covered with images of rural scenes, probably from Italy. The tables were draped with white table cloths, each with a wine bottle in the center. Kris smelled Italian seasonings with an undercurrent of garlic that made his mouth water. Kris spotted Peter, June, Sophia, and Barney in the far corner. Sophia waved at him.

He studied Peter and June as he walked toward them.

They don't seem godlike today. More tired. Almost haggard. I thought that that would not be possible. Gods and goddesses are always perfect, or at least that's the way they're shown.

Peter stood as Kris walked to the table. Peter shook his new friend's hand and indicated the empty chair next to him.

Cutting straight to the matter, Peter asked, "Are you ready to learn the rest of the truth, Kris?"

"I think so," Kris replied, a bit unsure suddenly of his decision.

"Good. We'll eat first. I took the liberty of ordering for you."

"Thank you."

The food arrived at that moment, interrupting the line of conversation. The rest of the truth will have to wait a moment, Kris thought.

Kris's plate of fettucine marinara steamed as he inhaled the fragrance. A smaller side dish contained baked zucchini seasoned with Italian seasoning. In the middle of the table, a loaf of fresh-baked Italian rested next to a bowl of seasoned olive oil. The others had the same meal, but Kris noticed that they ate sparingly. Peter cut a small slice of the bread. He broke off a small bite and dipped it in the oil then popped it in his mouth. Sophia ate a forkful of the pasta. She chewed slowly and sipped water.

Barney ignored the food and drank from his wine glass.

Though the food was not as stunningly delicious as that at the party, it still was tasty. Kris focused on the food while wondering why he was there. The others ate quietly.

Peter raised an eyebrow. "Would you care for a little brandy? I know it's a little early in the day. It's an excellent vintage."

"After last night's martini, I trust your taste. If you are having some, I will."

"I think a brandy would be in order for each of us. We can enjoy the moment before we talk."

Peter raised his glass. "To long life."

Twilight of the Gods

They all tasted the brandy.

The amber liquid was as warm as an Italian summer afternoon. Kris sipped it, savoring the taste of grapes with an afterglow of honey.

Sophia regarded Kris. "Does it meet with your expectations?" Kris realized that she had not spoken until then.

"It does. It is quite lovely, actually," he said, trying to sound knowledgeable.

She smiled.

"Now, if it is acceptable, let's begin our discussion. Kris could not imagine what they were about to discuss. But after the events of the party, he knew it would be unexpected.

Peter placed his empty brandy snifter on the table. "As you found out the other night, we are not as we appear."

Kris said, "I realize that now, but I just don't understand what I saw."

Peter smiled. "There are actually many of us. We pass as normal human beings who lead ordinary lives. We are from all over the world, and we represent every level of society."

"How many are there of you? Gods, I mean?"

Peter shrugged. "I'm not sure. We don't have a list, and we certainly don't do a census. But we can recognize one another."

"All of you are Greek and Roman gods?"

"Not just from those two groups. We have members that represent probably every religion you can think of, and probably religions you have never heard of."

Kris sat quietly. They seemed normal people now. So ordinary. Certainly not what he saw at the party. How could all of this be?

Peter said, "I can see from your face that you still don't really believe me."

Kris held his hands palms up. "I just feel like I am having some kind of psychotic episode. That you are not real, and I am just actually talking to myself. Even the party could have been a delusion. But then I think about what my mother would say." Kris scanned the faces. They were real.

"Yes, we are real. What you are experiencing, and what you experienced last night, is in fact reality."

Kris tilted his head. "Is there some way to prove any of this?"

"Ultimately? Perhaps not. But then again, how can you prove anything beyond a shadow of a doubt? After all, how do you know that you exist in the way you normally think you do?"

Kris shook his head. "Philosophers, and scientists too perhaps, have been trying for centuries to find a final proof for existence. It may not be possible to prove our own existence."

"Exactly. We are left with the inability to know whether or not we actually know anything." Peter paused. "There is a next step. If you are willing to take it."

Kris glanced at the door as though he were about to bolt from the room.

"Did you feel any ill effects from the other night?"

Kris shook his head.

Peter continued. "There is an intermediate version of the potion you took the other night. It lasts longer and allows you to settle in to the experience for a while. Then you can make up your own mind about the truth of all of this."

"What happens if I decide not to take the next step?" asked Kris, still uncertain. Was this rational? Or even sane?

"Nothing. If you decide not to continue, you simply go on with your life the way it was."

Kris wondered out loud. "What if I tell someone?"

"Do you really think that *anyone* will believe you if you did?"

Kris shook his head. "I guess not. I certainly wouldn't. Ok. Let's suppose I want to continue? Say I take this next step. How would that work?"

"You would take the next level of the potion. For a few days, you would be able to see the others who are around you. They, of course, would be aware that you know who they are."

"And then?" Kris wondered aloud.

"Then you either just go back to your own life, or you take the final potion and become one of us."

"Are there any side effects of the next-level uh—potion?"

"None at all."

Kris turned to Sophia. "Should I do it?"

She shrugged her shoulders. "Not everyone does. But I for one do think you should."

He exhaled and shrugged. "My mom would say 'Nothing ventured.' Ok. I think I will take this next step. But that doesn't mean that I will necessarily take the final step. I'll have to think a lot more about it."

Peter agreed, "Before you take the last permanent potion, you will learn a great deal more about this. Some of it you will figure out on your own. The rest of it we would tell you in the next meeting. So. Are you in?"

Kris suddenly felt the enormity of the decision. Here he was changing his whole life. Still, it sounded like the ultimate adventure. Like a superhero kind of decision.

"What the hell am I doing?" He realized that he had said that out loud. The faces around him were serious.

Kris spoke abruptly. "Ok. I'll do it."

Peter smiled and patted his shoulder. June tilted her head toward him, and Sophia planted a soft kiss on his cheek.

"Kris. I think you will just be blown away by it. Over the last few days as I have gotten to know you, I know you can handle this. Intellectually and emotionally, or I wouldn't advise it."

He gazed into Sophia's gray eyes. Gray-eyed Athena. He was beginning to understand why she affected him the way she did.

Peter handed him another silver-stoppered bottle. It was slightly larger than the last one. "You just drink. Like before. Now this time you will be able to control the experience. If it gets to be too much, or if it interferes with your life, you just blink twice, and you go back to seeing and experiencing life the old way."

"That's good to know. I have a feeling this is going to be overwhelming."

"It will be at first," Peter admitted.

Kris held the bottle, his hand trembling as he removed the stopper. He stared at the opening and sniffed.

"When you are in the state of heightened awareness, you will see beings from many religions and cultures. You may recognize some but not recognize others. Though they will all know who you are."

Kris asked, "How should I react to them?"

Peter answered, "That's up to you. Remember that other ordinary people cannot see their true selves either. They're only passing as normal. Just try not to overreact. You don't have to interact with them or even acknowledge them at all. They're used to that. Just go slowly and don't freak out. This is not a bad drug trip."

Kris breathed, slow and measured. "Here goes. As you said earlier, to long life."

He tilted the bottle to his lips as before, his head back slightly, the liquid flowing across his tongue.

He closed his eyes and focused as though he were beginning his meditation.

When he opened his eyes seconds later, before him sat Athena, Bacchus, Jupiter/Zeus, and Juno/Hera in all of their Olympian glory.

Despite being prepared, Kris gasped.

The four of them focused their attention on him.

Sophia asked, "Are you alright, Kris? you're little unsteady."

Kris shrugged. "Yes. Still a little blown away by this. But I can handle it. At least I can now."

Peter asked, "Are you ready to go home?"

"I think so." He blinked twice. To his relief, they returned to their ordinary forms.

Sophia, in her human form, raised her eyebrows. "It works, doesn't it?"

"Yes. At least when if it gets to be too much, I can just escape from the experience."

Sophia handed him a slip of paper. "If you need me, text me at this number. I'll get back to you quickly."

Kris glanced at the paper. "Ok. This is going to be the most amazing five days of my life."

Peter smiled knowingly. "That is an understatement. Your life will change forever in the next week."

Kris suddenly found himself at a loss for words. He bowed to the group instead. They responded with regal smiles.

Sophia arose. "I'll accompany you home."

"Thank you, Sophia," Kris said.

Even gods get tired sometimes, he thought as he took Sophia's arm. As the two of them made their way to the car, Kris glanced at the woman on his arm. Even more beautiful and more mysterious than when he first met her.

Chapter Six

As they rode back to his house, Sophia regarded him as he watched people on the sidewalk. The ordinary crowds of everyday people passed by, enjoying their evening activities. Then he blinked twice.

Among the ordinary people the most amazing figures walked down the streets. A man crossed the street wearing a toga with a purple stripe. A woman in a diaphanous yellow sari and a green veil stood on a corner. A huge brute of a man wore a Viking helmet and carried a massive gleaming sword. As Kris gazed enraptured, an Asian woman with a delicate figure, wearing little but flowers and leaves, floated by him and smiled demurely. A scintillating mist surrounded her. He blinked twice.

"Sophia, it's amazing."

"It is. Just try not to take in too much at once. It can be really stressful. Information overload."

Kris responded, "Ok."

"And you will probably need more sleep. Don't resist it."

He agreed. The Mercedes pulled up to the curb before his house.

As he emerged, Sophia leaned out. "I'll call you tomorrow. If you need me, use the text number."

Kris agreed, "I will."

Kris threw his jacket across the back of the sofa and headed to the bedroom. He collapsed across the bed, still dressed. In one minute he was snoring. The sun in his eyes woke him, and as he squinted, he thought about his dreams but then he realized the truth.

That was no dream. It really happened. My god. Or gods, I guess. Is this happening?? Am I just totally nuts, bonkers, psycho, high on drugs? Or did it happen. One way to find out.

Kris threw on a jacket and grabbed a cap. Too pretty a day to be inside. A fresh breeze greeted him and the birds sang in the waving trees. As he strolled to the park, he saw Mrs. Schultz playing with her grandson on the park bench. The two of them were feeding the squirrels. Normal day, normal activity. Then he blinked. Just then at the brownstone across the street, he saw a woman working in her garden, cutting flowers and placing them in a basket. He did a double-take. She was nearly naked, her alabaster skin draped with garlands of roses, her head crowned with ivy. She smiled at him, winked, and drifted toward the house. Her feet did not touch the ground.

Kris quickly blinked twice. She returned to her original form, an old woman in a shapeless housedress entering the house. She walked with a cane.

"Wow. Far out." Kris muttered.

He spent the rest of the day walking around the neighborhood, watching people. He had lunch at a diner. His waitress, a gum-chewing girl with tattoos and multiple piercings, transformed into an Asian woman wearing a garment made of iridescent material. Every move was like a choreographed dance, perhaps from Thailand (or more specifically Siam). Two blinks, and the gum-chewing waitress stood before him, eyebrow raised, waiting to take his order.

He climbed the steps to his house around 4:00, exhilarated but exhausted. He went to bed early, asleep as soon as his head hit the pillow. He had no dreams, at least none that he could remember the next day.

Sophia called the next morning just as he was finishing his coffee. "Did you sleep well?"

"I did. But after the strain of the day, of seeing all these new things, I was weary."

"Good. What you are experiencing is normal. I won't keep you. I think we are going to move up the schedule, if you don't mind. I talked to Peter and June last night, and they thought it would be a good idea. Is that ok with you?"

Kris asked, "I suppose. Does that mean that I need to commit to a permanent change?"

Sophia answered, "It would. They want to have dinner tomorrow instead of waiting several more days."

"That's soon." Kris felt his pulse, and he rubbed his wet palms on his jeans.

"Yes, it is." Sophia paused. "But it's really important."

The tone in her voice changed, became more intense. Her emphatic use of the word "really" made Kris nervous. His shoulders tightened.

"All right. I'll see you tomorrow night.'"

"Think carefully about the decision. It really is important."

"Is there a reason it's being moved up?" Kris asked. He clenched the phone.

"There is. You'll find out tomorrow. Enjoy your day. Observe everything around you."

The phone clicked.

Kris felt the beginnings of panic. Things were moving too fast. He was getting the bum's rush toward something unbelievable. And he only had twenty-four hours to decide.

Man, I need to talk to someone about it. Just about anybody I know would freak out about it. Except maybe Mike. He's done enough drugs that he doesn't find anything unusual. I think I'll call him in a little bit.

Kris had known Mike since high school when they played in a band together. Kris had gone off to college to be a teacher, while Mike dove into the rock star lifestyle. A couple of arrests for marijuana possession and a couple of bouts of homelessness followed. But Kris still kept up with Mike. Underneath the non-conventional lifestyle, Mike was still a good guy. Kris trusted him and knew Mike would not freak out when he told him about what had just happened in his life. He called Mike at noon.

"Hello," the drowsy voice was barely audible.

"Mike, it's Kris. You awake?"

"Uh, yeah, yeah," Mike replied yawning.

Kris apologized. "Sorry to call you this early in the day. I know you go to bed late."

"Nah. It's ok. What's going on?"

"I want to talk to you about something. Can we meet, maybe have a drink?" Kris suggested.

"Sure. How about we meet at five?"

"Yeah. See you then. Joe's Place?"

"Sure."

When Kris arrived at the bar, Mike had just ordered his second round. He summoned the barkeep with a wave of his empty mug, "Joe. Shot and a beer for our friend here."

"Thanks, Mike. How's the world treating you?" Kris asked, sliding into the booth where Mike sat.

"Better. I have a job and a place to stay. Life is good. How about you? You said you needed to see me. What's up? What do you want to talk about?"

"Well, as weird as it may seem, you are the one person I could think of I could talk to about this crazy stuff."

"Thanks, I think. I have experienced some weird things. And some of it has just been in my own head."

"Ok. I've met some new people, some really uncommon people. Like no one I've ever met. They have told me some unbelievable information. And it seems to be true."

Mike took a sip of his drink. He peered up at Kris through his long hair, expectant. "I've met some weird people in my life. Though I think some of them might have been just hallucinations!"

Kris laughed, took a gulp, and set his glass on the table. "Ok. Let me just say it straight. I have met some people who are not just people. They're gods." He watched Mike's face for his reaction.

Mike downed his second shot and squinted at Kris. "And by that you mean?"

"They really are gods. Roman deities. The real thing."

"And you're not on serious drugs? Tripping? Or having some kind of psychotic break?"

Kris shook his head. "No. I have seen them in their real form."

"Ok. How do you know it's real?" Mike said, buying into what Kris was saying.

"I took a potion that let me see them in that form. And I've seen other people who are gods passing as normal people." Kris downed his shot and took a sip of his beer.

"A potion? A drug? Some kind of hallucinogen? You know that sounds crazy, right? And you know I've done some crazy shit."

"Not that kind of drug. I know it sounds crazy. But I think that it's real."

Kris stopped. He held up his glass and pointed to Mike's. The bartender brought fresh drinks and then returned to cleaning the bar.

Mike sipped from the fresh drink and leaned forward. "What do they want from you? Why are they doing this to you? Is this some kind of cult?"

Kris shook his head slowly and shrugged. "I'm not actually sure why they're doing this. I'm meeting with them tomorrow."

"I hope it isn't a scam to get money. Or to get you to join a cult."

Kris responded, "I don't think it's anything like that," Kris assured his old friend, and maybe himself a little too, he realized.

"So what can I do? I have to say, it does sound like some crazy shit." Mike grinned.

"If they'll allow it, will you come with me tomorrow?"

"Sure. When? Where?" Mike agreed readily.

"I don't know yet. I'll let you know if I figure it out."

"This could just be the ultimate trip. They might be locking us both up in a rubber room before this is over."

"Could be." Kris sat back and shook his head. "I'll call you later when I figure it out. And when I clear it with them."

Mike grinned. "Let's hope this doesn't get weird."

"Too late. It's already that." Kris laughed.

Later when Kris asked, Sophia agreed to allow Mike to come, after she had cleared it with the others.

"You are sure your friend will accept what we tell you?" Sophia asked.

"He will. He is the most open-minded person I know."

"He's a musician like you, isn't he?"

"Yes. And a better guitarist than I will ever be. He's lived the musician's life as long as I've known him."

"That's good. His being a musician may be useful to us."

"When are we meeting?"

"The car will pick you up at 5. We'll have a drink and then perhaps dinner if you feel like it after the conversation."

Kris reminded her, "Mike will be with me."

The following day Mike arrived at the house at 4:30, dressed in dark slacks and an oxford dress shirt.

"Well dressed, sir," Kris complimented.

"Thanks. These are the clothes I wore when I was hunting for a job. These are actually the only decent clothes I own."

"Well, you pass muster. You want to go out and wait?"

Mike opened the door.

They stood on the front stoop and waited for the Mercedes to pick them up. After a short drive, Kris and Mike arrived at the Ritz Carlton. They walked through the lobby to the elevator. When they reached the floor, they knocked and Sophia opened the door. As they entered the room, Peter, June, and Barney stood to greet Mike. He shook hands with each. Mike glanced at Kris, eyebrows raised, a bemused expression around his mouth. Kris returned the expression. As they sat, Kris noticed that Peter and June still were exhausted.

Peter asked Mike, "What would you like to drink?"

Mike said, "Just a beer if you have it."

Peter opened a bottle, the amber glass beaded with condensation. He handed it to Mike with a chilled mug.

Mike examined the label on the bottle. "My favorite brand."

Peter smiled.

Sophia had already given Kris a glass with scotch and one ice cube.

Peter made eye contact with Mike. "Mike, what we are going to say may sound odd, but we assure you it's on the level. We are not trying to trick anyone."

Mike sipped from the frosted mug.

"I assume that Kris has explained to you what we have told him and what he has experienced."

Mike acknowledged, "He has. I trust him. If he says it's true, it is."

Peter answered, "Good. Now Kris, we must have a serious conversation here."

"I'm ready."

After a pause, Peter said slowly, "There is a reason that you are here. You were not chosen at random."

Kris raised his eyebrows, somewhat hesitant.

Peter examined Kris's face as he asked, "What do you know about your parents?"

"I know little about my real father. My mom never told me much. They never married. I think the relationship didn't last long."

"And your mother? You have told us a little about her and your impressions of her lifestyle."

"I know nothing about her childhood. She never mentioned her parents or her family. I always thought she might be an orphan."

"You grew up on a farm, didn't you?"

"We had a small dairy farm. My mother apparently inherited it, but I don't know from whom. She and my step father ran it."

Peter continued. "Ok. We are going to tell you about all of that. It will be shocking. Are you ready for the information?"

Kris compressed his lips. He felt an impulse to run for the door, but he glanced at Mike, who smiled and drank his beer. Kris said, "I suppose so," not sure at all that he was prepared for what he was about to hear.

He turned to Mike, "I'm glad you're here."

Peter tilted his head as he and the others watched Kris.

"Your father was someone unique. Extraordinary even. You are named after him. Like us, he had two identities."

"Ok. And?" Kris stopped, then he began again.

"So, you're saying he was a . . . god? Really?" Peter and the others waited motionless, staring at Kris. Mike sat, his mouth gaped open.

After a hesitation, Peter continued. "Yes. Your father was actually a Hindu god. Krishna."

Kris, mouth agape and eyes wide, exclaimed, "What?? Are you serious? How can that be?"

"The reason your mother had a dairy farm is that she was a Gopi, one of the milkmaids who followed Krishna."

Kris shook his head once. For an instant, he was speechless. "So wait, I'm the son of Krishna?"

Peter offered, turning to Kris, face serious. "Yes. We didn't think you were aware. But if you think about it, there's a reason you're a musician."

Kris answered slowly, "Ok. That makes sense, I guess. And, I've always wondered why my skin was darker than my mother's."

"Now, there is an important reason you need to know all of this now. The real reason you are here, the reason we are here."

"There's more?" Kris glanced at Mike.

Peter sighed. "Yes. As you may have noticed, June and I are not well."

Kris examined Peter's face, then peered at June. She sat quietly. "I have noticed the change. I thought you were just tired."

"Actually, it's far more serious than that. And not just for us."

Kris turned his attention to Sophia. "Are you sick too?"

"No. Not yet. But it's just a matter of time. For me, for Barney, for everyone like us."

"What is it? A virus?"

"I'm sorry to say, it's a little more complicated than that." She turned her face. "Peter, can you explain it?"

"I'll try." Peter offered turning his attention again to Kris, "I know you've studied myths and religions. You know about the Eastern concept of Chi, the energy that flows through the universe."

"You're right, I have read about that. It's like the Force in Star Wars."

"Yes. And it may be that George Lucas learned about that from Joseph Campbell."

"Makes sense. But what does that have to do with your being sick?"

"That Chi is our life force. And the flow comes from other people. The more people believe, the more the force flows."

"It's like Tinker Bell. People have to believe for you to live?" Kris suggested.

"Yes. The author of *Peter Pan*, J. M. Barrie, knew what he was writing about."

"I thought gods lived forever."

"Well, yes and no. Our force, our chi, can be passed on as our physical bodies die. As long as the energy is strong."

Kris exclaimed, "Ok. I understand! Now it makes sense. It's like Mr. Spock and his katra. He passes it onto McCoy."

"I believe that is correct. It may be that Mr. Roddenberry had the same idea in mind."

Mike stared, eyes and mouth open wide. Kris asked, "What do you think, Mike?"

"After this, I will never have to take drugs again!" Mike resisted the urge to laugh at the shocked expression on his friend's face. There was nothing funny about this.

They all sat quietly as Kris considered what Peter had just told him.

Finally, Kris asked, "What do you want me to do? I'm no one special." Then he remembered what they had just told him about his parents.

Sophia answered. "This is a real crisis. Not just for us. For the whole world, the whole human race."

"How is that?"

"As you know from mythology, there are gods for everything, for the trees, the flowers, everything. All of the nature deities, all of the gods who control it all."

"I know that all religions have that in common."

Sophia agreed "The energy flows both ways. We give our life force to the world, as it gives it back to us."

"Like the circle of life," Kris offered.

"Exactly. The problem is that, as people cease to believe, the energy stops flowing."

Kris asked, "You mean that people no longer believe in you?"

Sophia agreed, "Yes. And not just in us, but in any spiritual force or anything beyond the immediate physical world. The materialism of the modern world is actually destroying the energy that sustains it. That's why we see nature faltering. All of the stuff on global warming, the dying oceans, the pollution of the atmosphere, the extinction of species. It's all related to this."

"Our lack of belief is destroying the earth?" Kris asked, struggling to keep up with Peter's train of thought.

Peter continued. "Yes. Do know about the idea of Ragnarok in Norse mythology?"

"I've read about it. They talk about it in the Thor movies."

Peter agreed, "It's the idea that the gods will be destroyed and the universe will be destroyed. Supposedly a new cycle will then begin."

"Is that like the idea of the Big Bang?" Mike interrupted.

Peter turned to him. "Somehow scientists have discovered the reality of that idea."

Kris and Mike glanced at one another. Mike shrugged, overwhelmed.

Kris asked, "Doesn't Wagner include the idea in his Ring Cycle?"

"Yes. The German term that he uses is *Gotterdammerung*. The Twilight of the Gods."

"Unbelievable. All of that fits together."

"It all does. Carl Jung understood. As did Joseph Campbell. The Collective Unconscious does connect all living creatures."

Kris leaned back. His world was changing so fast that he felt light-headed and confused. Mike appeared stunned as he stared at Kris.

Finally, Kris exhaled and asked, "Now that I know all of this, what does it have to do with me? Or with June and you being sick?"

Peter paused. He coughed and put his hand to his face, covering his eyes. "I'm sorry. It is getting worse."

June touched Peter's shoulder. "Are you ok? Can I do anything for you?"

"I don't think so. I just need to finish telling this to Kris."

"What is it? What can I do?" Kris asked, feeling helpless.

As Peter slumped, Sophia continued. "We chose you for a reason. You are Krishna's son."

"You said that, but it's hard for me to believe. Besides, how does that help?"

"The only way Peter can get better, or June, or any of the rest of us, is to revive people's beliefs."

"You mean like a religious revival?"

"Not exactly. It's not like the revival that people have, speaking in tongues, dancing in the aisles. People, the human race, just need to have a sense of something beyond themselves, of a power that controls everything. Without that, the circuit's broken."

Kris glanced at Mike, his stunned disbelief evident as his eyes moved from Peter to Kris to Sophia.

Kris asked, "How do we do that?"

Sophia glanced at Peter and then picked up the conversation. "There is one way that might jump-start people, so to speak."

Twilight of the Gods

Kris asked, "And what is that?"

Sophia pronounced a single word, "Music."

Mike asked, "Music? You mean like songs, instrumental pieces?"

Sophia agreed, "Yes."

Kris sat back and sighed. "I don't see how that can help. That makes no sense. How can singing to people, entertaining them, get them in touch with some kind of spiritual power?"

Peter began to cough again, his face turning red. He gasped for breath between coughs.

Sophia bent over and examined Peter's face. "I think we need to stop for now. We need to get him home where we can treat him."

Sophia and June helped Peter to his feet. "Barney, call the driver. Tell him to hurry." Over her shoulder she asked, "Mike, Kris, can you help us get him to the car?"

They each took an arm and helped Peter to stand up and reach the sidewalk. The Mercedes pulled up almost immediately. The driver picked him up and put him in the back seat. June climbed in on the other side.

Sophia called to the driver as he closed June's door. "We'll be there right behind you," Sophia said.

Kris turned to Sophia, "Can I help?"

"Not right now, Kris. But you can do one thing. The most important thing you can do." Her gray eyes stared into his own blue eyes. He felt the force of her gaze.

She held out a flask.

"Is that . . .?" Kris stared at the small glittering object.

Sophia offered it to him. "Yes. It is important that you drink it. You can only really help once you have done that."

Kris felt hot, his heart pounding. "I don't understand."

Sophia held the flask steady and spoke slowly, pausing between each sentence. "I know. I'll explain later. But you need to drink it soon. It won't hurt you. And it may help save Peter. And everything else. I have to go now."

A cab pulled up, and Barney and Sophia got in. Sophia called to Kris as they drove away. "I'll phone in the morning and explain. Mike, I hope to see you soon."

The cab drove off, following the Mercedes.

Kris and Mike watched the two vehicles drive away. Mike turned to Kris. At first speechless, he recovered his wits.

Mike began slowly, "This is the most unbelievable thing I've ever experienced. I hardly know where to start to get you to explain everything."

"I actually don't know much more than you do. I'm happy you were there tonight," Kris said. "I'm grateful for you, man."

"I'm glad I was here too," Mike said, slapping Kris on the shoulder. "That's what friends are for, right?"

"Yes. And thank you. At least I know that these people are real, not just hallucinations."

"They may be real. The question is, real what?" Mike said with a grin. Then added in a bewildered tone, "So, you can see them the way they described?"

"Let's get a cab and go home," Kris said, shelving the conversation for the time being.

When they got back to the house and settled in, Kris explained what had happened to him recently.

Mike said, "I've seen Star Wars and Star Trek, so I know something about all of that. But I thought it was all just Hollywood fantasy."

Kris swigged his beer as he slouched in his chair in the study, and Mike sprawled across from him, his beer bottle dangling from his hand.

"Some of that stuff in the movies *is* Hollywood fantasy. But it's based on long traditions that go back to the beginnings of religion. Even before that."

"I know about the modern laws of physics and about the relationship between matter and energy. But I never thought about it being related to religion."

"Well, energy is the force that runs everything. In a way, it is like God."

"This all makes any drug I've ever taken seem boring."

"It may be that people take drugs because they've lost touch with all these ideas, the principles."

A glint of sunlight peeped through the blinds and touched the corner of the table.

Kris yawned. "The sun's coming up. We probably need to get a little sleep. Sophia will call this morning. After I talk to her and find out how Peter is doing, we can talk some more. You want to just stay here?"

"Sure, hardly any point in going home."

Kris walked to the bathroom, and when he returned, Mike was sprawled asleep on the sofa. Kris decided not to wake him up to go up to the extra bedroom.

Kris flopped on the bed and lay on top of the spread. He put his hands behind his head and stared at the ceiling. His head almost seemed to spin, but not like when he was in college. Back then, putting one foot on the floor would stop the room from spinning. But this was more than just excessive indulgence. His eyes drooped shut, but his mind whirled. It was too much. Too much to take in.

What do I do? Is this some kind of hallucinogen-induced state? How the hell do I know the answer to any of these questions? I guess I'll try to get a handle on it once Sophia calls. I sure wish Mom were here.

He rolled away from the window and dozed off.

Chapter Seven

The jangling phone jerked Kris from a dream of gods and goddesses dancing around him. He shook his head and squinted at the clock. After a moment, the time registered in his mind. Almost nine. He had only slept about four hours, but he felt rested.

He grabbed the phone and mumbled, "Hello."

"Kris, it's Sophia. Are you awake?"

"Kind of. Went to sleep late."

Sophia insisted, "We need to talk. Do you want me to come over? Or can we just talk on the phone?"

"Phone is ok. How is Peter?"

Her voice betrayed her concern. "He had a bad night. But he's a little better. We gave him some nectar, and that helped."

"Nectar?"

"Yes. You know about nectar, don't you?"

Kris answered, "I didn't know it was real."

"Yes. So is ambrosia."

Kris responded, "I guess all the stuff that I grew up learning as mythology is really real."

Sophia assured him, "It is. I know you will take a while to absorb all of this."

"Well, in that case, I need to know what to do. What's the next step?"

Sophia answered, "As I told you last night, you need to drink that last flask. It's the only way you can really help."

"I still don't understand why."

"In order to help Peter, you have to be one of us. And you can only do that by drinking that last potion."

"Then it will be permanent?"

Sophia acknowledged, "Yes. Then the power you have as Krishna's son will be available to you."

Kris paused, and then answered, "This is like a bad Hollywood movie."

"Actually, the movies are just a bad version of the real world. The world you have glimpsed so far." Kris detected a note of amusement in her tone.

Kris smiled. "Reminds me of The Matrix. I'm sorry. I still think in terms of movies."

"I understand. How does it remind you of that movie?"

"Welcome to the desert of the real. When Neo agrees to take the pill."

"Ok. Are you ready to drink the last flask? To see the real reality?"

"I'm choosing the red pill."

"Another Matrix reference?"

"Yes."

"Ok. Call me back when you have finished drinking it. Then I can tell you the rest of what you need to know."

Kris agreed. "I'll call right back."

He stumbled to the bathroom, feeling the pressure of his bladder. He regarded himself in the mirror. His blue eyes, dark curly hair, and mocha skin reminded him of who he really was. He had always hated his rounded face and his almost delicate mouth. Now he understood the source of his features. He had seen those features in mythology books, but he had not made the connection.

Getting ready to become a god, to save the world. But I still need to pee. The basic needs still apply.

He finished in the bathroom and flushed the commode. He stumbled to the kitchen and turned on the coffee maker. He made a strong cup of coffee. He was going to need the caffeine.

I guess this is my ordinary drug that helps me to cope with the world. Before I drink the other.

He slumped at the table and inhaled the fragrance of the steam that arose from the cup. As it cooled, he sipped the coffee, eyes half closed, savoring the flavor, but also delaying the next step. He was anxious. Taking the last swallow, he went to the living room.

Mike was still asleep on the sofa. When Kris walked in, he rolled over and squinted against the light. "Hey, buddy. Was that just a weird dream I had last night?"

Kris grinned and shook his head. "Nope. All real."

"My god."

Kris shrugged and laughed. "In a manner of speaking!"

Mike poured a cup of coffee and sat in front of Kris. "How are you? Did I hear you on the phone?"

Kris answered, "Sophia called. Peter's a little better, temporarily."

"What about that drink she gave you last night? Have you done it yet?" Mike wondered if Kris had chickened out at the last minute.

"No. I told her I would call her after I had."

Mike sat up on the sofa. "So you're actually going to do it?"

Kris was not sure if Mike was concerned or just curious. "The first two didn't have any side effects. Apparently, it's important that I do it."

Mike couldn't help but worry. He and Kris had been friends since high school. And Kris had stood by him through some rough patches in his life.

Mike sipped his coffee and said, "I just hope it's not something that will kill you or drive you insane. Bad LSD is one thing, but this is in a whole new category."

"You're right. I really don't have any idea what to expect. The last two were ok, but I don't know. That's why I want you to watch me take it. If anything weird happens, call 911."

"Could I get some more coffee first? If I need to leap into action to save your butt or something, I need some caffeine."

Kris laughed. Mike poured more coffee. He sipped and smiled into the steaming liquid.

Mike said, "I think that, after tonight, caffeine will be my only drug of choice." Mike tossed back the last swallow of coffee.

"You ready to watch me become the Hulk or something like that?"

. "I'm here for you, buddy."

Kris took out the flask and removed the stopper. He stared at the container and shook his head. *Mom, I hope you were right.* "Here goes. Long life, as Peter said."

He tilted his head back and drank the fiery liquid. As he swallowed, he sat down. He closed his eyes and slowed his breath. Meditation seemed appropriate at that moment. After a couple of minutes, he opened his eyes. Mike leaned across the table, examining Kris's face. Finally, he asked, "You ok?"

"I don't feel anything. I haven't grown any extra appendages. Feel like myself."

He rose slowly, a little dizzy. He breathed in and out, aware of his breath. He stepped toward the window, Mike following him. Kris opened the window and inhaled the cool morning air. A woman in a red warmup outfit jogged down the sidewalk. Normal enough. A hunched old woman in a faded housedress shuffled to her mailbox, letter in hand. Also normal. Maybe nothing had happened. Then he blinked.

The woman at the mailbox, now a voluptuous figure, wore a shimmering gown that seemed woven of sea foam green silk. She glanced up at him, waved, and floated up the sidewalk.

"I wish you could see what I just saw."

"I've dropped acid, but I don't think that can compare with what you're experiencing."

"I'm definitely altered. Do I seem odd to you?"

"Not any more than usual. But you always were one of a kind!"

Kris laughed. "I guess I need to call Sophia now. See what I'm supposed to do. Maybe I get some super powers. What do you think?" Not waiting for an answer, Kris dialed Sophia's number. "It's done. I put Mike on speaker so he can hear this."

Sophia asked, "Do you feel unusual?"

Kris shook his head. "No. Another beautiful day in the neighborhood. But one of my neighbors appeared to be a fertility goddess as she went to the mailbox. A goddess mailing her electric bill."

"You'll get used to that. At least it was a good thing to see! We are everywhere. Just think about how many religions there have been over thousands of years. That's a world full of deities."

Kris agreed. "True. Now we need to talk. Why have I done all this? You said that I can save Peter and June. And save the world on top of that? How?"

Sophia took her time in answering Kris, seeing how excited he was, she reassured him, "Just slow down. How many musicians do you know?"

Kris was confused by Sophia's last question. "Why do you ask? I do know a few, I guess. Not counting the ones that OD'd, went off the deep end, or just gave up music."

"Good. You are going to start a band." Sophia said.

Kris shook his head. "And what is that going to do? Save the world from bad garage-rock music? Or become the god of punk rock?" Kris couldn't help it. The whole idea seemed, well, outrageous, he thought.

Sophia continued. "I know this all sounds unbelievable. But I want you to be serious for a moment. I want you to think about music. Think about the impact it has on people's lives, about what Plato thought about music, and Pythagoras. Why was it emphasized in the Middle Ages as one of the four subjects associated with math? Why did the idea of the Music of the Spheres persist, starting in the Middle Ages or before? Why is music in all of the important events of our lives, especially in religion?"

Kris stared at the phone. "Wow! That is a lot to consider." He knew that the philosophical references were likely over his friend's head. He glanced over at Mike. Mike just shrugged.

Sophia insisted, "Just think about all of that. Talk to Mike about it. Ask any other musicians you know. I wouldn't mention the other stuff, if you know what I mean. Then I'll be in touch. Just don't wait too long. Peter's depending on you. I'm going to see him this morning. Then I'll call, probably about lunchtime." She hung up.

Mike grinned at him. "A band. You're going to save the world with a band? Really? You can't be serious. Like some kind of superhero music? And you are the son of a Hindu god? For real? You're going to turn into the guitar jukebox hero?"

"Beats the hell out of me. But something's going on. People keep turning into gods. It's like a real-life mythology book come to life. Or a bad Hollywood movie."

Mike agreed. "Or a really bad acid trip. Now the music stuff I can understand. It certainly has been a big part of my life. Yours too."

"True. And what she said about the Greek philosophers, the Spheres, the emphasis on music in the medieval curriculum, all of that makes sense."

"I guess so. Most of that philosophy shit is over my head." Mike answered, confused.

Twilight of the Gods

"I remember reading somewhere that listening to music actually changes your brain. It helps me concentrate when I'm working on something."

Mike agreed. "Music changes your brain. So, it's like a drug? I generally have some kind of music on from the time I wake up in the morning."

Kris sat back, his face serious. "Think about all of the kinds of music that are used in a religious context."

Mike scratched his head. "I do know something about that. A lot. From sitar music to Gregorian chant, shape note singing, Tibetan chanting. It's like every religion has its own soundtrack. The music sets the mood, gets people focused."

Kris held out his right hand, palm up, agreeing. "Maybe there's more than that. If music can actually change your brain, maybe it does have real power. Maybe all that mystical stuff actually does fit with what Sophia was talking about."

"Remember the line from the 60s song, 'We can change the world.' Might be true. The Woodstock Generation could still win."

They both laughed. "Far out. The Age of Aquarius is here!"

Mike sat up straight, his eyes showing his excitement. "We're going to start a band. Makes me feel like a high-school kid again. I know a couple of guys who might like to join us. One guy's a drummer. Another is good on the keyboard."

"Just don't mention the gods and all that stuff."

"No kidding. They'd run the other direction."

Kris laughed. "I think I want to talk to that guy from the other night. The one with the saxophone. I have a feeling he will fit right in. I love a band with horns."

Mike asked, "What kind of music are we going to do?"

"I have a feeling it's going to be real unique, maybe totally new. I think it's going to have a bunch of cultural influences if it's going to reach everybody."

"I can imagine a new kind of New Age, maybe Raga Rock meets Heavy Metal."

Kris sat forward, excited. "And with some folk influences. Paul Simon has done some interesting combinations. Do you know anybody who can play sitar?"

Mike shrugged. "I used to know a guy from India. He might still be around."

"Why don't we start trying to get in touch with some of these people. Maybe we can get them all together in a couple of days, see what we can work out. In the meantime, I'll talk to Sophia and see what she has in mind for the band to actually do. I'm still not clear on how all of this is supposed to work."

"Far out. Let's go get some breakfast. Then I'll start scrounging around for some of the guys."

Chapter Eight

They left the house after breakfast. Kris drove to Murphy's to talk to Sam about the saxophonist. When he arrived, Sam had just unlocked the door.

"A bit early for you, isn't it, Kris? You don't normally drink your breakfast."

"I just ate. Actually, I wanted to talk to you about that saxophonist from the other night."

"The one that was here when you met that hot chick?"

"That's the one."

"I see him pretty often. Actually, he'll be in here in just a bit. I owe him some money for the last gig he played in here. He ought to be here in about an hour if you can wait."

"Sure. Do you have any coffee?"

"Just put a pot on."

Sam brought him a cup of coffee.

Kris glanced around, the place remarkably altered in daylight. The sun streamed through the window blind, creating a band of light on which he could see dust motes dancing. The light hit the bottles behind the bar, creating a rainbow of hues that flickered on the wall.

I guess I have never been in here during the day, at least not this early. It's like I'm seeing the place for the first time. Maybe I'm just more aware because of what has happened to me. Maybe I see everything in a new fashion, not just people. Maybe the world has two personalities.

Two people came in and slouched at the bar. A man who obviously had not shaved that morning (or perhaps for several mornings) dropped to a stool and ordered a beer. Then a woman wearing a ratty fake fur and a maroon hat with a little veil on it sprawled coyly at a table in the corner. She ordered a Bloody Mary. She winked at Kris.

I have been where they are. I remember thinking of a beer and pretzels as the breakfast of champions. Sometimes leftover pizza and warm stale beer from the night before. And for company, a woman whose name I couldn't remember.

The door opened, and the saxophonist entered. As he glanced in Kris's direction, Kris blinked twice. The man changed form, and Kris shook his head.

The slender figure who stood before him had spiky hair, in a kind of Mohawk. He wore a loin cloth.

What was the guy's name? Native American. Played a flute. Oh yeah. Kokopelli.

The guy blinked twice.

I guess he sees me in my other form. I need to know how I appear to them.

"How are you?"

"Good. I heard you the other night."

"I remember. I saw you were talking to Sophia. I thought I might be talking to you soon. My name's Pele." They shook hands.

"I'm Kris. Do you know Peter?"

"I do. I hear he's not doing well."

"Not at all."

Pele said, "A lot of us are struggling. Sometimes I feel a little faint. It's like I am actually fading."

"Sophia explained it to me. She says that there may be a solution using music, so I'm trying to get a band together. Apparently, it can change things."

"I had heard a rumor about that idea being in the works."

Kris sipped his coffee. "Sophia, Peter, and June suggested it to me the other night."

Pele asked "What do you play?"

"Guitar. I have a friend, a normal guy, who also plays. He knows some musicians who might join us."

"Obviously, I play wind instruments, sax, flute, etc. If you get it started, I'm in. The guys I play with here aren't really serious. They just like some extra money. And a chance to play a little."

"Do you have a way I can get in touch?"

Pele reached into his pocket. "Here's my card. You can just leave me a text. I'll get back to you."

He regarded the card. Just a phone number and a picture of Kokopelli.

Kris smiled. "Nice."

"Most people don't even recognize the picture. Let alone understand why it's on there."

Kris glanced at the card again and smiled. "I'll be in touch in a day or two."

"Later. Long life."

Mike meanwhile had contacted the drummer and keyboardist. He also found a bass player. They agreed to meet in two days, on a Saturday, to start working on a sound and a playlist. They started brainstorming possible songs that they both knew, songs that the other members could learn. They sat in the study, each with a cold beer as they began to plan.

Mike asked, "What do you think about some of the Raga Rock songs from the 60s? Remember the music that the Beatles and some of the other bands did with the sitar and some other instruments and sounds? I think the Doors did some, and some other bands? that was Raga Rock. We can begin with those and then see what we can do with them."

Kris agreed. "That might work. I really want some kind of fusion of musical types to appeal to a range of listeners. I know some metal heads who would laugh if you brought a sitar out." He sipped from the amber bottle, then placed it on a coaster on the table.

Mike took a gulp. "You're right. By the way, the guy I know who plays sitar said he might be here. He has to get his instrument out of storage."

"I hope he shows. We really need that if we are going to have any Eastern influence in the music."

Kris sat back in his chair, hands before him in a steeple pose. "I thought about '*Gotterdammerung*' for the name of the band."

"I remember you mentioning that word. It refers to the gods?"

"Yeah. It's the German word for Twilight of the Gods."

"The word sounds cool. I think hard-core metal heads might like it just because it sounds tough."

Kris reached for his beer. "The connection to Wagner's opera might catch the attention of people who listen to classical."

Mike shrugged. "That's something I wouldn't have thought of."

"I think this might be an interesting experiment. Now I don't know if it's what Sophia had in mind. And to tell the truth, I don't know if it will save anybody. But it's bound to be fun. And it will beat the hell out of sitting around. I get bored with my life sometimes. At least this won't be boring!"

Chapter Nine

Saturday morning the motley crew of musicians came tumbling through the door. A couple of them carrying guitar cases, and Pele brought up the rear, a horn case in hand. They could have been in their late twenties, but a couple appeared to be in their forties. Or maybe it was just hard living. Jeans and tee shirts seemed to be the outfits of choice. Kris thought that they at least appeared to be a rock band. When they had settled in chairs and on the sofa, Kris stood.

"Hi, guys. I'm Kris. This is Mike." Mike took a sloppy bow.

Kris continued. "We're starting this band, see. It's gonna be a new kind of music. A blend of New Age, a fusion of styles, in other words. It's going to be different." Kris did air quotes when he said the last word.

The young keyboardist, who probably had played in the high school band, raised his hand before introducing himself as Jimmy. He pushed his black Buddy Holly glasses up on his nose before speaking.

"How different? I have heard a lot of kinds of music--rock, rap, big band, and so forth. What do you mean by fusion?"

"It's going to combine a bunch of cultural influences. A combination of Raga, Heavy Metal, a little classic rock, something no one has ever heard."

The bass player, calling himself Frank, interrupted Jimmy. "That sounds a little weird. Can all of that work? It might just sound like noise. People will hate it." Kris took stock of him. Mid-thirties, but with deep age lines in his face. His scalp showed through his scraggly gray hair. He flipped his ponytail back before sitting down. Yep, Kris thought. Hard living.

Kris faced him. "Weird? Maybe not. Just think of the people who have created new kinds of music. All music begins with the same basic notes, chord structures, tempos. We just go back to that. Then we create something new."

A small man sitting off to the side stood. Kris had noticed him earlier tapping on the table. Definitely a drummer, Kris thought. Handsome, high cheekbones, tanned face. Probably Hispanic. The man extended his hand. "I'm Carlos."

Kris shook his hand. "Carlos, glad you came."

"Do you have a band name?"

Kris responded. "I do. Mike and I thought about it. Gotterdammerung, Twilight of the Gods."

Carlos frowned. "That's a funny name."

Frank stroked his graying goatee. "I like that. It kind of sounds heavy metal."

Jimmy raised his hand. "Do you know the Wagner opera? We played 'Ride of the Valkyrie' at half time one year." He started to hum it.

Carlos sat up as he said, "I think I've heard that. Wasn't it in a Bugs Bunny cartoon?"

Kris smiled. "Sure. Kill the Wabbit. Kill the Wabbit."

"That's it. I always liked that cartoon. Elmer Fudd was funny."

"Ok, Any other questions before we start talking about music?"

Frank seemed interested, judging by his string of questions, "Once we get ready to play, where are we playing? What are we preparing for? I think this will be fun and all, but I want to play in front of people." He turned to the group for agreement. "And let's face it, making some money wouldn't be bad."

"I have someone who will set up all of that. Her name's Sophia, our manager. You'll meet her later. Meanwhile, I thought we might just listen to some music," Kris explained. "A combination of styles and types of music. Then begin to talk about how we can make it work."

Mike brought out a stack of CD's and played selections. He began with Ravi Shankar playing the sitar. "This guy was huge in the 60s. The Beatles owe a lot to him."

Frank said, skeptical, "I have heard of that guy. But that music is really out there. I don't know if Metal Heads will get into that."

Kris explained, "Just imagine it speeded up, with a strong bass line under it. Here is the Beatles with sitar included."

They listened to, the Beatles doing "Norwegian Wood" and "Within You Without You," both of which included sitar parts. Then Carlos Santana playing "Black Magic Woman."

Twilight of the Gods

The drummer grinned. "I was named after him. My old man went to Woodstock."

By the end of the evening, they all were talking about the music, the sounds and how to make it all work. Kris and Mike grinned as everyone left.

Pele stayed behind to talk. "Kris. This really sounds interesting. I can imagine the trumpet and the saxophone in some of those pieces. What do you think about doing a piece based on the Wagner? 'Ride of the Valkyrie' would be a wild opening number. It would certainly get the crowd going."

"Yes! That's amazing. Do you think you could work on that to play the next time?"

"Sure." Pele was full of enthusiasm. "A strong bass line under the horns with the sitar behind it all would be like nothing anyone has ever heard."

Kris agreed, excitedly. "Definitely. A real Aryan sound."

Pele tilted his head, eyebrows raised. "Really?"

Kris continued. "Sure. The Aryans came from India. Hitler distorted some of their ideas. The swastika was a holy symbol in Hinduism and Buddhism. The Germanic influence and the Hindu influence together could really kick ass."

Pele agreed. "The band name Gotterdammerung makes sense."

"I'm glad you like it. See you next Saturday. We all have a lot of work to do."

Mike and Kris popped two beers and made sandwiches. Kris made himself a peanut butter and jelly. Kris watched in amazement as his friend piled slices of bologna, cheese, and onion on two slices of rye. When they had finished, they carried the sandwiches and a bag of potato chips into the living room.

Mike gulped from his bottle. Remembering the earlier meeting with the musicians, he said, "You know, I think the guys might be willing to buy into this idea."

Kris swallowed a bite of his sandwich and drank a swallow of his beer. "It's a lot to take in. But I think we can make it work. And the music really could get people's attention. I don't know if that's what Sophia and the others had in mind, but I think it might be."

Mike stood, wiping mustard off his mouth. "I think I'll have another beer."

"Help yourself. By the way, I've been thinking. Where are you staying?"

"I've just been crashing with a buddy of mine. A guy I met in jail. I've been sleeping on his sofa. Since I got out, I really haven't had a place of my own."

"Why don't you just move in here? I have an extra bedroom. That way we can talk about the music and our plans whenever we feel like it."

Mike was clearly moved by Kris's offer. "Man, that would be amazing. You don't think I'd be in your way?"

"No"

"I don't have a lot of money right now. I sure do appreciate it. I'll stay clean and not get into any trouble. No drugs, no wild parties. Promise." Mike sounded earnest. And Kris believed him.

"It's a deal. Don't worry about money. I'd like the company. You can bring your stuff over tomorrow. And you can just stay here tonight."

"Grab another beer. Let's toast." Kris tossed Mike the bottle. He opened it and held it up. The bottles clinked. "Long life," Kris toasted before lifting the bottle to his lips.

Kris slept in the next morning. After his first cup of coffee, he called Sophia. She answered coughing.

"Are you ok?"

"I guess so. I didn't sleep well last night. I think I'm getting what Peter and June have. It's not good."

"I am so sorry. I have some good news. We got the band together. I think we have an idea for a sound that a lot of people will like."

"That's great! We've got to shake people up, make them feel the music. To see that their lives can be better. If we're going to change the world, that's how it has to start."

"We're going to practice again next Saturday. Can you come? I told them you would be our manager."

"I know nothing about managing a band. But I know some of the others who do. I'm going to call Peter right now. He'll want to hear this. Good luck getting ready for next Saturday."

Twilight of the Gods

Kris hung up the phone. He put a CD of Wagner's music in and sat back, thinking of Viking warriors and the great Hindu warrior gods, including Krishna.

He listened to more music and played along.

When Mike came home that afternoon, they drank a beer and listened to music. Guitars out, strumming and picking as they worked through arrangements. The music they were playing was derivative, but it was also unlike any of the originals. Their jam session was interrupted by the phone. It was Starr. Kris glanced at the clock. It was eight. They had been playing longer than he realized.

"Hi, Dad. How are you?"

"Really amazing. I have so much to tell you. But first, how are you?"

"Ok. A little down. I talked to my friend Jeffrey today. He's thinking about getting out of rehab."

"That is probably not good."

"He is just getting clean. When he gets that way, he gets too confident. Thinks he can handle it on his own. Then he's back to square one."

"Can you talk him out of it?"

"I've tried. He wants to come home Friday. 'Just for the weekend,' he says. I don't know if they'll let him do it."

"Well, if they do let him go home for the weekend, you can both come over on Saturday night. I have some pretty wild stuff to tell you. Also, I have gotten a band together, and we're having our first real practice on Saturday."

"That sounds good. Maybe it'll distract Jeffrey. What do you have to tell me?"

"I'd rather tell you face to face. It's not bad. Actually, it's pretty wonderful."

"I can't wait," she said, a happier tone in her voice. "Ok. Bye."

He returned to his guitar. The idea of the band was still intriguing, but the music and all of the events in his life mystified him.

We need something to let people know what we are. Who we are. Maybe we ought to have a theme song, an anthem. I need to do some research on Ragnarok. It's a great epic story. The destruction of the nine realms and the rebirth.

Kris decided that night before he went to sleep to hit the library first thing in the morning.

Chapter Ten

The next morning, Kris was at the library early, and Mrs. Dalton had just arrived.

"Good morning, Mr. Singer, you're here early."

"I knew you'd be here early. You always are."

"We try to serve the community. Are you here for anything in particular?"

"I have an idea for a poem. It's Nordic mythology. I need to know about the Ragnarok, the destruction of the universe."

Mrs. Dalton said, "It's been a long time since I read anything about that. You might start with *Bulfinch's Mythology*. I know there's a section in there about the Nordic myths. What about Campbell? We've talked about him before."

"Those are good places to start." Mrs. Dalton found the books on the shelves, and he sat at a table in the corner, notebook open.

The Bulfinch and Campbell were a good start. He wrote key ideas, names and events: The Tree of Yggdrasil, the Wolf of Fenrir, the Midgard Serpent, the Bifrost, the realms of Asgard and Jotunheim, the Norse gods and goddesses and the Frost Giants.

I've forgotten so many of the details We need something to represent us and what the band stands for. I hope I can put enough of the details in and that it will make sense when I'm done. Writing a song is not the same as writing a poem. I should be writing an epic instead of a little song. That's ok.

Mrs. Dalton stood beside him, smiling. "Did you find what you needed, Mr. Singer?"

Kris responded, "Yes, ma'am. I need to go get a cup of coffee and start working on the song I have in mind."

"Good. Let me know if I can help."

"Thanks. You are always so helpful."

Around the corner at the Java Jive, he ordered a mug of Sumatra coffee and sat in the back. The images swirled in his mind: the rise of the Frost Giants, the deceptions of Loki, the destructions of the Wolf and the Midgard Serpent. It was all so archetypal, so embedded in Western culture. Maybe the song would reach people, intrigue them.

Robert C. Covel

He began writing, sketching out ideas, scratching out lines and starting over. As he worked, the images and ideas from the Norse myths took over his mind. He saw the battle scenes, the heroic deeds of the Viking gods. Two hours later the song was finished, at least in rough form.

Twilight of the Gods
Gotterdammerung

From the frigid depths of Jotunheim
the wrathful Frost Giants emerge,
their vengeance sweeps across the realms
in a tidal wave of battle surge.

The Wolf, freed from its chains and lair,
rips living flesh with slavering jaws,
destroying life and bringing death
with mortal fangs and claws.

REFRAIN:
The Ragnarok brings destruction,
chilling Realms with frigid breath
unless the might of Asgard's gods
can halt the dark of icy death.

From Ygradrasill, great Tree of Life,
roots and boughs throughout the universe are spread,
from Niflheim and Jotunnheim to Asgard,
encompassing the span of Time and Space
of what is past and what to come.

The Midgard Serpent, tearing at the roots
lies, baring envenomed fangs.
Its earth-encircling deadly coils
ensnare the Hammer-wielding Hero
in agony from poison's bitter pangs.

REFRAIN

Twilight of the Gods

The Bifrost, glittering Rainbow Bridge,
in shimmering shards Kaleidoscopes
beneath the steel of armored hooves,
great steeds that bear the Giant foe,
shattering the paths of human hope.

Nine Realms that span the Universe
in Chaos and Discord clash.
The universal Harmony, its balance swept aside
by the Frost Giants' discordant violence,
as light and warmth of life implode
in blinding Apocalyptic Flash.

REFRAIN

The Dark and Cold of Death descend
into the Reign of Night.
But Hope remains to hear the strains
of Harmony once more,
a glimmer of new Light.

Then from the Dark and Silence
a Spark, a Note shall arise, restoring all.
Odin, the All-Father, awakening from sleep,
crescendo-ing of light and life
in Trumpet's clarion Call.

REFRAIN

The Ragnarock brings destruction,
The Gotterdammerung,
chilling Realms with frigid death,
until the light of Asgard's risen god
restores the living harmony
with the Voice, music's reviving breath.
Restores the living harmony
With the Voice, music's reviving breath.

Kris reread what he had just written. The rhythm might be a little off. But overall, he was pleased with it. It might actually work.

The rest of the week was devoted to playing guitar and working on the song. The music that he began to hear in his head reminded him of Wagner. They might need to get some tympani and a gong for the drummer.

Kris shared the lyrics of the song with Mike that night.

"That's really good. Explain some of the story to me. Unlike many," he laughed, "I'm not really up on Norse mythology, other than the fact that Thor kicked ass."

Kris filled him in on the basic story, the conflict between the gods and the Frost Giants, some of the other mythology.

Mike asked. "Do you have any ideas about the music?"

"Just a little. I can hear some big Germanic sounds like Wagner. But I can also hear the sitar under that, combining the two Aryan traditions. While the war in the song is from Norse mythology, I can also imagine the battles in the Bhagavad Gita. The two music traditions have to meet somewhere in the middle."

"Far out. I can't wait to hear that. I'm going to play around with it a little this week to see if we can at least come up with a melody."

"I'm hoping we'll have it down enough that we can play it for Sophia on Saturday."

"How's she doing?" Mike asked.

"Not very well. When I talked to her, she sounded really raspy and a little weak. She may have the same problem as Peter and June."

Mike shook his head. "Definitely not good. I'm not sure how this music idea is supposed to help."

"Me neither, Kris admitted. "I just hope it does. And after all they *are* gods. Hopefully they know something."

On Friday, the phone rang. Kris was playing his guitar, listening to Ravi Shankar and Wagner back-to-back. He turned down the volume and answered the phone. It was his ex-wife, Starr's mother.

"Hello?"

"Kris? This is Abigail."

"Hi, I haven't talked to you for a while."

"I know. I've been busy. Have you talked to Starr recently? Has she told you everything going on with her friend Jeffrey?"

"She has. I guess she called you," Kris said.

"Actually, I called her. She never calls me. She probably wouldn't have told me about him if I hadn't asked specifically how he was. I know they're just friends, but he's not good for her."

"You know her. Even when she was a little girl, we had to dig for information. She's a private person."

"True. But I worry about her. That guy is a loser. I wish she could find someone nice to settle down with." Abigail had stated that opinion before.

"I don't get involved in her personal life. And they're just friends."

"I still worry that she might be involved in something bad for her." Abigail said.

"Well she's supposed to be over here tomorrow afternoon. I have some guys coming over to play music, and Starr will be here. Jeffrey might be here too."

"I don't know that I want to see him, but I'd like to see her. Do you think I could drop by?"

"Sure. We're probably going to play about mid-afternoon. You can show up whenever you want."

"I actually have a date tomorrow. We're going to dinner and a movie. Will it be ok if he comes too?"

"Sure. Won't hurt my feelings. We'll probably be playing at 4:00. You and Starr will have some time to talk."

"Don't tell her I'm coming. She might not show if she knows. She just thinks I want to run her life. I'm just trying to help her. But she doesn't see it like that."

"I won't tell her."

"See you then."

When Mike got home from work, Kris told him about the phone call.

"So, your ex is going to be here with a boyfriend to talk to your daughter?"

"That's right."

"Wow. That has all the trademarks of a reality television show."

"I hope it won't be. For Starr's sake. You know, Abbie's actually a nice person. She's a good mom, even if she gets a little bit too nosy. Starr has to work at keeping Abby at arm's length."

"I'm just glad it's you and not me. I hope she doesn't mind the music."

"That shouldn't be a problem. When we were dating, we went to a lot of concerts, some pretty loud ones. She's only gotten conservative in her later years. She was actually pretty much a hippie. Like me. I just never outgrew it. She did."

The next day Kris and Mike began to get ready for the band. Kris made sure that he had chips and dip on hand, as well as beer and soft drinks. They decided to order pizza later when they wanted to take a break from practicing.

At 2:00 Starr called. Kris could tell by the tremor in her voice that she was about to break some news. She got right down to it. "Dad, I'm going to come by. And Jeffrey is coming. They let him out for the weekend. He has to be back tomorrow morning. I just hope it's not a disaster."

"I hope so too, Starr. Maybe being here will help him. Some of the guys have been through what he's dealing with, so maybe they can help. See you both when you get here."

Kris felt a little guilty not telling Starr that her mother would be there, but he decided to just let it be. Hoping it would work out.

The band members began to arrive about 3:00. They set up in the garage, and just as they finished, a van pulled up, and a small dark-skinned man emerged.

"Guys, I want you meet the sitar player. This is Sankar."

Sankar retrieved his instrument from the back of the van.

"That is one big instrument, like a guitar on steroids," Kris noted.

Sankar smiled. "It is. It's almost as big as I am." He placed large cushions on the floor and put the instrument on them. "I haven't played much in several months, Kris. I hope it doesn't sound too bad."

"We're going to kind of make it up as we go along, so you'll be a big help."

Once everyone had set up, Kris spoke to them.

"First of all, we have some people coming over. Or rather, I do. My ex-wife and her current boyfriend will be here, and so will my daughter with her friend who is in rehab. Sophia our manager will be here too."

As the band members were talking, the Mercedes pulled up, and Sophia got out from the driver's side. She had driven herself. She was casually dressed with her hair down across her shoulders. As she approached, Kris could see that her cheeks were flushed. She coughed as she walked up the driveway.

"Guys, this is Sophia. She's going to help us set up venues to play."

They introduced themselves. Frank and Carlos winked.

Sophia stood before the band, "Gentlemen, I am excited to hear what you are going to play. Your music is important to me, and I hope to help you be successful,"

An older Volvo pulled up, and Starr and Jeffrey hopped out. "Guys, this is Jeffrey. He's a friend of mine. I hope you don't mind I brought him."

Starr glanced at Jimmy, her eyebrows raised. "Don't I know you?"

Jimmy, glasses sliding down his nose, said, "I knew you in high school."

"I thought so! Small world."

Kris interrupted. "Starr. I wanted to tell you so you'll know. Your mom is coming too."

She cut her eyes over at Kris. "Really. Any particular reason?"

Kris shrugged. "She just wants to see you. Oh, and she will have her boyfriend with her."

Starr shook her head slightly. "I'll deal with it, Dad. I always do."

The band members took their places and picked up their instruments. Sankar sat on his cushions and picked up his sitar. He played a couple of runs.

"That is so cool!" Frank chuckled. "I feel like I have gone back to 1968."

"It is an ancient instrument. I'm glad you like it." Sankar said.

"I wrote a rough draft of the lyrics to a song I thought we might do. I envision it as a kind of anthem for the band, our opening number." He passed out copies to everyone.

Sophia perked up. "This is quite good, Kris. The gods will be honored."

"Do you have any music in mind?" Jimmy asked. "This all seems like Wagner. We might be able to adapt some of his sound."

Pele picked up his trumpet. "This might work as an opening." He played notes that recalled the opening to "Ride of the Valkyrie."

Frank played a bass run that answered the trumpet. The sitar added an exotic Eastern line, and Jimmy's keyboard brought the music back to the Wagner.

Sophia smiled. "That is going to be a magnificent opening for your performances."

They began to work on the music, each musician commenting as they played and listened. The combination of sounds was like nothing that Kris had ever heard. The Germanic sound of Wagner's music, softened by the exotic sitar, reflected the union of East and West.

Kris heard the sound of a car horn as a white Lincoln Navigator pulled into the driveway. Abigail rolled down the window and shouted, "Hi, everybody. I loved what I was hearing as I pulled up." She got out, and a man emerged from the passenger's side. "This is Randy Tragos, my boyfriend," Abigail said.

Kris examined the man, noting the carefully trimmed beard and the slightly up-tilted eyes. He smiled at Kris. Kris blinked twice.

Before him stood a distinctive figure. Two slight bumps, small horns protruding on his forehead above either eye, and a lascivious smirk across his face. Kris immediately recognized him as a satyr from Greek mythology. They had a bad reputation. The name Tragos certainly fit.

The man blinked twice, his smile broader.

Oh man. Do I tell Abbie? And if I do, how do go about it? She will think I am absolutely crazy. Or making up some outrageous story to ruin her new relationship. So now not only do I need to tell

Starr what's really going on here, but I also need to tell her mother. Maybe I really am going crazy. Or I will be before all of this is over.

Starr interrupted his reverie. "Hello, mother. It's good to see you. Mr. Tragos, it's nice to meet you. I'm Starr, Abigail's daughter."

He touched her hand and raised it to his lips. "Charmed, I'm sure."

Starr glared at Kris, eyebrows raised.

Kris regained his composure.

"Well, now that everyone is here, let's get back to the music."

They spent the next couple of hours playing parts of songs, each musician playing pieces that might somehow fit their new concept. Fragments from the Beatles, The Moody Blues, The Doors, The Electric Prunes all drifted across the afternoon. The musicians had certainly done their homework. As each musician played, Sankar played his sitar, trying to mimic the Western sounds with an Eastern undercurrent. It all worked.

At 6:00, Kris took pizza requests and called in the order. A half hour later they were eating pizza, drinking beer and cokes, and laughing as they talked music. Starr and her mother were in one corner engaged in an intense conversation. Abigail's date watched the two of them and then dared a glance at Sophia, who had daggers in her eyes. For once, the sly smile disappeared.

Jeffrey wandered over and sat beside Kris.

"Hello, Mr. Singer. I appreciate your inviting me over. I guess Starr has told you what I'm going through."

"She has. I know it's tough to deal with. I just hope you can keep it together. Not just for Starr's sake but for your sake as well."

Jeffrey glanced up at him and then dropped his eyes. "Yes sir. I'm going to try hard to beat it this time. I'm going back to rehab tomorrow. I like your band, by the way."

Kris smiled. "I'm glad you do."

"The music really is cool. Not just in the music itself but how it affects me. That first song was especially cool. I can identify with it. It's like we're all fighting this epic battle. There are gods and demons, and the battle could go either way. I guess my demon is drugs. I'm going to think about it this week while I'm in rehab. It might help."

Kris saw Abigail hug Starr. Apparently, their conversation had ended on a happy note.

Man, there are so many tensions here right now. All the problems with Jeffrey and how it affects Starr and her mom and me. And then Abigail's boyfriend. How and where did she find him? I guess I really can't tell Abbie. But maybe she'll see through him.

Mike came over, munching a slice of pizza and finishing a beer. "Kris, are we going to practice anymore?"

Kris turned toward the group and raised his arm. They quieted down to listen. "Everybody, Mike wants to work on the opening song again. I think he's right. If the audience buys into that, we can get them to accept the other music."

They put down their plates and drinks and then took their places. Sankar sat on his cushion and picked up his sitar. He played notes that were like the Wagner opening, but with a distinctly Eastern feel.

"That really is good, Sankar, Kris said. "What if we open with that and then shift to the horn and bass? Then the guitar and keyboard come in. Maybe the instruments can play back and forth under the words."

Then Kris glanced at Abigail and Randy. They seemed more involved with each other than the music. Their relationship worried him, but he couldn't get involved.

The band played a few minutes more and decided to quit for the night. As they were packing up their instruments, Sophia arose.

Kris asked her, "Do you think you are about ready to play somewhere?"

"I think playing in front of an audience will help us gauge how good our music really is. Does it reach the audience? Then we can go from there."

"I know that there is a little Battle of the Bands competition at a bar next weekend. Do you want to enter it?"

"Sure. Right, guys?"

"I'll sign you up tomorrow. I'll give Kris the details, and he can pass them on to you."

"Sounds good. Let's keep in touch during the week. If anyone has any ideas about the music, let me know. I want us to be tight next Saturday."

Abigail and Randy walked over, holding hands.

As they were leaving, Kris accepted Randy's offer of a handshake, but the glare that they gave one another made the handshake seem like two opponents touching gloves before a fight. Abigail did not notice.

Starr walked over, with Jeffrey following. "Dad, we're going to go too. I want to talk to Jeffrey before he goes back tomorrow."

"Ok. Jeffrey, fight your own demons."

Jeffrey answered, "Yes, sir."

As they walked to the car, Starr waved at Jimmy, who waved back.

After Starr and Jeffrey drove away, Sophia approached Kris. Mike had gone inside, discreetly leaving the two of them to talk.

"What did you think? Do you think the music will work?"

Sophia seemed rejuvenated, though the weariness still was evident in her eyes.

"Kris, I think that the blend of styles, the combination of cultures may be exactly what people need. The music is emotionally powerful. There is a physical energy to it. But it has an undercurrent of spiritual strength too. I think that union of the emotional, the physical, and the spiritual may be what we want."

"The crowd should be diverse enough to gauge the overall effect. I'm going to get Peter and June to come on Saturday. They really need the boost. And if the crowd responds well, that will help even more."

"I hope so," Kris said, crossing his fingers.

"I'm afraid that it's approaching a crisis. Unfortunately, conventional medicine can't do much."

Sophia left, and he went inside. Mike was sitting on the sofa, feet up, holding a beer. His eyes were closed. Hearing the door close behind Kris, Mike raised his head.

"So, she called this a Battle of the Bands. Is it a competition? Are there prizes?"

"I guess so. To me, that's secondary to the larger impact on the crowd. There's something much more important here than winning a few bucks."

Chapter Eleven

Kris spent a large part of the week listening to music and thinking about Saturday. He worked out the playlist. He knew they would only have a short amount of time to play to reach the audience.

On Tuesday, Kris called Starr. He was concerned about Jeffrey. He also knew that he needed to tell Starr at least something about what had transpired in his life.

"Hi, Dad. I'm glad you called."

"How are you?"

"I'm actually doing pretty well."

"Uh, how is Jeffrey?"

"Do you know, I think hearing you guys play the other night was good for him. He went back to rehab just as he said he would. I thought once he was out, he would not want to go back. But he seems more determined."

"Good. I'm glad to hear that. Listen, I want to have a little chat with you about the band and about Saturday night. Do you think we could meet and talk?"

"Sure. When?"

"Today at 6:00?"

"Absolutely. Where?"

"How about Murphy's. We can have a drink and talk."

"See you then."

Kris spent the afternoon listening to some of the Beatles' later music, followed by some Ravi Shankar and then Wagner. As he listened, the purpose of their music, and especially the song "Twilight of the Gods" was coming clearer in his head.

As he walked into the bar, Sam greeted him. "Well hello, stranger. Haven't seen you in a while."

"I know. Been really busy."

Kris had just finished his first drink when he heard Starr.

"Hi, Dad."

Sam brought Starr's chardonnay and Kris's scotch, and they held up their glasses.

"Long life."

"Same to you, Dad."

They each took a sip.

A couple of young men sat next to them, talking loudly about football. After listening to their debate about the SEC teams, Kris and jerked his head toward a table.

"Let's sit over here at a table where we can talk."

As they sat, Kris said, "I just need to fill you in on how the band came about. And about some other stuff."

"Ok?" her eyebrows raised.

"It's really weird. I don't want you to think I have lost my mind. It started when I met Sophia one night--" Kris said, pausing.

Starr interrupted, "I like her. She seems really rare in a way I can't define. I've never met anybody like her. Her eyes are like— an owl's eyes, like she looks through you!"

Kris agreed. "She is unique. Really--unusual. Let me ask you, do you know what her name means?"

"I think it's from Greek. Something related to wisdom?"

"That's it. It's actually a kind of alias," Kris explained.

Starr frowned. "So why does Sophia have an alias? Is she a fugitive? An illegal alien? A criminal?"

Kris took a sip of his drink. He put it back on the table and sighed. "The truth is, she's Athena."

"You mean, like the . . .?"

"Yes, the Greek goddess. And of course the owl is sacred to her."

Starr shook her head. "Ok, Dad. You said it was weird. But this is a whole new level. Why do you think that?"

"Trust me, I know it's true. And that is only the beginning," Kris said.

"So, there's more?"

Kris paused and took a sip of his drink. Then he told her about Peter, about June, about Barney. He did not tell her about her mother's boyfriend. She drank her wine and ordered another and drank that, as he told her the story of his new acquaintances.

He finished as she drank her third glass of wine."

"Wow, Dad. If anybody but you had told me this, I think I would have been out that door long before you finished. This really is the most incredible thing I have ever heard."

"I have actually questioned my own sanity."

He told her about drinking the potion and about being able to see the others in their true forms.

"I found out who my real father was."

Starr responded, "I knew that you had never known him, but you know now?"

"Yes. You know your grandmother had a dairy farm."

"I remember your telling me about your childhood on the farm."

"Well, she was one of the Gopis from Hindu mythology."

"One of the what? Remind me what that means."

Kris told her briefly the story of the milkmaids.

"And so, who is your father?"

"Krishna."

Her glass fell to the floor and shattered.

"What?"

"Yes."

"So, Krishna is your father?"

"And your grandfather. And your grandmother is a Gopi."

"So, you are saying I'm part divine too?" She stared, mouth open.

"You are. Have you ever felt a little unusual? Maybe in a way you couldn't define?"

"I have, but I always thought it was just the way you and Mom raised me. I always felt I should have been a member of the Woodstock Generation. But this is bizarre, weird!"

Starr shook her head, "I think I want a bourbon, straight up."

Sam brought her the bourbon, and she drank half of the fiery liquid in one gulp. She gasped as she put down the glass.

Kris then explained the rest of the story to her, the real purpose of the band, about Peter and June's declining health. Starr just listened quietly. Kris was not certain how much she was taking in.

He finished and sat quietly. They both stared into their empty glasses as though they were the source of answers.

"Dad, are you sure you haven't just gone off the deep end?"

"Believe me, I've asked myself that. But I really don't think so."

"I really have to absorb it. I don't even understand what that does to my life, to everything I have ever thought. My entire universe just got flipped and turned inside out."

"I know how you feel. Just don't freak out about it."

She stared at him a moment. "Is it ok if I leave now? I'll call tomorrow."

"Sure. Are you ok to drive?"

"I took a cab. Probably a good thing."

"I'll get Sam to call you a cab."

When the cab arrived, Kris walked her out and opened the car door. "I love you, Starr. Just let it all sink in. I'll talk to you tomorrow."

Kris walked back in and sat at the bar.

"One more, Sam."

"Sure."

"Your daughter ok?"

Kris sipped his drink. "She is. Thanks for asking." He paid his tab and went home.

Chapter Twelve

The next day passed quietly. Kris read more from the *Bhagavad Gita*.

Man, this stuff now is profound, deep. How the hell does Hindu mythology become family history? We spend our whole lives thinking the universe functions on a certain level, and then we wake up realizing that it's all an illusion.

Starr called later that afternoon.

"Hi, Dad. I told you I'd call. I still am reeling from everything you told me yesterday."

"I know. I figured that. I'm sorry."

"I can't even talk to anybody about it. Have you told anybody?"

"I told Mike. He was ok with it. But he's open minded."

"I don't know anybody that open minded."

Kris agreed. "He's had some pretty weird experiences, and all this does take some getting used to."

"I'm ok. It's just going to take me awhile. It certainly explains many things about my life. I know now why I always felt peculiar."

They were both silent for a moment before Starr said, "Well, I have to go. I'll see you Saturday. I hope you have a good week. Love you, Dad."

"Love you too. Are you sure you're ok?"

"I'm ok. See you later."

Well I hope she gets a handle on all of this. I hope that by Saturday she'll have a better grip on it, when she sees all of these people, knowing who they really are. I just wish Saturday would get here. I want to get on that stage and make the music happen.

Wednesday morning Kris woke to the sound of his phone. He squinted at the clock. 7:00.

Kris mumbled, "Hello."

"Kris. It's Sophia. I wanted to let you know that Peter's in the hospital. He just collapsed last night. They had gone out for dinner. He was already weak, and he just passed out in front of the restaurant. The doctor is one of us. They're giving him steroids, which will help for the short term. Obviously, it won't heal the real problem, but it will give his body strength for a while. I'm still hoping he can come on Saturday. I think that will help him more if the music goes as planned."

"I'll be right there," Kris assured her.

"We're all here. June and Barney. A couple of others you haven't met yet."

He dressed quickly and drove to the hospital. The nurse at the desk gave him the room number. When he walked in, he saw Sophia, June, and Barney. Sitting in the corner were two others, a man and a woman. He blinked twice. The woman was dressed in a long flowing robe that exposed one perfect breast. The man was wearing an ancient Egyptian outfit.

"Kris, this is Astarte, and this is Heka, the Egyptian god of healing. He's just getting the steroids. They're giving him a big dose to help the weakness. It's more than most people get at once, but he needs it. He'll get more the next three days as an outpatient. By Saturday he should be fully functional. The problem is that once the steroids wear off, there will be a big let-down. He may crash. So, it's important that the music helps him on Saturday."

Peter opened his eyes

"How do you feel?" Kris asked. The figure on the bed was the regal image of Jupiter, but a weak version, a fallen god.

"I have been better. I anticipate your performance on Saturday. I will be there."

"I hope you'll be in the front row. We'll make the magic happen. I hope I can be the fairy dust we all need."

The next two days passed slowly. Sophia called to let Kris know that Peter was responding well to the steroids. He was home and receiving the drug from a home health nurse, so he didn't need to exert himself going out.

Chapter Thirteen

On the day of the Battle of the Bands, Kris arrived at the venue a little before five. He entered through the back door and walked through to the stage. As he walked out onstage, he realized he had forgotten how big the place was. It had been a movie theater at one point, but the seats had been replaced with tables and chairs. The place probably had room for several hundred people. He was excited and nervous.

The last time I was here it was as a member of the audience. I need to talk to the tech guy about the sound and about lighting I have some ideas to make our opening more dramatic. I know that the opening number for a set is important, but that is doubly true for us. I just hope the audience likes the music.

The rest of the band members arrived, and they all stood on the stage together. They tuned their instruments, and by 6:00 they were set. The music was to start at eight, so they had time to settle in.

Sophia called Kris at seven. She was set to arrive at eight or a little after with Peter and June. "Peter's feeling good right now. He's high on steroids. I've got them sitting at the front so they can see clearly and hear. Barney and I will be sitting with them and a couple of other guys who are actually body guards, though I don't think that will be necessary."

At 7:30 Starr arrived. Kris had told the manager to expect her so she could get in. She was dressed up for the evening, a bright top decorated with flowers, faded jeans with flowers on the back pockets, and low-cut boots. Her hair was in braids with a head band. Kris smiled. She really is a member of the Woodstock Generation. She sat toward the back and waved at him.

The crowd began to enter at seven thirty. Kris saw a lot of young people, around Starr's age, and also a number of older people, more than he would have expected. The tables began to fill. They were certainly going to have an eclectic crowd. He saw Sophia enter. Peter and June followed her. They were dressed casually, but better than most of the other people in the audience. Peter wore a navy blazer with a white turtleneck underneath. June wore a navy dress with a stunning necklace. He hair was piled on top of her head with a small tiara. She certainly dressed for her true identity. Then Kris noticed the two large men behind them. He blinked twice.

He recognized both instantly from their attire. One, a blond giant, wore apparel appropriate to a Norse god. He held a hammer in one hand. The other, darker with curly hair and a full beard, wore a lion skin draped over his shoulder. Kris felt sorry for anyone who challenged those security guards!

At eight o'clock the first band came out to play, a punk band named Screaming Teddy Bears. Kris wasn't sure about the teddy bears part, but the screaming part of their name certainly was appropriate.

When the first band had finished, there was a break as the second band took the stage. As they tuned up, Kris recognized their music as more classic rock. They called themselves the Soaring Eagles, and from their playlist, Kris saw that they were essentially a tribute band for the Eagles. They would be a good band to follow. At least their sound fit in with the music that Gotterdammerung was playing.

The MC introduced the next band. Their lead guitarist stepped forward and began to play the opening to "Hotel California." The audience applauded and cheered as soon as they recognized the opening notes. Backstage, Kris sat and smiled.

He closed his eyes and listened. The guitarist was good, and the band's cover was excellent. They played "Desperado," and then the guitarist began another wonderful opening, the beginning of Santana's "Black Magic Woman." Once again, Kris closed his eyes and listened, smiling at the guitar's delicate sensuality.

I remember hearing them the first time. They opened for Janis Joplin. What a night that was! I had never heard of them at that time. This song is just hypnotic. Just like "Hotel California" it gives us a sense of the supernatural in ordinary life. I hope we can pick up that same idea and go with it. The audience has loved these two songs, so I hope they love ours.

The next song began, Eric Burdon and the Animals doing "Spill the Wine." Another of Kris's favorite songs, especially the flute solos, which he knew Pele loved. They finished, and the

Twilight of the Gods

audience applauded enthusiastically. After a couple of minutes, the band exited, the curtain dropped and Kris and the other members of Gotterdammerung took the stage. They set up quickly. Sankar put his cushions in front and sat, his sitar on his lap. He smiled and bowed to Kris. They heard the emcee announce them.

"And now a new band to the scene, they call themselves Gotterdammerung, the Twilight of the Gods. Their name comes from a Wagner opera and from Germanic mythology. Let's give it up for them."

The audience applauded. Kris breathed slowly. The curtain rose to a black stage. Then the spotlight hit Sankar. He began playing his Eastern version of "Ride of the Valkyrie." As he finished the well-known opening, another light revealed Pele playing the trumpet, and then Frank's bass picked up, followed by the keyboard.

The music changed, and Kris began singing their opening number. He finished the first stanza and the refrain. It sounded good. He could see the front tables, and the people seemed entranced. No one talked, as Peter and June were listening to the music.

He continued to sing, the music blending its Eastern and Western sound. He closed his eyes, feeling the music and the words. Mike was playing with his eyes closed, feeling the music. Carlos was playing the drums, attacking them like a Viking warrior. Pele swayed in time to the music as he played the Valkyrie themes on his trumpet. They played and sang, and Kris could feel the energy building between them as it flowed from the audience. They finished the last stanza and the refrain with its coda, and the audience began to cheer and applaud. Kris opened his eyes. The song was a hit with the crowd.

Kris could feel the audience response. He had been in a crowd like that before, had felt what they were feeling, but this was deeper. He wasn't sure if it was because of his increasing awareness from the potion he had taken, but the passion flowed from the crowd in waves, a blend of raw sensuality and sublime beauty. It flowed over him and the band. They were bowing, a little overwhelmed.

"Thank you. Thank you very much. And now we want to play a song you probably know, one of the Beatles' later songs, 'Norwegian Wood.'"

The crowd responded, and Kris could see some of them singing along. They then shifted into George Harrison's "Inner Light." Sankar's sitar touched the people in the audience. Kris saw them, eyes closed, flowing with the music. It was reaching them. Peter and June smiled, and they seemed serene.

They closed with Donovan's "Atlantis."

The audience response at the end of their set was overwhelming. "Thank you. Thank you so much. We are so happy that you like our music. We hope to see you again soon. Watch for announcements for our next performance. Good night."

They walked off stage, passing the next band. Later, they could not have told anyone what the last three bands played. Kris felt as though he was floating on the waves of sacred sensuality that he felt flowing from the audience.

Afterwards, the winners were announced. Kris was thrilled, but not really surprised, that Gotterdammerung won first place. After the audience's response to their music, he knew that they had at least surpassed the other bands.

The band members walked out on stage to more applause and cheers. They waved and bowed to the audience. The prize was a gift card to the music store that sponsored the event and a free recording session to record one number. It would then be played on a local radio station.

"Now we need to record a song," Kris said to Sophia.

"Yes. And it has to be the opening number. That is the one that will reach. People get it. I'll set up the recording session. We get that out there, get it on the radio, and then play more performances."

"Wonderful. I think some of us are going to go to Joe's and have a drink to celebrate."

Sophia answered. "I'm going to get Peter and June home. Enjoy your celebration."

Sophia left, and Kris joined Starr and the rest of the band as they headed to Joe's. They were so elevated from the experience on stage that the alcohol was redundant. As they lifted their glasses and toasted one another.

We really are feeling the spirit tonight. I have never felt like that, either in the crowd or on stage. It was all elevated. Sublime. Powerful. Now they just need to communicate all of that on a recording.

Chapter Fourteen

Kris slept in the following morning after a night of sensual dreams filled with dancing goddesses, fields of tall grass, dancing gnomes drinking wine, and the music from their set. Mike had left a note that he was going to visit a friend for the day. He went to the kitchen and made a cup of coffee. He carried his coffee to the front porch where he stepped into a bright, cool morning.

He enjoyed the morning, the beginnings of fall. A few leaves had begun to change, and the sky had a deeper shade of blue. *I love fall. There is a special kind of beauty at the end of the year. We tend to think of beauty as being at the beginning of things, the flowers of springtime and so forth. But the endings are beautiful too.*

The phone rang.

"Kris, it's Sophia."

"Kris said, "Hi, Sophia. How are you?"

Sophia answered. "Wonderful. Still feeling the effects of last night. I called this morning to set up your recording studio time. Your appointment is next week, Friday afternoon at 3:00. Can you let the rest of the band know?"

Kris floated through the day. He listened to the songs that they had played the night before, and also the music that the band before them had played. He read a little from the *Bhagavad Gita* in the afternoon and took a nap. For dinner, he made a stir fry and rice, adding curry powder and garam masala to give the food an Indian flavor. As he sat before his plate, he bowed before it, to Kali and Shiva, to endings and beginnings.

He called the members of the band to tell them about the recording session. They agreed to get together on Thursday evening to practice the song one more time. As he talked to each, Kris could hear the joyful tone in their voices. They all felt transformed by the moment. Now if they could just hold on to that feeling until Friday.

He slept peacefully that night, no dreams that he could remember. The next morning, he lit some patchouli incense and sat to meditate. His breath settled quickly, and his mind drifted. His thoughts shifted from the performance to the upcoming recording.

Twilight of the Gods

Emotions floated by, worries about Starr, thoughts of Abigail and her new boyfriend, concern for Peter and June. He let the thoughts and feelings drift with his breath, like a cloud of incense.

On Thursday afternoon, the band arrived to prepare for their recording. The excitement was palpable as they set up.

"Has anyone ever done anything like this?"

Everyone shook their heads.

"So, this will be a big deal for everyone. Let's play tomorrow like people's lives depend on it. When this gets played on the radio the first time, I want people to turn it up. I want them to call the radio station to request it. Let's be that good."

The two-hour practice was focused and fulfilling. They talked about each element of the song, about when each instrument came in, about how to get the most dramatic effect from the lyrics. They played it through one last time.

As the last note faded, Jimmy grinned behind the keyboard.

"That was epic!" He pushed his glasses up on his nose.

Kris glanced over. Mike was smiling, one eyebrow raised.

"Well, bud. You made all this happen. It's a good thing you have friends in high places."

The next morning Kris awoke early, clear headed and relaxed. He lit some incense, this time burning a stick of frankincense and a stick of myrrh. The frankincense reminded him of his Catholic upbringing. The combination of the two had to be auspicious, he thought, as he sat on his cushion. He sat for a half hour, focusing on his breath. He could hear "Twilight of the Gods" echoing through his mind.

Just like Lady Madonna. Listen to the music playing in your head.

They left at 2:00. Mike put his guitar case in the back seat, and Kris put in a CD of the Beatles. They listened to the music quietly, each lost in thought.

Chapter Fifteen

They arrived at the studio at 2:20. The address was a small house in a rundown neighborhood.

The houses on the street needed attention: repairs, paint, and TLC. It had been painted sometime recently, a bright yellow. A sign in the front yard "Grace Notes Recording Studio" let them know that they had found the place.

As they entered, a young woman at the front desk asked, "May I help you?"

Kris paused. Her flaming red hair and green eyes captivated him.

"Uh, yes. I'm Kris Singer. We're here to record a song."

"I'm Maureen O'Kelley. Mr. Burdett will be right with you. Follow me, please."

As she led them through, Kris appreciated her dark green dress which fit over her hips.

"You can wait for him here." She smiled at Kris, her upturned eyes regarding him.

Soon after she left, the door opened again. A dark-haired man entered.

"I'm John Burdett. You belong to the band Gotterdammerung?" He had a slight French accent.

Kris and Mike introduced themselves.

"We have bass guitar, lead guitar (Mike here), drums, keyboard, and sitar. And I do the vocals."

"Sitar, huh? I don't think I've ever actually seen one. Other than seeing Ravi Shankar play in a video. We can arrange the studio to accommodate you. We have drums already set up. We also have a keyboard."

He led them to the studio. "Would you like some water or coffee? Maureen can bring you some."

She brought two bottles of water. "Mr. Singer, have I seen you somewhere?"

"I don't think so. I certainly would remember if I had met you."

She smiled and winked.

As she left, Mike said, "I'd say she might be interested."

84

Twilight of the Gods

"May be. She certainly is fascinating."

The rest of the band arrived and set up. Mr. Burdett arranged microphones and made a place for Sankar to sit in front.

In twenty minutes, they were ready to record.

Sankar played the opening notes, his sitar resonating. Pele's trumpet picked up the melody, and the song filled the room. In a few minutes, they had played through the piece. Mr. Burdett gave them a thumbs-up. "Let's listen to it."

They listened to the playback.

A couple of places were a little loose. Jimmy was a second late in one part, and the bass was not quite loud enough.

"Ok. Do you want to play it once more?"

"Yes. We want it perfect. I think we can play it perfectly this time. Is everybody relaxed? Let's make this one work."

They played the song again.

"Let's listen to it again."

Burdett began the playback. Kris noticed that Maureen was in the booth. She smiled, her eyes closed as the music played.

"What do you think, guys?"

They paused.

Frank said, "Perfect. I don't think I have ever played better."

"I agree. That is the best keyboard I have ever played."

"I think that I would not have minded having Ravi Shankar hear me play that."

Maureen asked, "Mr. Singer, that is some of the most beautiful music I have ever heard. Who wrote it?"

"Thank you. I wrote the lyrics, and Mike did most of the music with contributions from everybody else."

"I'm impressed." She smiled at him.

John Burdett said, "I'll get the CD ready for you. It should be ready in a couple of days."

"Thank you." Kris shook his hand.

They packed up their instruments and walked out together. As Kris walked out, Maureen stopped him.

"Would you like to have a drink sometime, Mr. Singer. I'd love to talk to you about the song."

She handed him a sticky note with a phone number on it. "Call me."

As they got in the car, Mike said, "Told you. That is one hot babe."

"She is lovely. I'll certainly call her."

When they got home, Kris called Sophia.

"We were wonderful. I'd say inspired. We only did two takes, and the second one was perfect, if there is such a thing."

Sophia was pleased. "I'll get in touch with the people I know at the radio stations and let them know to expect to hear from you. We need to make copies of the CD. I know each of you will want one, and we need to have several to use for publicity. This is where it becomes work."

After he hung up, he called Starr.

"Hi, Dad. How was the recording session? Do you feel like a big star?"

"It went really well. We only did two takes. I can't wait for you to hear it. The receptionist was nice. I think I'm going to meet her for a drink."

"That's great, Dad. It's about time you have someone in your life."

"We'll see. I'll let you know when I get the CD. We'll probably all get together to listen to it and celebrate."

Mike left to meet a friend for dinner, and Kris sat in the study, savoring the moment. He could hear the music still.

Twilight of the Gods

Chapter Sixteen

Tuesday morning Kris received a call from the recording studio. When he said "hello," a vaguely familiar voice responded, "Mr. Singer?"

"Yes."

"Oh, hello. This is Maureen from Grace Notes. We have the CD of your song. I listened to it. It sounds wonderful! I have never heard a song quite like that. It really touched me. I wanted to ask you. Would it be ok if I had a copy of it?"

"Absolutely! I guess that makes you our first fan. And I'm a fan of yours. I'll come by today and pick up the CD."

"That would be good. If you come by about 11:00, that's when I take my lunch break."

"Great!"

Kris glanced at the clock. He had about an hour or so to get ready.

He decided on khakis and a blue oxford shirt. Dockers with no socks. He wanted his appearance to be casual. But nice.

"Hello, Mr. Singer," Maureen said when he walked in. I was just listening to your song again. I can't get it out of my head. It's like I'm listening even when I'm not."

"Please call me Kris. So, I guess the song is like 'Lady Madonna'."

He tried not to stare at her dress, another green dress. As before, the color set off the color of that gorgeous hair, those striking eyes.

Man. That décolleté is killing me. Need to keep my eyes up. But those amazing green eyes make it easy.

"I went ahead and made a dozen CDs. I know you all want a copy. And copies for radio stations. Does that work?"

Kris responded, "That's wonderful."

Maureen smiled. "If people are like me, they're going to be calling in and requesting it. I may wear out my own CD copy of it."

Kris asked, "Are you ready to go to lunch?"

"Sure. I'll just let Mr. Burdett know."

She popped her head in Burdett's door.

"Mr. Singer's here. We're headed to lunch."

"Ok." Mr. Burdett peeked out the door.

"Have a good lunch. Maureen, take your time. I've got everything covered here."

"Thanks."

Star of India, the little Indian restaurant Maureen had chosen, had a serene ambiance. There were only a few tables, and it was comfortable and quiet. Kris could hear music playing low in the background. Ravi Shankar. Perfect.

They ordered pita sandwiches with black beans, avocado, and bean sprouts. Maureen ordered green tea, so Kris did too.

"I love this place. I come here a lot for lunch. The food is good, and the atmosphere is so tranquil that it's like a meditation session. I feel renewed when I go back to work."

"I can certainly feel that. How long have you been working at the recording studio?"

"About a year. Before that I did various jobs. I was a secretary at a law firm. That was awful. Seeing these people at their worst, being screwed over by bosses, having injuries from accidents that insurance companies wouldn't cover. I couldn't stand it."

"You shouldn't hate your job. I couldn't work for a place that went against my values. That's bad karma," Kris said.

"I certainly agree with that. You're retired, aren't you?" Maureen asked.

"I am. I was a teacher. I taught for almost thirty years."

"What'd you teach?"

Kris responded, "English. I loved it."

"I think that has to be one of the most rewarding ways to earn a living. If you can stand the kids."

"It wasn't the kids that caused the headaches. It was parents. And sometimes administrators and colleagues. The kids were great usually," Kris said.

"They just need someone who believes in them," Maureen said.

He continued. "Do you know the Pink Floyd song 'Another Brick in the Wall' It's pretty much my theme song. I always felt sorry for the kids. They were at the mercy of teachers who didn't understand them."

"I understand you have a daughter."

"I do. Her name's Starr. She lives here in town."

"So, you're divorced?"

"Yes. Abigail and I have a pretty good relationship. I see her occasionally."

"That's important. Just because two people change and can't live together anymore doesn't mean that they have to hate each other."

"I think so too. It makes it easier on Starr. She doesn't have to choose between us."

Maureen responded, "I don't have any kids. I was married for a while. But we just grew apart. He doesn't live here. I hear from him occasionally, but he's remarried and has kids."

"So, you never remarried?"

"No. I just don't want the attachments."

Kris agreed. "I just never found anybody I wanted to live with for the rest of my life."

She checked her watch. "I probably should be getting back. Mr. Burdett is good at handling things when I'm gone, but he'd rather do the technical and creative stuff and leave the phones and so forth to me."

They walked back to the office. She seemed comfortable not talking as they walked. The afternoon sun warmed them, and the birds sang among the bright leaves.

"I've enjoyed this. Would you like to go out for dinner some time?"

"I'd love it." She smiled at him. "That was a lovely lunch. I can't wait to go out."

"Are you available Friday night?"

"I am."

"We could go out for a drink and then dinner."

"Great. What time?"

"Seven?"

"Here's my address." She handed him a post-it note.

"See you then."

She leaned over and kissed his cheek. He felt her breast brush his hand.

Chapter Seventeen

Kris did not remember driving home. Maureen had just reignited a glow within him. A woman with that kind of intuitive intelligence and that much vitality! And she liked his music.

When he got home, he floated into the study and put the CD in. The music burst forth from the speakers. It really was good.

Funny that hearing it from the speakers objectifies it. I feel as though I just bought a new CD from my favorite band.

The band met that night to listen to the CD and celebrate. Kris volunteered to order pizza, and others were bringing salad and snacks.

Kris decided to call Starr too. He knew she would want to join the party. He also wanted to tell her about Maureen.

Everyone was there by six. As they walked in, Kris gave each one a copy of the CD. The label said, "'Twilight of the Gods' by Gotterdammerung. Grace Notes Recording Studio."

Each man examined the CD as he gave it to him. It was a touching moment, a connection.

When they had all arrived, Kris opened champagne, a surprise that he had planned for that moment. He poured the sparkling golden liquid into the glasses and passed them around.

The men from the band, Sophia, and Starr all stood around him.

"Let's have a toast. Here is to our music and to the power of music to change the world."

"Long life," Sophia responded, toasting the band as they drank.

"Now let's listen." Kris popped in the CD and turned up the volume. The first notes of the sitar gave him chills, and everyone had shivered. Then the clear notes of the trumpet touched them. They listened, eyes closed. The music had a noticeable effect on Sophia like a revitalizing drug or a magic potion.

As the last notes faded, Mike raised his glass. "To the music, and to Kris who made it happen."

"Hear, hear!" They all lifted their glasses toward Kris. He pointed to Sophia, "Sophia is the one who really is the muse for this."

"Thank you, Kris. I'm going to get these CDs out to the radio stations. Everyone out there needs to hear this."

The pizza arrived, and they all ate. By 8:00 people started to leave. Tomorrow was a work day.

Starr patted her father on the back. "Dad, I'm so proud of you."

"Thank you, Starr. I wanted to tell you that I have a date Friday night."

"That's great. With whom?"

"Her name's Maureen. She's the receptionist at the recording studio."

"That's nice," Starr said, a bit curious. "So you like her, huh?"

"She's pretty special. I think you'll like her too."

The band members drifted out, thanking Kris.

Before she left, Sophia said, "Kris, I just want to tell you again, I think this song is amazing."

"I just hope it does what it needs to."

Sophia agreed. "I actually know Maureen. I'm not surprised you two connected. You have a lot in common. Have fun. I'm going to the radio stations tomorrow to talk to their program managers to get them to play this. I'll let you know when it's going to be on the air."

Kris and Mike sat in the living room eating the leftover pizza and drinking a beer.

"That is absolutely incredible, Kris, to hear our music on a CD."

"I agree," Kris said with a grin.

Sophia called on Thursday morning. "Kris, the song is playing this morning on a program called New and Notable."

"I know that program. That station plays a wide range of music. A perfect place to release our CD."

"It is. I have a couple of stations who have promised to play it later too. Hopefully that will to get your recording some attention. We can talk about playing live gigs at venues around town. And then talk about releasing a complete CD."

"You really have it all planned out, don't you?"

"I do. I think we have to think big. I'm even thinking about awards, maybe even a Grammy."

"Now that's beyond big."

He called the other band members, Starr, and Maureen.

All of the musicians thanked him and promised to listen. Starr shrieked with excitement when he told her. "That's amazing, Daddy! I gotta go. I need to call everybody I know. I want all my friends to call and request it."

Maureen thanked him and promised to tell Mr. Burdett as well.

Kris thought, to have our CD about to be played on the radio, and to have the prospect of a hot date with Maureen, all at once. This is unbelievable. Almost more than I can take in.

The announcer on the radio station introduced the song.

"This next song is from a new group here in town called Gotterdammerung. If you are an opera fan, you will recognize the band's name from the Wagner opera. The song's title is "Twilight of the Gods,' which is a translation of the band's name. The CD is from Grace Notes Recording Studio. I called the studio, and the receptionist said that the song has a strong influence from Raga Rock from the 60s. You might remember some of the late Beatles' music with George Harrison on sitar. So, here's 'Twilight of the Gods' from Gotterdammerung."

Kris sat in the study, radio turned up. The notes blasted from the speaker and shook the books and furnishings as he listened. Again, the song seemed to be by someone else. And it was good. Really good.

"That is a powerful song from a new group. We hope to hear more from them. This could be a whole new movement in music. So, listen for more from Gotterdammerung. Let us know what you think."

We're on the radio. I hope people like it. I hope they call in. I hope Starr's friends like it and that they call the radio stations. And I really hope Maureen liked it.

The next day the song played on two other stations. The first station had been deluged with calls (Kris surmised that Starr's friends might have had something to do with that).

Sophia called. "I know someone at the paper who writes about music. He's going to mention it on Saturday. He's a fan of Wagner and knows something about Norse mythology. He heard the DJ call it Raga Rock. But he knows that the original term for Twilight of the Gods, in Old Norse, is Ragnarock. So, he's calling your music Ragna Rock."

Kris laughed. "I'm going to use it when I call radio stations or venues. That kind of term could really help us to proliferate the music. It can catch on. People love catchy labels."

"I'll talk to you on Monday."

"Thanks, Sophia."

Chapter Eighteen

Kris spent a large part of Friday talking to the band members. They all wanted to talk about the music on the radio, about the response, and about the new term Ragna Rock. Kris told them about Sophia's plans, including the mention of a Grammy. That last detail overwhelmed them.

At 5:00 Kris dressed for his date in a sport coat, mint green shirt, and a tie with a dark green stripe. He figured that Maureen would probably wear green, and he wanted her to see that he paid attention to such details.

She opened the door when he rang the bell, and he almost gasped.

She had on a forest green velvet dress with a gathered bodice. Her upturned eyes were highlighted by green eyeshadow, and her lips lined in a dark red lipstick.

"Well, aren't you dapper, Kris?" She smiled.

"And you are stunning, to say the least."

She smiled and winked. "I try to please."

"I thought we might go to an Italian restaurant. They have wonderful vegetarian and vegan options."

"I love Italian. Pasta and red wine are great combinations."

At Papa's Pasta and Pizza, the hostess guided them to a table and handed them menus. Kris admired the décor. The restaurant was less formal, more family oriented than the restaurant where he had met with Peter and the rest. He sat back in his chair and smiled as the server took their drink orders.

"What would you like to drink?"

"Cabernet for me," Kris said.

"I like Cabernet too. I drink chardonnay sometimes too. Let's just get a bottle."

"Why not? Live life with passion."

The waitress soon returned with the wine and two glasses. Kris tasted it and found it to his liking. The waitress then poured Maureen's wine, then filled Kris's glass.

Maureen held up her glass. The dark red liquid caught the light, and it glinted like rubies.

"Here's to us and to music. Long Life," Maureen said, raising her glass.

It's funny how I hear that toast everywhere now. I wonder how Maureen knows it.

They touched glasses and sipped the wine.

He ordered linguine marinara, and she ordered the vegan pizza. The both ordered a salad with balsamic vinaigrette dressing. "When you can get delicious and healthy together, that's a perfect combination."

"I agree," Kris said, taking a bite of salad.

They enjoyed the salad, sipping their wine. Then their entrees arrived.

Maureen's small pizza covered with marinara sauce and fresh basil over sautéed vegetables smelled delicious.

As she took the first bite, she commented, "Calling this pizza is a massive understatement."

They ate quietly, savoring the food.

As they finished, Kris put down his fork. "I'm glad you didn't mind not talking while we ate."

Maureen said, "Food this good deserves complete attention. It should be savored. Not many people seemed to understand that attitude."

As they finished their entrees, the waitress asked them, "Do you want dessert?"

Kris shook his head. "I don't think so. After that salad and entrée, dessert would be redundant. And I'm so full I don't know where I would put it. I would like a cup of coffee, if you don't mind."

The waitress brought two cups of coffee in delicate porcelain cups. The cups rattled in the saucers as she placed them on the table.

Maureen breathed in the fragrance of the coffee and then sipped. Kris did likewise.

"The perfect end to a lovely meal." They finished the coffee, and then rose to leave.

As he drove back to her house, Maureen commented on hearing the song on the radio.

'It really sounded good on the radio. And of course, Mr. Burdett was delighted that they always mentioned the recording studio when they played it."

"It was unbelievable hearing it. Sophia told me that there will be a brief review of it in tomorrow's paper," Kris said proudly.

At the door, Maureen said, "Kris, thank you for a lovely evening. I hope to see you again very soon." She leaned over and kissed him. He had hoped to kiss her, and he was pleased that she took the initiative. The kiss lasted a moment, and he felt the tip of her tongue touch his lips in that instant. It aroused him.

"Sleep well, Kris. Talk to you soon."

"I'll call you," he said stepping back as the door closed.

He did not sleep well. That little kiss gave him dreams such as he had not had since adolescence.

The review in the next day's paper was positive, which pleased Kris. The reviewer picked up on the term "Ragna Rock." Kris was especially happy to see that detail: any kind of tag like that would help listeners to remember the song and the band.

Sophia called about the review. "I think I can set up some venues for the band. There are small clubs always searching for talent."

"Good idea, Sophia. Now that we have a little publicity, we need to get out there so people will remember us."

"I think there is an opening in Midtown for next weekend. Do you think you can be ready?"

"I think so. We have a playlist. We can cover a lot of other songs. Most of the stuff we know are standards, the Beatles, Moody Blues, Eagles, Santana."

"That's good. Kris, you need to think about writing some more songs. The mythic ideas give you a whole vein of material to explore. I think you know enough about various cultures' beliefs to do some really good songs. Remember, our ultimate goal is to get the listeners back to a more believing mode, to see the world beyond just materialism and hedonism."

"I get that," Kris agreed, his mind already working on lyrics.

Kris sat down to think of song ideas. The Norse mythology gave him some ideas. He started writing potential titles that might turn into songs. "Loki's Deception," "Ice Giants' Revenge,"

"Rainbow Bridge to Asgard." They all sounded like possible songs, maybe more Heavy Metal.

My poem "Persephone and Hades" would be a great potential song. The idea of lust and violence, of love gone wrong. A definite possibility. The story of Krishna and the milkmaids. Funny that that is a family story for me! So many stories. Just about every great myth and story from every culture is a song.

He talked to Mike that night about the song ideas.

"These are great possibilities. I know that other bands have used mythology. Led Zeppelin uses the image of Icarus on their albums, and their song 'Ramble On' uses ideas from Tolkien."

"That's true. And those Tolkien ideas go back to Wagner and the Norse mythology."

"You said you have a poem with Persephone and Hades. We might be able to do something with it since you already have the poem."

Kris handed him the poem.

Persephone and Hades

I.
In dappled glades and verdant meadowlands,
she dances with the breeze to satyr's pipes.
She celebrates Demeter's fertile joy
with golden innocence of nymphs and fauns.
The effervescent light, which concentrates
her form with lingering caress, enchants
the blossoms: turned to dancing butterflies.
Companion to the virgin deities,
fair Artemis and gray-eyed Athena,
Persephone delights the woodland gods
with grace and beauty, delicate and pure.
The god of death, dark Hades, watches her,
concealed in desperate shadows from her sight.
His eyes, like glowing embers, watch her steps,
attracted to her innocence, her life,
as darkness longs for light or cold for warmth.

The clouds obscure the sunlight, casting shade;
the notes transpose to darker minor key.

II.
Exiled from Mount Olympus' sunlit peak,
denied divine companions, desolate,
he rules the realm of disembodied souls.
His throne of glistening obsidian
arises like a solitary peak
that dominates the subterranean plains.
The somber endless caverns occupied
by countless generations of the dead:
the shades in endless waves of loneliness
like swirling leaves before the restless wind.
Around the vortex of his single throne,
the maelstrom of distraught mortality,
he sits among the multitudes, alone.

III.
Driven by desperation, Hades skulks,
enchanted by Persephone, he waits,
entices her toward his yearning grasp.
His offered courting gift a fragrant fruit,
the pomegranate, tempts her innocence.
Down twisting tunnels, sunlight left behind,
her suitor guides her soft uncertain feet
to subterranean realms where she will reign.
Her radiant effulgence splits the dark,
like lightning parts the midnight thunder clouds.
Her marble throne with filigree of gold
festooned with emeralds, its opulence
shines forth like moonlight glow behind the clouds.
Her wafting floral fragrance fills the air
reminding mortal souls of summer bliss.
The proffered pomegranate in her hand,
cut fruit like a transected human heart,
the juice flows forth and stains her fingertips.
Its royal tincture tempts the thirsting dead

Twilight of the Gods

who pause before her opalescent throne,
like Hades, smitten by her vibrant life.

IV.
Demeter kneels before the mighty Zeus;
the lightning-bearer grants her fervent wish,
releasing fair Persephone to her
for half the year, the other half to stay
with Hades as his queen, the penalty
for tasting morsels of forbidden fruit.
Her reign beside the Despot of the Dead
is interrupted by her mother's plea.
Her joyful face dispels stark winter's clouds.
Once desolate, the world rejuvenates,
enchanted by her gracious touch and smile.
The flowers spring beneath her tender feet
as nymphs and fauns rejoice for her return.
But Hades grieves beside her empty throne,
the underworld, twice desolate, despairs,
awaiting her return to rule again
beside her Dark Lord, Monarch of the Dead.

Mike read the poem slowly. When he finished, he grinned. "There are a lot of good images in there, and you can pare it down to the essentials. I can hear the last line with the idea of the Dark Lord, Monarch of the Dead as part of the refrain."

Kris agreed, excited to begin. "I'll work on that first, and then think about some of the others."

"This could be an incredible concept album. It could really go somewhere. What an amazing first album that would be." Mike smiled.

"I think Sophia would love that."

"And the band too."

"I'll get to work on some of the songs," Kris said.

"We can include them in our playlist as you finish them, and then think about recording them."

The next day Kris began to think about the Persephone and Hades song. It needed a catchier title. Maybe something like

"Desire of the Dark Lord." Then he needed to cut it to the most dramatic parts. To get down to the two sides of the story—the beauty and innocence of Persephone and then the dark brooding side of Hades. The Yin and Yang of the story.

He had just finished work in the afternoon and opened a beer when the phone rang.

"Hello."

"Dad. Something's happened to Mom."

"What, Starr? What happened?"

"She called me a little while ago. She's on her way to hospital."

"Why? What happened?"

"It's that guy she was dating. He beat her up," Starr's voice trembled.

"Oh no! Where are they taking her?"

"The Midtown hospital."

"I'm headed there now. Can you drive?"

"I'm ok. I'm leaving right now. I'll see you there."

Kris grabbed his keys. He left a note for Mike and drove to the hospital, his mind whirling.

Starr was already there when he arrived at the Emergency Room. She was in tears.

Kris hugged Starr. "Hey, darling. Are you ok?"

She sobbed. "Yeah. I haven't been able to see Mom yet. They're working on her. I don't know what condition she's in. A nurse said that she's not going to die, but she has some pretty significant injuries. The nurse said she'd let us know as soon as she knew anything."

They sat together on a sofa. Starr still was crying, but the sobbing had subsided. Kris sat stone faced.

I can't believe this happened. I guess I should have expected it. I know from what I have read in mythology about satyrs and what they're capable of. I don't know what I could have done. Told Abigail what he was? Like she would have believed that.

A nurse came out.

"We have Mrs. Singer stable. She is sedated, but you can see her briefly. She may be asleep already, but I know you're worried."

She led them to the room and pulled back the curtain to allow them to enter.

Starr gasped as she saw her mother. Her face was bruised, both eyes blackened and her upper lip split. She had one arm in a sling. An IV tube dripped into a needle in her other arm.

"Mom? Are you awake? It's Starr. Daddy and I are here."

Abigail mumbled and opened her bruised eyes slightly. "Starr. Kris?"

Abigail moaned and closed her eyes.

The nurse stepped forward. "I think the sedative has kicked in. She'll sleep for a while. As you can imagine, she's in a lot of pain. We still need to do some more tests. We need to do some x-rays, and we need to be sure there's no internal damage."

"We'll wait outside. Let us know what room she'll be in," Kris said, putting his arm around Starr.

"Oh, God, Daddy," Starr sobbed. "I can't believe that guy could do that to her!"

"I know, Starr. Sometimes people can do really dreadful things. But at least she's still alive."

"I hope she doesn't have any internal damage."

"They'll know as soon as they do the tests. I guess we just have to wait." They walked to the waiting room. He decided to call Sophia. She would know what to do. After all, she was the one person he knew who knew who and what this guy really was. Kris went outside to call. He did not want Starr to hear the conversation; he was not ready for her to know what he knew about her mother's attacker.

When Sophia answered, Kris blurted out, "Sophia, my ex-wife is in the hospital from being beat up. That guy you saw her with is responsible."

"I am so sorry, Kris. I thought I should warn you about him. But I could see from your expression that you knew who, and what, he is."

"I did. But I really couldn't tell Abigail. She would not have believed me anyhow. She would just have thought I had lost my mind. I don't know what to do now."

"Have you talked to the police or anyone about it?"

"I haven't. I assume that they were notified, but I don't know for sure."

"Obviously you can't tell them what he really is. They probably won't find him anyhow. He'll just disappear, move somewhere else."

"So, nothing will happen to him?" Kris exclaimed.

"No. It will happen again. It's in his nature. You know that from your studies in mythology. They don't have their reputation by accident."

"Ok. I guess I'll just concentrate on helping Starr deal with it, and Abigail to the extent that I can."

"Not much else to be done there. And don't forget you have the music to focus on. I know this is important to you, but the music has more profound importance."

"I haven't forgotten. I'll try to get this behind me. I have some really good ideas for songs. We will be practicing to get ready for the next concert."

"Good. I'm going to see if I can get some other radio stations interested in your single."

I hope to get some of these other songs done and ready to perform soon. Mike and I are talking about a concept album eventually."

"I have that gig set up in midtown for next weekend."

"We'll be ready. I need to get back to Starr."

When Kris walked back into the waiting room, he saw two police officers talking to Starr. She was even more distressed.

"Hello, officers. I'm Kris Singer, Abigail's ex-husband."

"Hello, sir. I'm Officer Bennett, and this is Sergeant Bailey. We're sorry your ex-wife is apparently the victim of domestic abuse. We're just trying to find out who did it and to get any details we can to track him down."

"Daddy, I told them about that guy she was dating."

"Do you know him, sir?"

"No. I just met him once. I think she introduced him as Randy Tragos. That's all I really know about him."

"So, you don't know anything about their relationship? Or where we might find him?"

"I'm afraid I don't."

Sergeant Bailey asked, "Miss, do you know anything about what led up to your mother's assault?"

"My mother called me after it happened, she just said he got mad at my mother. Then he apparently just went off on her."

Kris said, "He beat her pretty badly."

"Thank you for your help. When she's better and feels like talking, we need to get more information. We'll be in touch."

Starr responded, "Thank you, officer. I hope you can find this guy and get him off the streets."

Kris hugged Starr. "We just need to concentrate on helping her to recover. And let the police do their jobs."

Kris walked up to the desk.

"Is there any indication when Abigail will be in a room?"

"Soon, sir. She just went to radiology. From the x-rays, she apparently has no internal injuries other than the broken arm. She should be in a room within the next half hour. I'll let you know when they get ready to move her."

Twenty minutes later a nurse entered. "Mr. Singer. Mrs. Singer is going up to room 312 in just a couple of minutes. If you wait five minutes or so for them to move her and get her situated, you can go up."

"Thanks."

They entered the room just as Abigail was being transferred to the bed. She was conscious and whimpering as the orderlies moved her. "We're sorry. Can we get you anything? The nurse should be here in a few minutes to give you something for the pain."

Abigail just shook her head. Her swollen lips and bruised eyes and face brought tears to Starr's eyes again.

"Oh, Mom! I can't believe he did this to you!"

"I know. I can't either. I certainly had no idea he was capable of this."

Kris approached the bed, "Hi, Abbie. I am so sorry you are going through this."

"Thank you, Kris. Thank you for coming," Abigail wheezed.

Kris squeezed her hand. "Please let me know if I can do anything."

Starr touched her mother's hand, "Mom, the police were just here. They're searching for him. They said they want to talk to you."

Abigail whispered, "I told the nurse to tell them to come back by today. The longer they wait, the less chance they have of finding him."

"Abbie, do you know why he did this?" Kris asked.

"He got mad at me. I didn't want to do something, and he just hit me."

Kris glanced at Starr. He could tell from Abbie's tone that there was more to the story than she was willing to tell with her daughter in the room.

The nurse came in.

"Mrs. Singer. I'm going to give you something for the pain. I'll put it in the IV." She scanned Abigail's bracelet and then injected the medication into the IV.

"You'll be sleepy in just a couple of minutes. I'll be back in to check on you again. You just rest."

Abigail drifted off, while Kris and Starr sat quietly, each absorbed in their own thoughts.

The police returned a little later. Abigail was still in pain, but she was conscious. One of the officers asked, "Mrs. Singer. Could we get information about what happened and about any information you might know about the man who did this?"

"I'll tell you what I can. Starr, do you mind stepping outside? I'd rather you not hear."

"Do you want me to leave too?"

Abigail shook her head slightly. "You can stay if you want to, Kris. It might help."

"Ok, Ma'am. Could you tell us what happened?" Officer Bennett took out a pen and a notebook.

"I will. Kris, some of this is a little embarrassing."

"It's ok, Abbie. Just tell them everything."

"We had just gotten back from dinner. He wanted to stay over. We had retired for the evening. We had just, uh, you know. And I went to the bathroom."

Kris could see her blushing, even through the bruises.

"And then what?"

"I came back to bed. A few minutes later, he wanted me to do something else. I told him I didn't want to, that it would hurt."

"And?"

"He tried to force me."

"Are you referring to sodomy?" Officer Bennett asked, his pen paused over the notebook in which he had been writing.

"Uh, yes."

"Then what did he do?"

"When I said no, he hit me. I resisted, and he hit me several times. He grabbed my arm to turn me over. That's when he broke my arm."

"Did he stop?"

"I started screaming from the pain. That's when he left. Then I called 911."

"Do you know where he might have gone?"

"No. He said he was staying in a hotel downtown, but I don't know which one."

"Is there anything else you can tell us about him? Where he works? Any place where we might be able to find him?"

"I'm embarrassed that I know almost nothing about him. I can't believe I could be so naïve. I just acted like a dumb kid with a crush."

"That's ok, Ma'am. People sometimes make mistakes."

Abigail glanced over at Kris. He could see the shame on her face.

"Thank you, Mrs. Singer. We'll continue to try to find him. If you think of anything else, please call. Here's my card. We'll be back in touch later."

They left, and Starr reentered the room.

"Can they do anything to find him?"

"I don't know. I really wasn't much help, I'm afraid. Kris, I'm sorry you had to hear that."

He walked over to the side of the bed and touched her cheek.

"It's ok, Abbie. I really do understand."

"I can't believe I could be so trusting. Or that I could be so wrong about him." She winced, perhaps from the pain.

Kris agreed. "Sometimes there are things about people that we couldn't possibly know."

Chapter Nineteen

A couple of days later, Abigail was released from the hospital. Kris and Starr picked her up at the hospital. They stopped at the pharmacy and got her prescriptions for pain medication filled.

They took her to her living room and helped her into her leather recliner chair with her feet elevated, Starr heated some soup and made her a grilled cheese sandwich.

"Do you remember making me chicken noodle soup and grilled cheese when I didn't feel good as a little girl?"

"I do. It's funny that you're doing it for me now. Things have a way of turning upside down."

"I'm glad to do it. I think I'll stay here for a couple of days if that's ok."

"I would really appreciate it. I could use the physical help, and I would love the company right now."

"Is there anything I can do for you?"

"That's sweet, Kris. If you don't mind, you could go to the store for me and buy a few things."

"Just give me a list. I'll go right now."

She wrote the list on a pad. "I need milk and bread. And some more soup. Get me some Tylenol. And if you don't mind, a bottle of Chardonnay."

"I'll be right back. Do you need anything, Starr?"

"I don't think so."

He drove to the store, his mind in a whirl. So much had happened recently.

He returned from the store and put away the groceries. "I hope you don't mind, Abigail. I bought you some chocolate chip cookies from the bakery. I know you like them."

"That's sweet. I could sure use a little comfort food right now."

"Thanks, Dad. We're going to be ok. I'm going to try to spoil Mom a little."

"Good. I think she can use it."

When he returned home, Kris called Maureen. He knew that, after their date, she would be expecting a call. He didn't want her to think that he was blowing her off.

"Hi, Maureen. It's Kris."

"It's good to hear from you. I was afraid I had scared you away with that kiss."

"Nothing like that. Just a kind of family emergency." He told her about Abigail's assault.

Maureen sighed. "That is really awful. I actually had a similar encounter once. But in my case, I got away before it got bad. Like you said, sometimes you don't know who people really are."

"I have had occasion to discover that recently." After a pause, Kris said, "I know this might not be a good time to ask, but I was wondering if you wanted to go out again."

"I think that would be lovely. What do you have in mind?"

"I thought we might go to a movie. Or maybe a concert. Whatever you would like."

"A movie would be fun. But I have another idea."

"What is that?"

"How about if we just watch a movie on On Demand? I could make dinner. We could just have a quiet evening together."

"I would love that!"

"How about Friday night? Are you available?"

"I think I could be available. Why don't you come over about seven? We can have a glass of wine and then eat. I don't know what movies are available, but there's always something to watch."

"See you then," Kris said.

Kris called Starr the next day.

"So, how's our patient?"

"She is healing. But she is so ashamed at what happened. She can't let herself off the hook. She just keeps saying, 'I can't believe I could have been so wrong about him'."

Kris responded, "I hope she will get over that. It's hard sometimes to realize that people aren't who you think they are. Sometimes we don't really even know ourselves."

"I know that's right."

"Let me know if I can do anything for you or your mom. By the way, how's your friend Jeffrey?"

"I talked to him yesterday. He seems much better. The rehab really seems to be working. He asked me if you had written any more songs."

"I'm working on some. We have a gig next weekend."

"So how are things otherwise?"

"I actually have a date this Friday."

"Wonderful. With whom?"

"The receptionist at the recording studio. We went to dinner one night. She's cooking for me, and we're going to watch a movie."

"Sounds like fun."

"I think so too. I'll talk to you soon."

Chapter Twenty

Kris bought two bottles of wine to take Friday evening, a chardonnay and a cabernet.

As the door opened, he held out both bottles, "In vino veritas."

Maureen extended her hands to take the bottles. "I'll drink to that. Please come in," she said, leading him in.

As she led him to the living room, he watched her walk. She wore a black skirt, which fit tightly across her bottom, and a white blouse with ruffles down the front.

"Do you want some wine?"

She returned with a glass of red wine for him and a glass of white for herself and sat next to him on the sofa and held up her glass.

"Long life."

He smiled. "And to you."

"How is the recording industry?"

"We are staying busy. The little PR we got from your recording has brought in some more clients."

"It's always nice to be a positive influence. The band has a gig next weekend. I'm trying to write some more songs. Mike and I are even talking about the possibility of an album."

"If the songs are anywhere close to the first one, you will have an amazing album."

"I've got some ideas, I think. More mythology. It could be an interesting concept album."

"I can't wait. If it's ok with you, I'd like to be there at your gig next weekend."

"I'd love to have you there, to have a friendly face in the crowd."

"I better check on dinner. I've got a stir fry on. It has mushrooms, bell peppers, bean sprouts, and edamame in it. I'm serving it over rice. For dessert, I've got some peach halves that I'm putting in the broiler, topped with brown sugar. I hope you like it."

"That sounds great. You could open a restaurant," Kris raised his wine glass.

"I would just rather serve an exclusive clientele," Maureen said with a wink.

He followed her into the kitchen, glasses in hand.

"Would you top off our glasses, please?"

He refilled her glass and handed it to her and then filled his own.

"I think it's done. Would you hand me the plates, and I'll serve dinner?"

She heaped a mound of brown rice on each plate and a scoop of the steaming stir fry vegetables over the rice.

"Here you are, sir."

He sat at the table.

He leaned over his plate and inhaled the steam. "Smells delicious."

"I hope so. I aim to please." Again, that smile.

He picked up the chopsticks and took a taste of the vegetables. "Delicious. You used curry seasoning."

Maureen smiled. "I did. I somehow knew that you would love curry. I hope it's not too spicy."

"It's perfect. I'm afraid my cooking is fairly boring. You use wonderful spices."

"I like to be a little adventurous in my cooking. Who knows, you might learn a thing or too!"

They ate slowly and quietly. Again, he appreciated her willingness to eat in silence without feeling awkward. They finished the main course. Maureen went to the kitchen, and in five minutes brought out the broiled peaches with brown sugar.

"That smells delicious!"

She handed him his plate with a dessert fork. "Would you like to eat dessert in the other room?"

"Yes. That would be lovely."

They returned to the sofa and savored the delicate fruit.

"Don't you love fruit?" Kris took his first bite of the peach.

"I do. I don't care much for desserts. Too sweet usually. But fruit has a delicate flavor that is so honest. The brown sugar makes it a bit more decadent. And again, I like to try new recipes."

"Fruit has a kind of sensuality that you can just savor. And this is wonderful. The brown sugar adds a touch of sweetness and extra flavor."

"True."

After they finished the fruit, Maureen put the dishes in the kitchen. She asked, "Do you want to see what's on the television? I think there are some good movies on."

"Absolutely."

Maureen refilled their glasses. They turned to the on-demand movies. They settled on a romantic comedy.

"I enjoy movies like this. They're predictable, but sometimes that can be a good thing."

Maureen said, "Life gives us surprises sometimes. Predictability's reassuring. But I also like surprises."

"Life gives us both."

As they watched the movie, Maureen moved over on the sofa and settled against Kris. They finished the last sips of wine. Maureen smiled at Kris, her eyes half closed. He bent toward her and tasted the wine on her lips.

"Veritas?" She smiled as she asked.

He kissed her again. She touched his lips with her tongue. He felt his heart quicken as her breath warmed his lips. He held her to him and kissed her more passionately, the passion returned. She turned and pressed her breasts to him. He pulled her tighter, her softness against his chest.

"Let's go to the bedroom." He followed her down the hall. She pulled back the comforter on the bed and sat on the edge.

"Kiss me again."

He sat next to her and pressed his mouth to hers, their breath blending as they kissed.

She stood and took off her blouse, then unbuttoned his shirt. He reached down and unbuttoned her skirt. She stepped out of it. Her silk bra and panties were a sea-foam green with lace.

Kris beheld her as she lay on the bed. Like a fertility goddess. Large breasts, full belly, wide hips. Just perfect. The promise of sensuality. A Celtic goddess, an Earth Mother.

Their lovemaking was passionate. He touched her, his hands knowing how to please. Their breath, their touches, every motion in synch. As he entered, they moved together. He gazed into those stunning green eyes. They reached their peak together. They shuddered together, then collapsed. Kris felt his heart slow. They lay beside one another, the sheet across them.

"Kris, I knew this is how it would be. We're a lot alike. More than you know."

"What do you mean?"

"I know you. I mean I know who you are."

He raised up on one elbow. She lay on her back, her red hair cascading across the pillow.

"What do you mean you know who I am?"

"I know. I know who your father and your mother are."

"How could you know? I don't understand." He raised up on one elbow.

"Because I'm like you. My father was mortal. But my mother is a Celtic fertility goddess." She turned toward him and smiled.

"Oh, my god. I actually thought of you as an Irish deity."

"Exactly. No better expression. Though goddess might be more appropriate."

"When did you know?"

"The instant I saw you." She shrugged her white shoulders.

"How did I not know?"

"With those who are only partly divine, it's harder to see. It takes practice."

"That explains so much. No wonder I felt the passion." He touched her cheek.

"Yes. And of course, I felt it too. I knew that this would happen." They lay quietly for a moment. Then Kris raised up on one elbow.

Kris asked, "I suppose you know about what happened to my ex?"

"I do. That so-called man she was with is no good. I am not one bit surprised. Those creatures are especially good at finding vulnerable victims. And, of course, they usually get away with it."

"Apparently he's going to get away with this. I don't think the police will ever track him down."

"Probably not."

They lay quietly, comprehending the new level of their relationship.

"You know it's amazing. Abbie ends up in a relationship that begins passionately and then becomes violent. Then our relationship goes a totally opposite direction."

"Relationships are always complicated, and especially when you have this additional level of complication thrown in."

"There are certainly lots of stories in mythology that show that."

"Myths are stories, but they are real. And so are fairy tales, by the way."

Kris frowned. "What do you mean?"

"Fairy tales. They're real."

"Oh. I guess that makes sense too."

"It does make sense. I hope you sleep well and that the fairies bring you sweet dreams."

The next morning, they had a sleepy-sensual follow-up. Afterwards, Maureen called from the kitchen, "Do you prefer coffee or tea this morning?"

"Normally I would have coffee, but I'll have whatever you're having."

"I'm having mint green tea."

They sat in the breakfast nook and watched a robin searching under red and yellow leaves for its breakfast. Maureen's purple silk kimono tied at the waist, revealing most of her cleavage. Kris wore a red terrycloth robe that she gave him.

"You do look lovely this morning," Kris said.

She sipped her tea. "Satiation does wonders for one's appearance, don't you think? Or is it the perfect case of beauty being in the eye of the beholder?"

"I'm not sure. Either way I love the view. What are your plans for the day?"

"Not much. I want to do a little cleaning. Then I'm just going to read a little and listen to some music. What about you?"

"I think I'm going to work on a song. Last night gave me an idea. I want to write a love song about Krishna and Radha."

"What a great idea," Maureen said enthusiastically.

"You're the muse for this one, you know."

"I love being that. I hope that I can continue to be a-musing!"

He laughed and leaned across the table to kiss her.

Chapter Twenty-One

Kris prepared breakfast when he got home, made a cup of coffee, and sat in the study to eat and work on the song. He heard the flute as the primary instrument in the song, perhaps the voice of Radha as she danced for Krishna. The sitar would play Krishna's motif, and the two instruments would communicate with one another. He could hear the music in his head and could envision Radha dancing and enticing Krishna to join her. The dance would eventually peak and turn into a passionate love embrace.

Kris worked on the poem all morning. The lyrics were easy. The images filled his head as the god and the milkmaid danced. The ending of the song evoked the Kama Sutra. As he wrote the last stanza, he thought of Maureen and the night before. He read the song and smiled. It's good, he thought to himself.

Krishna and the Milkmaids
Milkmaids
With flowing hair and flashing eyes, they dance.
They guide their lowing herds to verdant fields.
They sway like wafting breezes over grass,
their laughter like the blossoms opening.
The gopis sing, their gentle voices lilt,
chanting and enchanting as they swirl
among the grazing cows they twist and turn,
entrance the gentle god who watches them.
Refrain
The harmonies of joy, the sacred choreography
enchants, entices lovers, opposites entwine,
becoming one, the blissful unity
of Kama Sutra's mystical embrace.
Krishna
He plays his flute, touches the apertures,
the notes drift like the butterflies, touching Radha's ears.
She pauses, turns, and smiles at his gaze.
She swirls, her iridescent dress flashes in the light.

She moves, responding to the notes he plays.
His soft breath whispers to his bamboo flute
that weaves a spell, the choreography
for Radha and the milkmaids' joyful feet.
Refrain
Milkmaids
Encircling her dance, attendants swirl,
their flashing feet and flowing arms entice
her devotee to join her in the dance,
to play his notes, to move to her embrace
within their circle's unifying charm.
The dancers and the dance combine and lift
and drop together on the sacred notes
that fade to stillness on the whispered breeze.
Refrain

He decided to call Pele about the flute part of the song.
"Pele, this is Kris."
"How are you? How are the songs coming along?"
"The songs are good, and so am I. I have a question for you. Can you play pan pipes?"
Pele laughed. "Absolutely. Actually, one of my favorite instruments. I pretty much play any wind instrument. What do you have in mind?"
Kris told him about the song and the instrumentation he had in mind.
"That sounds inspired. I can already hear the music in my head as you describe it. Do you have the lyrics done?"
"I need to work on some of the rhythms and a couple of word choices. I have to be careful at the end. I want the images to be sensual but not too explicit. I just want a balance in the song. The relationship between Krishna and Radha is very important."
Kris could hear his excitement. "It sounds like you're well on your way. I think I'll play around with the ideas and see if I can come up with some music that will fit the images. I'll call you back later and play it for you. We can connect the music and the lyrics later."

"Great. Then we can share with the rest of the band. I need to talk to Sankar about the sitar parts too. If I can give him what you come up with, he can do his melody. Then the rest of the music will fall into place."

Kris called Starr while he was taking a break. "Hi, Dad. How are you?"

"I'm well. I just wanted to check on your mom."

"She's better. Her bruises are healing, and her arm is getting better. The pain is subsiding."

"Have you heard from the police?"

"They came by this morning. They had more questions for mom about the man who assaulted her."

Kris asked, "Have they tracked him down?"

"No. They think he's left town. They actually can't find any record of this guy. They think his name might be an alias. They don't have any record of him, no driver's license, no credit cards, nothing."

"I must say, I'm not surprised. I don't think we'll ever hear from him again. He'll go somewhere else and find another victim."

"I just empathize with mom. She feels so naïve. It will be awhile before she ever trusts anybody again. Speaking of which, how was your date?"

"We had a great time. Maureen is an exceptional woman."

"I can hear from the tone in your voice that it really was a great time. I'm not going to pry. I hope she is someone special for you."

"She may be. Tell your mother I called. Let me know if I can do anything for her or for you."

Kris returned to the song. As he thought of Krishna, he also thought of Shiva and Kali, the two sides of creation and destruction.

The two sides of passion, the positive and negative, the creative and destructive, are everywhere. Maybe music can find a balance. Maybe it's about the real harmony of the universe.

Pele called back.

"Kris, I want you to listen to this. I recorded it. I can hear this as being the voice of Radha, the rhythm of her dance. What do you think?"

Kris put his phone on speaker and sat to listen. The pan pipes were the perfect instrument for the part. Their delicate breathy sound perfectly represented the voice of Radha's passion for her divine lover.

"That's beautiful, Pele. It's like you're inside my head. I can't wait for Sankar to hear it. I think I'll record it from the phone to play for him."

"Better yet, tell him to call me, and we can get together to work on it. It's always better to collaborate when you are face to face. The music has to communicate, and the instruments need to talk to one another."

"Great idea. We need to get the band together to practice before the midtown gig. If you two could have those parts worked out, maybe we could get this song ready to play."

"A world premiere of a new song to go along with the other single. More good PR for the band."

"Let me know how it goes with you and Sankar. Here's the number."

Kris knew that those two would come up with beautiful music. He then called the rest of the band to set up a practice for Monday evening. He thought they might need to practice more than once, especially if they were working on a new number. Their first performance after being on the radio needed to be good. He hoped that people who heard "Twilight of the Gods" on the radio would have expectations of their music. The phone rang. It was Maureen.

She asked to his delight, "Are you busy?"

"No. I worked on the new song a good part of the day. Pele and Sankar are working on their music together to represent Krishna and Radha."

"I can't wait to hear what I inspired. You never know who the music can inspire."

"I think I have some idea."

"We might do our own little Kama Sutra dance." Kris heard a sensual giggle.

"Do you want to come to our rehearsal tomorrow night?"

"I'd love it."

"I think I'll invite Sophia to bring Peter and June."

"Great idea. What time?"

"We're meeting about six. You could come early."

"I usually get off work at five. Could I bring Mr. Burdett?"

"Of course. We would be nowhere without him."

Kris made sure he was ready for the rehearsal. He replenished the beer and wine stock, called for pizza to be delivered, and cleaned up the house. Maureen walked in a little after five. Mr. Burdett followed her.

Kris met them at the door. "Hello, Mr. Burdett. Welcome."

"Please call me John, Kris. I'm excited to hear your band again. Maureen said you have a new song to play tonight."

"It's still in the beginning stages, but I'm hoping that we can have it ready for next weekend."

"Great," Mr. Burdett said.

A few minutes later Kris glanced out the window. The Mercedes stopped in front, and Sophia stepped from the front passenger seat. The driver opened the back door for June and then for Peter. The three walked to Kris and shook hands.

"Welcome to my humble abode. Peter, June, your health seems much better than the last time I saw you."

June bowed slightly. "Thank you, Kris, we are feeling much better. Your music is already helping us."

"If that's true, I hope that tonight will be a booster shot for you."

"Sophia said you have a new song for us."

"It's about Krishna and Radha."

"A song with a family connection?" June asked.

Kris agreed. "Yes. I hope the song is worthy of the subject matter."

The band members arrived and set up to perform. Sankar and Pele were evidently excited.

"Kris, could we begin by playing our two parts?"

I think that would great, Sankar. I've heard some of what Pele was working on. I can't wait to hear your part."

When everyone had settled, Kris told them what he, Sankar, and Pele had been working on during the week.

"As they are playing their parts, I want each of you to think of your own instruments. How can you add to the pan pipes and the sitar to create a beautiful, powerful sound? How can this song represent that powerful love theme between Krishna and Sadha?"

Pele began. His opening was haunting, a breathy call for love and tenderness from the milkmaid Sadha. When he had finished, there was a pause, and then Sankar played. His music echoed Pele's, Krishna answering the call for love. Then the two alternated, playing quietly and slowly at first, then picking up the pace and the volume. The initial tenderness became stronger, more passionate. It crescendoed, then receded, the final strains echoing to silence.

"Well, what do you think?"

Carlos spoke first. "I can hear those Indian drums in the background."

"The bass can go right under those drums. I can hear all of it together."

Jimmy played a riff on the keyboard. "This can be both the flute and the sitar, bringing the two instrumental lines into harmony with one another."

"Perfect, guys. The harmony is exactly what we need. Now let me share the lyrics I have written right now. I can play with the rhythms a bit to make the words fit to the music."

He handed out the words to the song. Everyone read quietly. When Maureen finished, she smiled at Kris, eyebrow raised. And then she winked. He had little doubt of the effect the song had on her. The flush on her face spread down across her bosom.

Peter said, "Kris, this is inspired. June and I are honored that you have written this, at least in part because of our own situation. The words convey the beauty, the harmony, the depth of feeling that the world has lost."

Kris bowed deeply to Peter. "I am the one who is honored. Thank you, Peter."

Mike exclaimed, "This is amazing. I know a little of the story of Krishna, but you capture not just the story, but the real passion, the spiritual depth of the story. Let's get to work. Let's make this song work for the weekend."

By Saturday, they were ready for their performance at the Midtown Music Hall. "Krishna and Radha" was tight, and "Twilight of the Gods" was even better. They had agreed to open with that again, as they had with the Battle of the Bands. It had become their anthem, their theme. Most of their playlist was covers from the Beatles, the Moody Blues, and other with similar sounds. The new song would come close to the end of the set.

The rehearsal was good. Each song they played was tight, and they felt confident about the performance.

When they finished, Sophia said she wanted to talk to the whole group. "I think that you will do well tomorrow night. If you will just leave your instruments here, I'll make sure they are delivered and set up for the performance. That way you won't have to worry about that."

"Just like having roadies to do the work for us. Cool." Mike grinned at Kris.

Sophia continued, "And I will also take care of getting you there tomorrow. Can everyone be here tomorrow by five o'clock?"

They agreed, and the band members departed.

Kris bowed slightly to Sophia. "Thank you. We'll do everything we can tomorrow night to be worthy of your care and attention. We'll try not to sound like a garage-rock band."

"I know you'll do well, Kris. We all believe in you."

Sophia, Peter, and June left in the Mercedes. Kris waved, and June responded with the customary royal wave.

Maureen moved to him. After they kissed, she said, "I think I'm going to go home tonight. I am really tempted to stay, but you need to sleep."

Maureen kissed him again.

"Sweet dreams."

"Dreaming of you."

After Maureen left, Kris sat in his study with a glass of Glenfiddich on the rocks. He knew that Mike would probably be out late. He popped in the CD of "Twilight of the Gods" and closed his eyes. It was good. He could not wait to record the new song. He listened to George Harrison's "Within You Without You," and the Beatles' "Norwegian Wood." Finally, he listened to the song "The Lonely Shepherd." They had practiced it that night for the first time, but everybody knew it. They were probably going to close with it.

He finished his drink and went to bed, hoping to sleep. He dreamed of Maureen dancing with Krishna as George Harrison played sitar.

Kris woke just as the sun was rising. Mike had gone to bed.

Kris lit incense, choosing patchouli, and sat on his cushion. His mind whirled at first, music blending into music. Eventually, it settled and cleared. He only sat for twenty minutes, but he arose refreshed. A good way to start the day.

He made coffee and made a stir fry with rice for breakfast. He sliced mushrooms and chopped a bell pepper and seasoned it with curry and garlic. He put another small skillet on a burner and poured coconut oil in it. He sliced a banana and chopped an apple and added the fruit to the sizzling oil. When it had browned, he removed it from the stove and poured the fruit onto a plate and sprinkled cinnamon and nutmeg over it. The aroma as it cooked reminded him of Krishna and Radha as they danced. Breakfast had just become a sensual experience.

At 10:00 a rental truck pulled up. Two young men knocked on the door. "We were told to pick up some musical instruments to take to the Midtown Music Hall."

Kris gestured, "Back here."

They followed him. "Just be careful with them," Kris warned.

One of them said. "We're musicians. We know."

They carried each item with great care, probably more than the owners would have.

When they had loaded the last guitar case on the truck, one of the movers turned to Kris. "We heard your band has a great sound. We'll be there tonight. Have a good day."

"Thank you. I hope you enjoy tonight."

The day passed slowly. Kris attempted to read, tried to watch television, but mostly he sat and stared at the sun on the trees.

The members of the band arrived early. Maureen arrived a little later. She was dressed conservatively, jeans and a modest top. She gave Kris's hand a squeeze and kissed him on the cheek.

The musicians chattered excitedly. Jimmy asked, "Kris, is she sending a bus for us?"

"I don't know. I thought maybe taxis, but a bus would make more sense. Whatever it is, it will get us there. We can trust Sophia."

At five minutes to five, Mike exclaimed, "Oh. My. God!"

They ran to the window. Three black stretch limousines stopped in front of the house.

"Unbelievable!" Jimmy exclaimed, "I feel like I'm on the set of *The Godfather*."

The drivers stepped out and opened the passenger doors.

"Well, are we ready?"

They exclaimed, "Oh yeah! Let's do this!"

"Mike, Pele, and Jimmy, why don't you get in the first car. Then Frank, Carlos, and Sankar. Maureen and I will bring up the rear."

Trying not to be over-eager, they walked to their transportation, wondering how the evening could top this.

Chapter Twenty-Two

Sophia, Barney and Peter and June were waiting outside the concert hall as the limos arrived. As the drivers opened the doors, the passengers emerged, half expecting red carpets and throngs of adoring fans.

Sophia stepped forward as Kris and Maureen climbed out of the limo. "Kris, your instruments arrived. They have been set up as you usually do. Everybody just needs to make sure that the setup is correct. You probably need to talk to the tech crew to be sure that the lights and sound are going to be right."

Kris walked through the front door, feeling like royalty. He strolled down the aisle toward the stage, The place seemed huge.

On the stage the instruments were where they should have been. The band members picked them up and held them, gazing out across the empty seats. For a moment, no one spoke. It was an important moment for all of them.

Kris talked to the sound and light people. He made sure that the lighting would be right for the opening number. He also made sure they understood that Sankar would be sitting on a cushion in front, so the lighting and microphone had to be adjusted for that.

The doors opened at 7:30. Kris glanced out from behind the curtain, hoping not to see a mostly empty house. Finally, at 7:45 he worked up the courage.

My god! The place is filling up! There are still quite a few empty seats. But it's going to be a respectable house.

The band gathered in a circle at 7:50. Sophia, Peter, and June stood to one side. Kris saw Barney standing behind them.

"Ok, guys. This is it. We are ready for this. There are people out there who are ready to hear us. They want to hear our music. Remember, the music is the only thing that matters. As long as we are in harmony, and the music is in harmony, everything else falls into place. Are we ready?"

A collective "Yes!" from everyone.

Sankar went out and sat on his cushion, picking up his sitar. Pele picked up his trumpet. The others took their places behind the curtain. Mike put his guitar strap over his shoulders, and Frank touched the strings of his bass, moving up and down the guitar neck, eyes closed for a moment. Jimmy stood at the keyboard. The stage went dark. They heard the crowd fall silent.

The announcer's voice, "Ladies and Gentlemen. Gotterdammerung!"

As Pele played the opening notes to "Twilight of the Gods," the spotlight hit him. The audience applauded. Then Sankar answered the trumpet music on his sitar. The second spot light. Even more applause. And then it began.

Kris could not believe the response to the first song. The crowd applauded, cheered, stomped. They loved it. As he was singing the song he had written, he squinted to get an idea of the size of the crowd. The place was nearly packed. The band members smiled at one another as they played.

From then on, song after song, all of the covers they had practiced. Sankar received huge applause for "Within You, Without You." Kris heard some people singing along to "Norwegian Wood," which surprised him.

Each song received more applause. Kris felt himself buoyed up by the audience response. The waves of applause swept across him like a tidal wave, carrying him along. He remembered the Battle of the Bands where all of this had started. The feelings of passion, the energy from the crowd. That had been amazing at the time. But it was nothing compared to this. This was raw passion, almost lust. But above it, pervading through it was a more sublime feeling. More spiritual somehow. Each song raised the level of feelings.

They finally reached the moment for "Krishna and Radha."

"I hope you enjoy this next song. It's important to us. It's a kind of a spiritual love song about a Hindu god, Krishna, and a milkmaid named Radha. Their relationship is very important in Hinduism, and their love represents an ideal that transcends just the religion. It's about the kind of love that brings people together. The kind of love that can change the world."

Pele put down his trumpet and picked up the pan pipes. The high, breathy notes drifted out across the audience. They were suddenly quiet, mesmerized by the sound. Then Sankar's sitar responded, Krishna singing to the milkmaid who danced before

Twilight of the Gods

him. Pele went over to stand next to Sankar, and their instruments communicated as they played.

Kris began to sing. He could see people in the front row moving to the music, like lotus blossoms drifting before the breeze. Their faces were turned up to him, eyes closed, smiling. The music and his voice flowed outward across the many faces. The music was having the effect they needed.

Then on impulse he blinked twice. The result was so unbelievable that he almost stopped singing. Among the people in the crowd, he saw figures in togas holding elaborate chalices. Among them he saw Peter, June, Sophia, and Barney in their Olympian aspects. Dancing around them were bevies of maidens festooned with garlands of flowers, and fauns playing pipes like Pele's. One group of young women, dressed in saris, danced in a circle around a young man also in Indian clothing. He danced in turn with each of them, touching each as he smiled, his face familiar to Kris.

In another section Kris recognized Egyptian clothing, their dance more formal, more ritualistic. At the center of the dance were a man and a woman. Kris recognized them by their dress. The woman wore a headdress that resembled the crescent moon. The man's headdress had two ram's horns, one on either side. Isis and Osiris, another great love story from mythology. Other groups were sprinkled through the crowd. Kris recognized Nordic gods and goddesses, many dressed for battle. One group of warrior women bowed to him. Undoubtedly, they had recognized the allusion in the opening number. Many figures he did not recognize, their clothing unfamiliar. He saw one female figure in front, one breast exposed, her dress familiar to him: Astarte, the fertility goddess who had received a disapproving stare from June.

The song drew to a close. Kris sang the final words, the words about love everlasting, love beyond the flesh and beyond life into eternity. The song about Krishna and his love for the lovely milkmaid. The final notes of the pan pipe and the sitar blended. The harmony drifted to silence across the audience. They stood for a moment, the dancers paused like statues, hypnotized by the lyrics, the melody, the effect of the music. Kris stood before them, microphone raised to his mouth, not sure how to respond to the silence, the stillness.

And then the audience erupted. Wave upon wave of applause and cheers. The divine faces in the crowd regarded him, knowing that he saw them, knowing that he knew. Many bowed to him, a slight bending of the neck. He bowed back. The rest of the band bowed to the thunderous response to the song. The crowd quieted.

"Thank you. We are honored by your applause. This song is an instrumental, and you may recognize it. It's called 'The Lonely Shepherd.' It features our horn player, playing once again the pan flute. Pele, if you please."

Pele began the opening melody, picked up by the rest of the band members. While Pele played the pipes, Jimmy played the trumpet part, reminding him of his high school band days.

The final notes played. The audience began its response to the music once again. Kris closed his eyes and felt the waves of emotion, the passions that the music had evoked. As a finale, they played the opening to "Twilight of the Gods," Sankar playing the opening bars, followed this time by Pele's trumpet. Those notes faded, leaving the crowd satiated with emotion. The curtain dropped. Kris exhaled and smiled.

The musicians laughed, and Maureen hugged and kissed Kris. He knew he was soaking wet from the performance.

The musicians shook hands, hugged. They were complete, a unit. They had shared an event that seemed nearly incomprehensible. Maureen stood behind Kris with a hand on his shoulder.

Sophia walked onto stage. Kris could see Peter, June, and Barney standing just offstage. With Sophia walked a man in a suit, slightly out of place at a concert.

"Kris, I want you to meet someone. Kris Singer, this is Homer Apollonius."

"Hello, Sir," Kris said.

"I'm happy to make your acquaintance. I enjoyed the performance. You have a unique sound. I represent a recording company, Pantheon Records. We would like to talk to your band about a recording contract."

Twilight of the Gods

Kris stared in disbelief. He mumbled, "That is wonderful!" He shook the man's again, trying not to appear too excited.

Before they left the stage, Gotterdammerung had a recording contract. They talked about their ideas for new music, and Kris talked about some of the other songs he had in mind. The executive for Pantheon seemed impressed with the idea of a concept album.

Later, when everyone went home, Kris sat in a quiet house. He had told everyone that he would talk to them tomorrow. Tomorrow would begin a new chapter in their lives.

It's all about the music. All religions have music at the center. The Twilight of the Gods. There is no twilight, no ending. Every twilight is followed by a new dawn, the beginning of a new day.

Chapter Twenty-Three

The CD, entitled *Twilight of the Gods*, was scheduled for release on Valentine's Day. Their performances at various venues had received a good bit of attention from the press.

Mike called to Kris one morning. Kris had just finished his meditation and was drinking his coffee as Mike was watching television.

"Kris, have you seen the news this morning?"

What's up?"

"I just happened to be flipping through the channels and saw that conservative news channel talking about our music."

Kris put down his coffee. "No kidding! That's great."

"Not necessarily. Some evangelical has started a campaign against us. He's calling our music 'the Devil's music.'"

Kris sighed. "I guess I should have seen that coming. I knew we were going to push some buttons. I just hoped it wouldn't be a big deal."

"So now what do we do?"

"I don't know. Just hope that the publicity doesn't hurt us. Someone said that there's no such thing as bad publicity. Other bands have had controversies, more than I can think of. At least we're getting reactions. Better than being ignored, I guess. I can imagine what the reaction at our release party will be. Probably a circus."

Kris was correct about the response to the release party. Sophia and the executives from Pantheon had wanted to make a splash with the party, so they had booked a large nightclub and invited many celebrities, the media, and political figures to the party. They spared no expense, wanting to make it one of the events of the year. It was to be a black-tie affair, with fancy hors d'oeuvres, an open bar, and champagne for a toast. The highlight of the evening would be the band playing some numbers from the album, culminating with the CD's title cut, "Twilight of the Gods."

That evening the band members dressed up. Kris wore a tuxedo, which felt odd, but Sophia had insisted.

Maureen wore a dark green dress, more conservative than her normal dress, but still not exactly demure. The bodice was not décolleté, and the hem line was to the middle of her knee.

Starr dressed in a simple cotton dress with an empire bodice that would have not been out of place at Woodstock. She had a garland of yellow flowers on her head.

The other musicians were less formally dressed. As they stood in the living room waiting, Mike and Frank tugged at their collars, loosening their neck ties. Carlos shrugged his shoulders.

"I don't know if I can play drums wearing this monkey suit, man."

"When we get up there to play, we can shed some of this stuff. When we first get there and when we first go in, hopefully the press will be there to take pictures."

Mike tugged at his collar once more. "I can handle it for that long, I guess."

"I know you can. Guys, I need to talk to you about tonight before we go. Take a seat."

They sat down, and Kris stood in the middle of the room.

"We know there has been some controversy about our music."

"What's with that, man?" Carlos asked, his hands raised.

"As you know, some people think our music is against their religions." Kris explained.

"So, do you think there will be trouble tonight?" Mike turned to Kris, his eyebrows raised.

"I hope not. But if there is, we need to be prepared. I've heard that there may be some protestors there tonight. And it's important that we react properly. Let's not give the negative press any more ammunition."

"How do we react?" Mike asked.

Sophia stood and faced Mike, who had asked that question. "The best way to react is probably not to react. Almost any other response will be the wrong response. Just walk through the crowd and keep focused."

Jimmy raised his hand. "Do you think there will be any violence?"

Sophia, her face serious, answered, "I hope not. We have our security. And of course, the police will be there too in case it gets out of hand."

Kris moved up to stand next to Sophia. "Let's just focus on what we are doing tonight and why. Keep your mind on the music. That's what all of this is about. Right? The limos are here. Let's get in a circle here and focus our energy."

They gathered around and placed their hands one on top of the other. For a moment, they were silent.

Kris asked. "Who are we?"

"Gotterdammerung!" They shouted as their hands rose upward.

"Let's go. Twilight of the gods. Let's enjoy tonight."

They paraded out to the black limousines that awaited. Kris, Starr, Maureen, and Sophia got into the lead car. The others rode behind them, two to a car.

As the cars left the curb and headed to the club, Kris turned to Sophia.

"I really hope we're not heading for trouble"

"I don't know, Kris. But you know the kind of violence that religious extremism can provoke."

Kris agreed. "The human race certainly has a history of that! Violence provoked by religion."

"One of the sad ironies of the human race." Sophia shook her head, the tiara moving slightly.

"I was a little surprised that our music would evoke this kind of response. We're just a band. And not a famous band either."

"Of course, the message of your songs is meant to touch people." Maureen shrugged.

"And sometimes people don't really want to be touched. Especially when it is their beliefs that are being touched." Her startling gray eyes flashed.

Maureen looked puzzled, "I don't understand why they are so adamant about their beliefs. We aren't challenging them. Why are they so insistent that our beliefs are evil?"

Sophia shrugged her shoulders. "Human beings can be such odd creatures. So often they are so short-sighted that they don't see the possibility of more than one correct perspective on any issue."

"I know," Kris agreed. "In order for me to be right, everyone else has to be wrong."

"The universe is just not one-dimensional. It reminds me of the believers of various minor cults who were sure that the earth was flat." Maureen shook her head and smiled.

Kris asserted, "We live in a world of modern science, of relativity, quantum mechanics, string theory, so many other scientific theories. How can religious beliefs be so out of step with everything else?"

Sophia responded, "That's a good question, Kris. The problem is that so many religions accept one idea, one text, one truth as the last word. Period. Then they stop thinking. That last word becomes Word, with a capital. And then that's it."

"So, they are blind to everything else?" Kris wondered.

"Apparently. Monotheistic beliefs forget that they are the culmination of a long history of spiritual growth. They can only see back along the path so far."

"I always heard that hindsight was 20/20." Kris raised an eyebrow.

Sophia paused, then explained, "Actually, hindsight tends to be myopic. People only see back so far. They can't see over the horizon, so they assume that nothing else exists in their past. Spiritual myopia can be worse than blindness."

The limo slowed. "Well, we're here, Kris. And it's a mess out there. I hope the other guys are ready for this."

A crowd awaited them, a roar erupting as the limos stopped. "There they are!"

At least a hundred waited, most carrying signs. As the cars stopped, the crowd enfolded them. Sophia reached over and touched Kris's shoulder.

Kris saw three vans from the three local network television affiliates. And then he saw the cable news channel van. "For better or worse, we're going to make the news." He glanced at Sophia.

"I think it will be for the better. With any luck, this will make national news. These protestors may end up being the band's best friends!"

Kris stared across the crowd of sign-carrying protesters. Most were younger people, neatly dressed and well groomed. Kris noticed a couple of men with long hair and beards, decidedly like Old-Testament prophets. Despite the differences in appearances, the protesters all had one trait in common, their signs. He could read messages "The Devil's music." "One God, one belief, One Way." "Your way is the way to Hell."

They waved their signs, shouting the slogans scrawled on their signs. Moving among them were television cameras and reporters putting their microphones in people's faces.

"Well, are you ready to face the rabid masses, Kris?" Sophia touched his shoulder.

"I think so. I just hope no one hits me."

The driver opened the door for Sophia first, and then for Maureen and Kris. The protesters moved just enough for the doors to open and for Sophia and Kris to exit the limo. They were close enough that Kris could smell their breath and body odors. The camera crews pushed through the crowd. Sophia stepped to the front and to the microphones. "What is your reaction to the crowd tonight? How do you react to the comments about the band's music?"

Sophia smiled at the cameras. Kris knew how startling that smile could be.

"We are thrilled at the response and at the crowd that has showed up here tonight. We're confident that once people listen to our music they will understand the message of love and understanding."

As the two imposing men moved through the crowd, the protesters continued to shout, but they moved to either side. Kris thought of Moses in the book of Exodus, parting the Red Sea.

Kris, Sophia, and the other band members walked toward the door untouched.

As they stepped inside the front door, they breathed a collective sigh of relief.

"I don't think that any of them wanted to face those two guys," Kris said, pointing to the burly figures ahead of them.

They entered the doors of the club, and the crowd closed behind them, as they walked to the ballroom to set up for the event. The ambiance was impressive, as Kris knew it would be. The tables covered with white table cloths and decorated with gold statuettes of gods from various cultures made a definite statement about the theme for the evening. Kris saw images of Greek figures (including a statue of Athena that was amusingly incorrect), Egyptian gods, a statue of the Hindu god Ganesh with his elephant head, and other images of divinity.

"The table decorations are stunning, don't you think?"

He glanced at Sophia. She smiled. "Divine, aren't they?"

He grinned.

The crowd were dressed in formal attire, for the most part. Around the edges were some less well-dressed people. Kris recognized them as the musicians and other figures in the industry. A couple of them raised goblets of champagne.

The band members moved to one side of the crowd and took three of the tables, in awe at the attention.

"Man, Kris, isn't this awesome?"

"Yes, Jimmy. A long way from where any of us started."

Mike proclaimed, "You got that right! I went from being basically homeless to this. I'd say music has already transformed my life."

Kris saw the television cameras filming the crowd, focusing on the local celebrities. He spied one or two politicians talking to reporters. He turned to speak to Sophia, but her chair was empty. She stood with the cable-news reporter, talking and smiling. She gestured in the direction of the band, and the camera followed her gesture. Kris had the presence of mind to raise his goblet.

After another glass of delightful champagne and some of the finger food, a man wearing headphones approached Kris.

"Mr. Singer. Would you and the rest of the band follow me? We need to get ready for your performance."

"I'll see you after the performance," He said, kissing Maureen on the cheek.

They walked to one end of the ballroom where a curtain had been erected. Behind the curtain was a raised stage. Their instruments and the sound system were already in place.

"We already did a sound check, and your instruments are in tune. We thought that might be best."

Kris spoke to the tech person. "Thank you. We do appreciate it."

Sankar sat on the cushion in the front. "This is so comfortable. I would like to take it home for my meditation area!" He picked up his sitar and touched a couple of notes and then strummed a chord.

"Mr. Singer, are you ready? We're about to pull back the curtain."

Kris turned back to the musicians, "Ok, guys. This is it. Ragnaroc!"

They all raised their fists in salute.

The MC announced to the audience, "Ladies and gentlemen, the reason for tonight's festivities. Gotterdammerung!"

The curtains drew away on either side, and Kris saw the crowd moved to the edge of the stage, applauding. Many raised their goblets and drank to the band.

"Thank you for being here. We hope you enjoy the music and that you like the CD. This has been an amazing journey thus far, and we hope that the quest for peace and understanding through music continues." The crowd applauded Kris's words.

Kris blinked twice. As with their last gig, he saw numerous groups representing various cultures and religions. So many costumes. The Egyptians, the Hindu gods, the Nordic warrior gods, Greek and Roman deities a microcosm of human civilizations cheering and applauding. The effect was overwhelming, like an image all the gods from all the religions.

They started with two Beatles songs, "Norwegian Wood" and "Within You, Without You." The audience recognized the two songs and applauded when each began. Sankar's sitar solos received special attention. He smiled broadly at the attention.

They then played a couple of Moody Blues songs, including "Nights in White Satin" and "Legend of the Mind." The audience loved the flute solos, and Pele waved to their response.

Finally, they played Kris's song about Krishna and the Gopis, the milk maids. The sitar solos flowed through the music, and Kris saw the people in the front swaying slightly, their eyes closed. The band members swayed as they played, their eyes closed as well, mesmerized by the sensual spell of music. At the end, Kris introduced Sankar, followed by the other members. The audience applauded enthusiastically for each as they were introduced.

"For our closing number, we are going to play the CD's title cut, 'Twilight of the Gods.' The title, incidentally, is a translation of our band name Gotterdammerung. We hope you enjoy it."

Pele began, his trumpet playing the opening notes of Wagner's "Ride of the Valkyrie." The sitar came in behind that, and the other instruments surrounded those sounds, blending the sounds of East and West in harmony. Kris began to sing, the song of Ragnaroc, the myth of destruction and creation.

The audience stood transfixed. Kris felt the tension as he sang, drifting on the harmony of the instruments. The audience felt the same uplifting effect, as the room seemed in slow motion. He sang the last refrain of the song, and the final notes of the sitar drifted to silence. For a moment, the room was silent. Kris stood with the microphone still at his lips, unsure of how to react.

Then the audience erupted in wild applause and cheering. The uproar continued as the band members bowed, their faces betraying their amazement. As the applause quieted, Kris turned to the band.

"Ok, guys. 'My Sweet Lord'."

They played the George Harrison song, a hymn to all the gods. As Mike played George Harrison's guitar solos, Sankar played underneath with the sitar. The audience swayed to the music and song along with the chorus of "Hare Krishna, Hare Rama." The music united the audience and the musicians as they all swayed together and sang together.

Another eruption of applause ended the experience. As the musicians stood together and talked, Kris felt the energy. The members of the audience stood in groups drinking one last glass of champagne and laughing. The television cameras panned the room, and Kris saw the reporters doing their closing segments on the evening.

"A great evening, don't you think?" Sophia walked up on stage with Maureen beside her.

"That was the most amazing experience of my life." Kris said as he kissed Maureen, her face beaming. "I can't wait to see how this gets covered on the news. I hope the demonstrations don't get too much coverage. I'd hate to see it turned into a circus."

Sophia agreed. "But the controversy may have been what brought the cameras. So, it could end up being a good thing."

Maureen patted his hand. "You just need to trust the music."

"You're probably right. Maybe it will help sell some CD's. People will want to know what all the fuss is about."

"And of course, Kris, the important thing here is for people to listen to music. The world needs healing." Sophia's face was serious.

"I never forget that. Selling CD's and getting famous would be fun. But the other is most important. The fame just serves that purpose."

"Are we ready to go?" Everyone had packed their instruments, and they were waiting for a signal.

"Yes. Where do we want to go? Let's celebrate," Kris suggested.

Mike said, "How about Sam's bar? That seems appropriate."

"Good idea, Mike. Absolutely. This all started there, so we need to go there to celebrate. I'll see everybody there." Kris walked to the awaiting limo, Sophia on one arm and Maureen on the other. Starr walked behind them.

They arrived at the bar a half hour later. Sam was thrilled to see them.

"How'd it go?" Sam asked. "I know you had to knock them dead. Did you?"

"It was amazing, Sam. We need to turn on the news. The television stations were all there, including cable news." He glanced at the clock. "It's almost 11. Let's see if it's on this soon."

Sam turned on the television to the ABC station. After the headline story about political scandal, the anchor began coverage of the night's event. "And tonight, a local band called Gotterdammerung became the center of controversy with the debut of their new CD "Twilight of the Gods."

Everyone cheered. "Man, we're famous. Our band name was just on the news!" Mike raised his glass.

The picture shifted to the protestors and a close-up of Kris and Maureen emerging from the limo. Then a shift to Sophia talking to the reporter.

Twilight of the Gods

Maureen turned to Sophia as they watched. "You are a natural in front of the camera.!"

"Thank you, Maureen."

The news story then shifted to the band's performance. The camera showed them playing the CD's title cut, followed by the audience's thunderous response.

The reporter on the scene, staring into the camera, said, "A local band might be on its way to stardom. Despite the controversy and the protest, their music may make a difference on the music scene. The world may be a better place because of their music.!"

"Yes!" Kris stood up and held his glass high.

"Gentlemen. Ladies. I salute you. Ragnaroc!"

They all raised their glasses and toasted "Gotterdammerung!"

Kris sat down. "Well, Maureen, Starr, Sophia. It has been a memorable night."

Maureen agreed. "I think that things will never be the same after this. Get ready."

"Maureen's right. We are on the road to change." Sophia smiled, her gray eyes pensive.

Chapter Twenty-Four

Kris flipped to the news early the next morning, eager to see if the news coverage continued from last night. He flipped to the local ABC channel first, then the other network news coverage. All of the local channels had similar coverage of the night before. Most of the coverage focused on the demonstrators, which Kris expected. Each story, however, had a brief clip of the band playing. The CBS story included a close-up of Sankar playing his sitar, a serene smile on his face as he played his opening section to "Twilight of the Gods."

Kris smiled as he sipped his coffee.

Not bad. The demonstrators did us a favor. I guess the old saying that there is no such thing as bad publicity is true.

Kris put the CD in and turned up the volume as he did the morning dishes and straightened out the study. He had enough distance from the music now that he could be more critical.

As he was dressing, the phone rang. It was a publicist from Pantheon. "Mr. Singer? Have you seen the morning news?"

"I have, Kris said, "It's a little surreal to hear my name mentioned and to see the band."

"Have you watched the cable news coverage?"

"I haven't. I wasn't sure that the national news would find it worthy."

"Well, since the cable news is based here, they did actually cover it. And of course, that went national."

"Did they focus on the demonstration?"

"They did a little, but the reporter commented on the new kind of music you play. She apparently has followed the local stories, because she used the term 'Ragna Rock' that someone used when you won that competition."

"That's great! I hope we get more coverage like that. Speaking of that, do you know where we are playing next?"

"I know that you have one gig set up in a couple of weeks. If your CD starts selling, we may be able to think beyond local performances. I'll let you know if we get any nibbles."

"Thank you for calling. Keep us informed. Maybe our CD will make us all some money."

"That's why we are in business. Have a good day."

Kris made a second cup of coffee and turned on the cable news. In a few minutes, the story about the concert popped up. The opening of the story covered the marchers with their signs; the coverage moved inside and showed a couple of clips, one similar to the network coverage, but then a shot of the crowd swaying to the music as they played "My Sweet Lord."

With microphone in hand the reporter spoke into the camera.

"Baby-boomers and other music enthusiasts will remember this song that George Harrison made famous. The influence of Indian music and culture followed the Beatles when they returned from India. The term used for that kind of music was Raga Rock. But this new band, Gotterdammerung, is calling their music Ragna-Rock after the Nordic term for the end of the world. Viewers might want to watch this new talent. We may see the beginnings of a new movement. This is Joan Jackson, CBN Headline News."

"Wow! Just wow!" Kris sat back and shook his head. He grabbed the phone and called Maureen at work. Before she could say hello, he asked, "Have you seen the news?"

"Hi, Kris. You bet we have. It's all anybody is talking about. And to think that the demo you made was done right here!"

"I know. And if it weren't for that, I wouldn't have met you."

"I feel the same way. I hope it means your CD sells."

"I do to. I just talked to a publicist from Pantheon, and they seem pretty psyched about the coverage."

"They should be. They can make some money off this album. And the coverage may mean more business for them too."

"I'll just be happy to sell some CD's and to make a little money."

Maureen laughed. "I think you are going to do better than that."

"I don't want to get my hopes up too much."

"You want to come over after work and have a glass of wine?"

"Sure. Let me know if you hear any more news about last night."

"I will. Love ya. Bye"

The CD sales took off the next week. The cable news coverage got the attention of music lovers, and the coverage jumped over to the entertainment channels on television. Kris could barely keep up with the phone calls. People from Pantheon called him daily, and the other members of the band were like children at Christmas. A local television morning show host called Kris to set up an interview, and the cable news did a follow-up story on the band's newfound success; the images of the debut party and protests was interspersed with a video clip that someone had made of their battle of the bands concert. Kris felt at the center of a whirlwind.

Two weeks after the band's debut, Kris had settled into a new routine. Maureen helped him with correspondence, and he answered phone calls as promptly as he could. On Friday night, she came over to his house, and they ate a quiet meal. They were both exhausted from the activities of publicity.

"Are you as tired as I am?" Maureen sat on the sofa, wine glass in hand and head back.

"I don't think that I have ever been more tired. This is exciting. I don't know how people who are really famous do all of this."

"They don't. They have staff. That's why people joke when they say 'I'll have my people call your people'."

"I guess that's what it takes." Her red hair spread across the sofa back, her tired expression an image of sensual exhaustion.

"Do you want to go to bed?"

"I do. I may be too tired to walk there. Could you just teleport me?"

"I'd carry you like Rhett Butler if I weren't so exhausted myself."

"Let's just lean on each other and maybe we can make it."

They collapsed on the bed and were instantly asleep.

The phone woke them. Kris jolted awake. The clock said 4:05. His first thought was "Who died?"

He mumbled into the phone. "Hello?"

"Mr. Singer?" the voice asked on the other end.

"Yeah." Kris said.

"This is John Burdett at Grace Notes. Is Maureen there?"

"One moment. Maureen, it's John."

Kris handed her the phone, and she held it to her ear, eyes still closed. "Hello?" she mumbled.

"Maureen, it's John. I'm sorry to wake you. Listen, someone tried to burn our office last night. The police are here, and I would appreciate if the two of you would come down here as quickly as you can."

In shock, Maureen turned to Kris, "Kris, someone just tried to burn down our building!"

She hit the speaker button on the phone so Kris could hear as John continued, "The police have him in custody. He was carrying a sign from the demonstration. He said something about hellfire and getting rid of the Antichrist."

"So, one of those crazy-eyed people we saw in the crowd?"

"Apparently."

"We'll be there as quick as we can," Kris said, kicking off the covers.

John said, "I'm sure the police will want to talk to you."

Maureen, eyes suddenly wide open, said, "That's crazy!"

"I know. People are nuts."

"I guess we need to get going," Maureen said.

"I'll make coffee while you get ready," Kris said. Heading to the kitchen, while Maureen stumbled to the bathroom.

"I just need to brush my hair a little. I must look a fright."

"You're fine. But do what you need."

He returned in five minutes with coffee, and they drove to the Grace Notes studio. When they arrived, police and firemen were everywhere. Red and blue lights flashed like a scene from a television crime drama.

John stood on the sidewalk, frantic and confused as they walked up to him.

John introduced the officer next to him, "Chief Johnson, this is Kris Singer and my administrative assistant Maureen O'Kelley."

"I'm sorry you had to get up so early. This is a mess, but it could be a lot worse. The guy in the back seat of the patrol car over there apparently tried to set the building on fire. Fortunately, he didn't have a very good throwing arm. He tried to throw a Molotov cocktail through the window, but it just hit the brick below. It just burned the front of the building a little."

Kris saw glass shattered on the sidewalk and a black fan-shaped pattern that scorched the brick below the plate-glass window.

"Wow! I can't believe he was still here when you arrived."

"Someone was driving by on his way to work and saw him throw the bottle. The guy called 911, and when the fire department arrived, the arsonist was standing here with his sign, shouting. Do you recognize him?"

Kris and Maureen walked over to the patrol car and peered in the window. The man glared at them. His unkempt hair and scraggly beard framed his belligerent face.

"I saw him at the demonstration, like an Old Testament prophet. I don't know what book of the Bible he's from. The Book of Crazy, I guess."

Chief Johnson said, "I guess that's all we need you folks for right now. We're going to take him in and book him. I'm sure they'll do a psych eval on him. I can't imagine they'll find him sane."

John apologized, "I'm sorry you had to get up so early."

Maureen shrugged her eyes sleepy. "I'm just glad it wasn't more serious."

John answered, "Me too. You can go back home if you want. I can handle this right now."

"Ok. Call me later and let me know what's going on."

"I will. I'll just need to get someone to clean up the mess once the police and firemen are done here."

He turned to Kris. "Thanks for coming, Kris. I can't believe that people are reacting to your music this way."

"People just don't like to think their beliefs or ideas are threatened."

"I hope this isn't the beginning of a real mess."

"Me too. Talk to you later."

They drove back home quietly, Maureen drifting to sleep almost instantly. When they arrived, Kris woke her. She walked in the house and headed back to bed.

"You go ahead. I'm going to have another cup of coffee and watch the news. I'm sure the fire will be covered."

Twilight of the Gods

The fire was the lead story. As Kris turned on the television, the blond reporter was interviewing Chief Johnson.

"Chief Johnson, do you know what happened here?"

"Apparently, the suspect threw a Molotov cocktail at this building. Fortunately, he missed the window. He was still at the scene when we arrived."

"Do you have a motive?" The reporter asked.

"From his comments, he was upset at a demo that a band made at this studio."

"Do you know the name of the band?"

"Yes. They're called Gotterdammerung. It means Twilight of the Gods. They just released their first CD."

"Is this related to the story that we covered with a protest related to that band?"

Chief Johnson shrugged. "Apparently, the suspect was at that protest as well. A band member identified him."

The camera panned the scene as the firemen were preparing to leave. Kris saw a glimpse of the patrol car, the man still glaring from the back window.

He turned off the television and sat quietly, sipping his coffee and meditating on the situation.

Maureen got up a couple of hours later. She wandered into the living room, rubbing her eyes.

"Hey, Babe. Did you get your nap out?"

"I feel better. But that was not a good way to be wakened."

"It was on the news, of course."

"Did they say anything new?"

"No. Just what we had already heard. There might be some more on the evening news."

"It still just seems surreal. And over some songs."

"I know. But people take music seriously. And especially the music we're doing. It challenges their beliefs. People don't like that."

"I can see that is true. I just hope that this is not the beginning of something."

"We just have to wait and see. But we can't stop now. It's too important."

Maureen made another cup of coffee and sat in the kitchen with it as Kris started breakfast. At 9:00 the phone rang. It was Sophia.

"Kris, I guess you know the news."

"John called us at 4. We went down there. Then I saw the news coverage."

"I think this might actually be a good thing in the long run. The music is getting people's attention. They're listening. Now we just need to guide their thinking."

"I just hope people don't show up with guns next time."

"I know," Sophia said. "But we knew this idea was going to be controversial. This might just give us more publicity. It could help CD sales which means even more people will be listening."

"I hope the success doesn't come at too high a cost."

"I understand, but failure would be an even greater cost. I talked to Peter, and he agrees."

"I guess I'm just starting to really understand how important this project is," Kris said.

"Top priority importance, Kris. Don't forget that. It probably sounds exaggerated, but the human race could be depending on what we're doing. We need people to wake up, to believe again. And not just on the level of protesting or throwing bombs. The music can wake them up. That may be what this is. But people are sometimes cranky when you wake them up."

"I don't mind the protests, but I would prefer not to have any more bombs."

"I'm going to let you go. Call me if anything else happens. If I hear anything, I'll call you." Sophia hung up.

Kris said, "I think Sophia is worried. But she says we need to do what we have been doing."

The story was on the news for a few more days, with follow-up stories on the bomber, his background, his mental state, and the progress of the investigation. One television channel included interviews with people's reactions. Most of the comments expressed shock at the bomber's actions. One young man, evidently a college student, expressed the general sentiment, "Just because he doesn't like someone's music doesn't mean he can

144

bomb a recording studio. I don't like country music, but I'm not going to kill someone. I'll just change the radio station."

In the interests of fairness, the reporter also included a person who represented the other side of the issue. Kris recognized the man as one of the protesters from the street that night before the party. He had been carrying a sign with a religious message.

"We don't approve of their anti-God message. We have a right to express our opinions too. Violence may not be the answer, but sometimes it's necessary to get people's attention. God is on our side."

After four days, the story disappeared. Other significant world events took center stage again, the usual wars, famines, and political unrest.

The band's CD began to sell. The sales people from Pantheon Records called Kris. The CD was getting nationwide attention. And in two weeks it made the Billboard charts.

Kris couldn't wait to tell Maureen at work. "Hi, Babe. You won't believe it. Our CD is on the national charts!"

"I just saw that. John got the information. Because he's in the business, he gets that kind of info. You should have seen the expression on his face. He will probably have a martini for lunch today!"

Kris laughed. "I could have two. This could be just what we have been hoping for. I know Sophia, Peter, and the rest will be pleased. People are listening to the music. And they're talking about it."

"The best advertising of all—word of mouth. One protest and one failed bomb attempt, and the CD gets noticed. Wow. Just wow."

"I need to call the other band members. We should figure out how to take advantage of this. And maybe turn some of the protestors into believers."

"That's a tough challenge."

"I know," Kris said. "But that's the point of the music. We're not just doing this to push one CD or to make money."

"You're right of course. But you have to agree that making some money isn't bad."

"Nope. It's good to be able to eat. Speaking of which, you want to come over to eat tonight? And who knows, we might celebrate a little extra!"

"I just got a tingle. I think that's great. I'll be there after work. Bye, love."

When they heard the news from Kris, the rest of the band members were giddy with delight. Jimmy in particular was so excited that Kris was afraid he would hyperventilate and pass out before he could get off the phone. The others were slightly less excited, but Kris knew that everyone felt the same optimism.

That evening Maureen went to Kris's house to cook.

"What would you like for dinner, Kris?"

"You know, since I have met you, my diet has totally changed. I used to eat stir fry and brown rice with beans. That was pretty much every meal. Now every meal is an adventure."

She smiled. "I know. Your diet was about as bland as beige. You ate healthy, but it certainly was limited."

"I have really discovered fruit. Sautéed bananas with coconut oil. Baked fruit with spices and marmalade. Fruit and chopped nuts in my stir fry. So many new adventures!"

Maureen agreed. "The music, our relationship, our food—all of our experiences have blended into a more delightful swirl of sensuality."

"Maybe that's the way it's supposed to be."

"People's lives are so drab, downright unimaginative. Their food is boring, they don't see the beauty of the world. No wonder they have forgotten how to believe."

Kris shook his head. "Or their beliefs have become angry and destructive."

Maureen's face was serious for a moment. Then she smiled.

"True. But we don't have to buy into that. Let's celebrate our lives. Let's just put some peaches in the oven, slice some bananas with them, and swirl marmalade over it. And then we can sprinkle some chopped walnuts over it. We can just have dessert for dinner."

"Great idea!"

As they ate, they talked about the music and its reception. Kris confessed his worries about the protestors and their violent responses.

"How do you think we can get some of the protestors to see that we are not the enemy?"

Maureen shrugged her shoulders. "Maybe we need to examine the music they listen to, the music they perform in church, in their temples, their mosques, their synagogues. Music is one of the experiences that religions share."

Kris leaned over and kissed her full on the mouth. Wide-eyed, Maureen responded to the kiss, as the marmalade made their lips sticky, sensual.

"Wow!" Maureen exclaimed.

Kris grinned as he stared at her. "You are brilliant! That is perfect. There are so many songs we can do. Leonard Cohen's 'Hallelujah' is perfect. The images are biblical, but the passionate undertext shows another side. I could write some songs with biblical texts as a basis. Song of Solomon would be a perfect song for our purposes. The images are so sensual, and the song is supposed to be about the love of God and man."

"I can actually hear it. The sitar would be perfect for that."

Kris drank a swallow of wine, the ruby liquid dribbling down his chin.

"Sorry. I get a little carried away."

Maureen dabbed his chin. "That's actually kind of sexy."

"Maybe I should just pour the whole glass down my front."

Maureen dipped her index finger in the ruby liquid and licked it. Then, maintaining the eye contact, she dipped once more and touched the hollow at the base of her throat.

She smiled at Kris. "Or maybe you could just pour it on me. Talking about all these sexy religious themes is getting to you, I can see."

"Maybe. Would you like to go into the other room and be dessert? I mean we could continue dessert!"

They both laughed loud.

"Now that is a classic Freudian slip. I think that both might be in order. Like something out of *Tom Jones*."

They refilled their glasses and retired to indulge in their just desserts.

The next day Kris called their contact Anita Wright at Pantheon and told him about their plan.

"Kris, that sounds like a great follow-up CD." Anita said. "You could solidify the base you already have with your first recordings and then expand to get larger interest. You might even get cross-over from pop and rock to the religious charts."

Kris sat with his phone to his ear, pondering that possibility.

"Do you think it's possible?"

"Of course. Everything in business is about marketing. How you package the product and sell it. Whether it's music, clothes, or cars, it's all in how you market the product to the target demographic."

"I can see that. I just never thought of music that way."

"You are the musician, the artist. Leave the packaging and marketing to us. I'll pass all of this on to Mr. Apollonius. I know he will approve."

"Will do. I have some songs to write. And others to arrange so we can cover them with a twist. I'll keep you informed."

"We can make this big. Keep us in the loop."

After they hung up, Kris sat with his phone in hand. He shook his head. This could be amazing. Then he called Maureen and the band members.

Chapter Twenty-Five

A week later, Kris had a date with Maureen to celebrate the band's success. Kris arrived at Maureen's house a little early. She opened the door smiling.

"Hello there. Aren't you lovely?" Kris took a step back to admire her.

"I bought this today for our date. I wanted to impress you."

"I am impressed! You are gorgeous in that."

"Come on in."

He stepped inside and they walked to the living room.

"Do you really like it?" She twirled for him. Her dress was a delicate sea-green color. It was just slightly décolleté and fitted at the waist. The skirt was pleated and stopped just short of her knees. Her red hair in gentle waves framed her face, highlighting her eyes. Her makeup gave her a mischievous appearance as she winked at him.

Kris stared. The dress was designed to show off her generous curves, and it succeeded admirably.

"You make me to want to stay home tonight. But you probably wouldn't be wearing your dress for long."

She laughed. "You naughty boy. But there's always afterwards. Dessert maybe!"

"Sounds yummy."

"You clean up well yourself, speaking of that."

"I decided that I could dress up a little. Though now I wish I had dressed up more." He wore a navy blazer and tan slacks with a light blue oxford dress shirt and a subtle paisley tie.

"I'm sure you will be the best dressed man there."

"I had better be if I'm accompanying you."

"Where are we going?"

Kris answered, "I know a little club that has a band tonight. I've made dinner reservations. We can eat and then dance."

"What a lovely date! You really know how to charm a girl!"

"That is the idea. Since you are so charming, after all!"

"Are we ready to go?"

"Excellent idea. We have 7:30 reservations. We can have a glass of wine when we get there."

He walked her to the car. The sun had just set, and the cool breeze stirred Maureen's hair. Walking behind her, Kris could just smell her perfume, a floral scent with a touch of musk beneath it. The fragrance was subtle but sensual. As he opened the car door, she eased into the seat. "Thank you, kind sir."

When they arrived at the club, the band was just finishing their set up. Now that the band had begun to make a name for itself, musicians recognized him. The hostess escorted them to their table, which was tucked into a corner not too far from the dance floor.

"Your server will be with you shortly. Enjoy your dinner."

"This is nice, Maureen. The décor is beautiful, and I love the table setting. White table cloth, linen napkins, elegant silverware. You chose well." She bent over the single flower in the small vase. "And a real rose, not silk or plastic."

"True beauty, like you."

The waiter arrived and took their drink orders.

"Do you know the singer, Kris?"

"I do. I've heard this band a couple of times. They do a lot of classic rock and some of the stuff from the 60s like we do, some of the later Beatles, Moody Blues. I enjoy them."

"This is sounding like a perfect evening." Kris reached over and squeezed her hand.

The waiter returned with their wine. Kris raised his glass, the deep ruby liquid glinting in the soft light. "To you, my dear. And to divinity. Long life."

They touched glasses and drank, Maureen licking a drop of wine from her upper lip.

Kris watched at the other couples celebrating. He saw one couple who seemed a little frail, the man evidently caring for his fragile wife, ordering for her and listening carefully to her quavering voice. Another couple closer to the band were younger and louder. Kris noticed the woman laughing as she drank her martini, evidently not her first. The man leered at her and touched her shoulder, sliding his hand toward the top of her breast. Kris glanced away.

The waiter returned to take their orders. They ordered the vegetarian lasagna with a side salad and fresh fruit for dessert.

"I'll get your orders in. I'll check back in a bit to see if you want more wine."

The band began to play. They started with the Beatles, "I Wanna Hold Your Hand," which segued into "She Loves You." Kris reached across and squeezed Maureen's hand. "I remember them on the Ed Sullivan Show. My little sister was crazy about them, and I had never heard of them."

Maureen laughed, "I could hardly hear them for all the girls in the audience screaming. I was one of those girls who thought Paul was dreamy."

"My sister thought so too. I didn't really get into their music until later when they got past some of that pop music. And of course when they discovered Maharishi Mahesh Yogi and Transcendental Meditation, and LSD, that's when I really liked them."

"And just imagine. If you hadn't heard that and George Harrison playing the sitar, where would you be today?"

"Isn't it funny how things work out."

"Someone said, 'There's a divinity that shapes our ends.'"

"I think it's true. And it led me to you." He squeezed her hand again.

Their salads arrived, followed by their lasagna. The salad was called a Heart Salad on the menu. On a base of hearts of romaine, it included hearts of palm, artichoke hearts, and cherry tomatoes with Raspberry vinaigrette dressing.

Maureen took her first taste of the salad. "This salad is delicious. And the sweet dressing is such a nice complement to the tartness of the lasagna sauce."

They ate quietly, savoring the flavors and textures. The waiter removed their salad plates, and then later returned for the lasagna plates. They both ordered another glass of wine to have with dessert. They ordered a plate of mixed fruit for dessert. The waiter brought their fruit and their wine.

"I love fruit. It is so simple and sensual at the same time."

Kris took a bite of strawberry, which tasted like summer sunshine.

"I know. I think it's interesting that the Bible shows that the first sin was eating fruit. A fascinating way to show our sensual natures."

The band began to play a Moody Blues song, "Nights in White Satin."

"Would you like to dance?" Kris asked.

"Absolutely. This is one of my all-time favorite songs."

Kris guided her to the floor and put his hand on her waist. She moved close and took his hand. They closed their eyes and moved, not so much dancing as swaying to the flow of the music. Kris hummed to the music, inhaling the fragrance of Maureen's perfume, lost in the moment.

The band finished the song and then moved into "Late Lament," the poetic piece that followed "Nights in White Satin."

Maureen shivered, as Kris held her close. She whispered, "This has always been such a profoundly moving piece for me. It reflects so much of human life."

"I know. The Moody Blues does that to me too."

The music finished, and they returned to the table.

Kris raised his glass. "Here's to Days of Future Passed."

"Long life." They drank.

The band began a faster number, "Old Time Rock and Roll." The young couple got up to dance. The young woman was a little unsteady on her spiked heels as they danced, gyrating and clapping her hands. The man held one hand and kept one hand on her waist, until she moved away. She twirled and laughed, momentarily losing her balance. Her date caught her and held her again. He laughed pressed her close, his hand sliding down her back to the curve of her bottom. The woman stared up into his face and kissed him open mouthed.

Kris and Maureen sat and observed the couple. They glanced at one another. Kris shrugged. "I guess he thinks he's going to get lucky tonight."

Kris shook his head. "But she will probably be passed out before they get home."

"For that guy, it won't matter much to him."

"I know." The man leered at the woman he held up. Then Kris blinked twice. He recognized the man.

"Are you ok, Kris?"

"Yes. But I just recognized him. That is the guy who assaulted Abigail."

"I think you are right. Of course, he changed his human appearance. But he can't change who, and what, he really is."

The man glared at Kris. He leered. Kris knew that the recognition had been mutual.

"Let's just pay and leave, if you don't mind. They paid their bill and walked to the parking lot. As they were approaching the car, they heard loud voices and laughing. The man and his date walked behind them, the man guiding his intoxicated date to a red Corvette. He waved at Kris.

"I know you," the man said as he smirked at Kris.

Kris turned to unlock the car door.

"How's your wife?" Kris heard a laugh as the man asked the question.

Kris turned toward him. "None of your business, you son of a . . ."

"Come on, Kris." Maureen touched Kris's hand.

He opened the door for Maureen and walked to his own door as the man approached.

"I didn't mean to hurt her, you know."

"I don't want to hear it. Go away, you bastard, or I'm calling the cops."

The man pushed him, and Kris fell back against the car and then stood up again. As he stood, the man laughed. As the laughing figure reached toward him to push him again, Kris hit him in the eye.

"You bastard," the man snarled and hit Kris in the face. Blood from Kris's nose streamed onto his shirt as the man walked to his car and sped from the parking lot, tires squealing.

As he crawled into the car, Maureen exclaimed, "Oh Kris! Are you all right?"

He took his handkerchief out and put it to his nose. "I'm ok. I've had worse than that. I'm just glad I hit him. He'll have a black eye in the morning."

"Can you drive?"

"I'll be ok. I just need to stop the bleeding. I don't want to ruin my jacket."

Kris started the car and drove home. Kris held his handkerchief to his nose, Maureen, biting her lip. By the time they got home, the bleeding had stopped.

"I'll get you some ice," Maureen said as they walked through the door.

"Thanks. Get me a couple of paper towels. I just want to make sure I don't get blood on anything." She took the handkerchief and put it in the sink with ice water. She gave him paper towels and a plastic bag with ice cubes.

He sat in a chair in the kitchen leaning on the table.

"I can't believe all that happened. I'm sorry I ruined our date."

"That's fine. It's not your fault. You tried to walk away."

"He just wouldn't let it go."

Maureen touched his shoulder. "They never do."

"I'm not a violent person. But when he talked about Abigail with such absolute contempt, I just lost it."

"I'm actually impressed that you defended her. That was really heroic of you."

"I just feel like I made an idiot of myself. I know it didn't really do any good. It didn't help Abigail, and it won't help his other victims. Probably including that poor drunk girl he was with."

She walked over behind him and put both hands on his shoulders. She bent over and kissed the top of his head. "Sometimes just taking a stand is important. Chivalry is not dead. And you are my knight in shining armor."

He turned his face toward her. She kissed him.

"My hero. Shall we go to bed?"

"Just give me a towel to put on my pillow. This is not exactly how I saw the evening ending."

"I know. You will receive your reward for your heroism at a later date. It will be worth waiting for."

Chapter Twenty-Six

Kris and Maureen sat in her apartment and sipped their wine on Friday afternoon.

"What do you want to do for dinner?" Maureen asked.

"I thought we might go out. I know we just ate out, but I thought we could have dinner with Starr and Jimmy, if you don't mind."

"I'd love that, Kris. You can tell her about your heroic deeds."

Kris touched his nose, which still hurt. "Why don't I call her and see if she'd like to have dinner with us? She usually doesn't do much on Friday evening."

Maureen put down her glass. "Great. Where would you like to go?"

"How about something new? I was thinking today about Indian food. Let's go back to Star of India. I'm in the mood for something a little spicy."

"Great. I love that place."

"I'll call Starr, and then we can make plans."

When he called Starr, she was thrilled.

"We'll pick you up at 7:00."

"I'll be ready, Dad."

Maureen made the reservations.

They picked up Starr and Jimmy and arrived at the restaurant. As they entered, Kris inhaled, the air redolent of curry and other fragrances that made his mouth water.

"This was a good choice. I'm starving just smelling all of that."

"Me too, Dad. Thank you both for including us."

Maureen said, "We're glad you could come."

As they waited to be seated, the sound of sitar music began, and they smiled and closed their eyes.

A young woman in a sari approached. "May I show you to a table?"

They followed her, the music drifting around them like lotus blossoms.

The waitress walked over to take their orders.

"Do you know what you want, Maureen?"

"I know that they have a spicy vegetable dish with lots of curry."

"That sounds good."

Starr closed her menu. "I'll have the same."

When the waitress returned with their water, Kris said, "We have a friend who plays sitar. As a matter of fact, he plays in the band I play in."

"What is your friend's name, if you don't mind my asking?"

"Sankar Sridaran."

"Of course! I know him. He comes in here. He told me he was in a band."

"We love his music. You should come hear us play some time. What is your name, if you don't mind?"

"I'm Lakshmi."

"I'm Kris. I am glad to meet you."

"Likewise. I should go check on your orders. If you will excuse me."

Kris said, "I suppose we shouldn't be surprised she knows Sankar. I know the Hindu community is tight knit. Of course, it revolves around the temple. I went to the temple with the family of one of my students one time. I felt as though I were in India."

"That's fascinating."

"It was. Especially to see young students there. It's odd to think that they come from such an almost alien culture and during the week they have to 'pass' as the expression goes."

Starr smiled. "I knew a couple of Indian kids in one of my classes in high school. They were cool. Some of my friends thought it was funny they wouldn't eat beef. Other than that, they fit right in."

"I remember them. A couple of them were in band."

Maureen said, "Must be odd for them to feel so almost schizophrenic, to live in two worlds. By the way, I need to tell you about your father's chivalric deed the other night."

Kris grimaced.

"What do you mean, Maureen?" Starr asked, puzzled.

"We ran into that guy who assaulted your mother."

"Oh! I hope you beat him up! Or called the cops."

Kris shook his head. "He left too fast for me to call."

Maureen touched his shoulder and grinned. "But he did give him a black eye! I was so proud of your dad!"

"And I got punched in the nose for my trouble."

. "Well, you are my hero anyhow. I'm proud of you, Dad."

"As long as the two ladies in my life are proud of me, I'm happy."

Jimmy smiled and held up his water glass. "Mr. Singer. To chivalry!"

They all raised their glasses and drank. Kris could feel himself blushing. Fortunately, at that moment, Lakshmi returned with their food.

"Enjoy. I'll return to check on you." Lakshmi bowed slightly and left.

Kris took the first forkful of the vegetables. He chewed slowly, savoring the curry and other spices. Starr took a forkful and chewed. Kris pondered the moment. Maureen, savored the food, eyes closed with a slight smile. He thought of the Cheshire Cat.

As Kris took the second forkful, he became aware of a table across the room. A brown-skinned man sat with two young women. The man wore a loose white shirt and linen pants. The man had large brown eyes and a neatly trimmed mustache. The women wore saris, one a delicate green and the other a soft yellow, like tropical blossoms.

The three of them smiled at Kris when they became aware of his gaze, somehow, the man familiar to Kris. Then he blinked twice.

The man's face was beautiful, sensual. His skin was no longer brown, but a cerulean tint that reminded Kris of the heat of a summer afternoon. He turned and smiled at Kris, his dark eyes glowing. The two women also gazed at Kris, Starr, Jimmy, and Maureen, their expressions friendly, seductive.

Of course. He was at the concert. I remember him. I think those women were with him I know I have seen his face in a picture. Or somewhere.

The young man raised his graceful hand, palm up, in a gesture of welcome.

"Kris. Do you know who they are?" Maureen asked, her eyebrows raised.

"I ought to."

"Yes, you certainly should. Especially him."

The man and the two women arose from their table and flowed toward them.

The man addressed Kris, "Hello. It is good to see you. We enjoyed your music. You are talented musically, but the spirituality in your sound is beyond technique."

Kris bowed, acknowledging the compliment.

The man gazed at Starr, His dark eyes peering into hers. She dropped her eyes. The man then touched Maureen's out-stretched hand. Instead of shaking her hand, he leaned over and touched his lips to her fingertips, his mustache brushing her skin. Kris saw her skin flush across her face and over her breasts.

"Please allow me to introduce myself. I am Krishna."

Kris stared at him, mouth open. "You are--?"

"Yes. Your father. I am pleased to see you."

Kris sat quietly, considering the man before him.

"I know you are at a loss right now. Sophia told me who you were. And of course, I know Maureen slightly." He turned and bowed to her. She returned the bow, eyes lowered.

"Please allow me to introduce my companions. This is Akashleena. Her name means Star. And this is Kamala."

The two women bowed slightly, smiling at Kris with eyes lowered.

"Who is this delightful young lady?" he asked, indicating Starr.

"This is my daughter, Starr."

"Of course. Also a star. I knew about her." He smiled at her, as she gazed at him, silent.

Kris said Starr. "This is, uh, your grandfather."

She still stood speechless.

"Your mother was a lovely woman, Kris. We shared many beautiful hours together. And of course, you are the result. I have followed your music since you began the band. I am pleased that you share my love of music and the spirit behind it."

"Thank you. I'm honored. I am so pleased to meet you, to know who you are. I have always wondered who my father was. My mother never told me much."

"I knew her as Radha. She was one of the milkmaids. I know you must know the stories that have come down through the mythology."

"I do. But I had no idea." Kris stopped.

"Of course, you did not. I am pleased that we finally meet. We are leaving, but I wanted to speak to you. I'll see you at your next performance. I know that you will fulfill your promise. I'm sure we will talk more later."

He turned to Starr. "I can see your grandmother's beauty in your face. I'm sure we'll meet again."

He gestured, palm up, fingers out, a graceful benediction. They turned toward the door and flowed out.

Kris turned and stared at Maureen. "That was—amazing. So, you knew?"

"I did. But I knew you would meet him when you were ready. Now you know why you are the person you are."

Lakshmi returned with their bill.

Kris asked her, "Do you know that man?"

"Yes, sir. He comes in here frequently. And always with new women."

Kris smiled. "I will tell Sankar we met. We enjoyed our meal. Thank you."

"Namaste."

"Dad, that was unbelievable. I'm still speechless."

"I know. I can barely comprehend it myself. We'll talk later when we've had time to let it sink in."

The four of them left the restaurant, emerging into the twilight, the stars beginning to twinkle in the heavens. The breeze touched the leaves on the trees, dancing to the sensual touch of the evening air. Kris could almost hear the distant strains of flute music on the whispering breeze.

Chapter Twenty-Seven

The next afternoon Kris began to work on the new song. He made a peanut butter sandwich and opened a beer. He found his King James Bible and sat down to read The Song of Songs. As he sat in the study munching his sandwich, he read, amazed at the imagery and the language.

He took a swallow of the cold beer and shook his head.

This is amazing stuff. I know we never read this in church! If we had, every adolescent boy would have had to go immediately to confession. This is the Bible?! It's more like the Kama Sutra. Theologians try to explain away the sensuality by calling the relationship between the soul and God. But it is so frankly sensual, so erotic! It reminds me of that statue by Bernini, Ecstasy of Saint Teresa. What a great song this will be. I can imagine Krishna's Gopis dancing to it.

He read the poem as he finished his lunch. Even the peanut butter sandwich and the beer seemed a new sensual experience, not exactly the wine and fruit in the poem, but certainly more delicious as he focused on each bite, each swallow. He read the poem twice more and began to take notes on images and words that he could use. He went to the computer and found a recording of Ravi Shankar's music to inspire him as he began to write the opening verses of the song:

Rose of Sharon
"Oh, my love, he kisses me
and his lips are honeyed, soft.
 His breath like perfume, like sweet incense
carries my heart aloft.

My love fills my soul like the bees' honeycomb,
his sweetness food for my heart.
His passion a garden of plenty
from which I would never depart.

Kris realized that he had sat reading The Song of Solomon and working on the song for two hours.

Not bad. This is definitely not church music. Though maybe it should be. Too bad we don't get to see more this side of the Judeo-Christian tradition. We get the fire and brimstone without the passion and the other fire, the fire of creation. And procreation for that matter.

He typed up what he had written so he wouldn't lose it. His study had gotten to be such a mess that important pieces of paper tended to disappear if he placed them on any surface. One day he would clean up the desk. But not right now.

By the time he and the band met to practice, he had finished a rough draft of the lyrics. He printed out copies and handed them around. Starr was there with Jimmy, and Kris handed her a copy as well.

"I'm working on a new song. I want to know what you guys think. It'll need music to go with it, but I know that you can do that."

They sat reading quietly. Mike moved his lips as he read, and Kris could see Sankar swaying slightly as he read. He could already hear the music in his head.

"What do you think?" Kris asked.

"This is pretty far out stuff," Mike said.

Jimmy said, "I like it. It sounds familiar, but I can't place it. Is this from some Indian text?"

Kris saw Sankar smile with just the slightest shake of his head.

Kris answered. "Actually no. It is Middle Eastern though."

Jimmy inquired, "Where from?"

"The Bible."

"You're kidding! Where?" Frank sat with his mouth open.

"Old Testament. Most of it is from the Song of Solomon. I just used a lot of the images and the feelings and modernized it a little into a love song."

Sankar acknowledged, "It does feel very much like a Hindu text. Maybe from The Ramayana or a story about Krishna."

"I actually had Krishna and the Gopis in mind as I was writing it."

"That's amazing, dude," Mike said laughing out loud. "I may have to go back and reread some of the Bible. I didn't know stuff like that was in there. We sure didn't hear it in church. Especially in the Baptist church I went to!"

"I know. And that is the point of our music. We want to educate people, to show them that there is a lot more to their beliefs, and other people's beliefs than they know."

"So that is what we're going to do in our next CD?"

Kris glanced at Pele. "I was thinking we might call it *A Joyful Noise*. It comes from Psalm 100, which is about singing to God. We can show people that all religions do that."

"That's a pretty tall order," Carlos said. "Do you think we're up to it?"

"Think about our first CD. We can do anything we want."

Mike said, "We've got some work to do."

"Sankar, do you think you can do some music that will reflect the Eastern feel of this song?"

"I think so, Kris. I was hearing it in my head as I read it."

"I know," Kris said, smiling. "Listen to the music playing in your head, as the Beatles said."

"Great, we need to think of some songs from other artists that we can cover. Songs that people can relate to. Any ideas?"

Mike raised an index finger. "How about that Cat Stevens song 'Morning Has Broken'? That's a religious song, isn't it?"

Jimmy spoke up, "We still sing that in church sometimes. Didn't Cat Stevens change his name and stop singing?"

"You're right," Carlos said. "He converted to Islam and changed his name to Yusuf Islam. In effect, we get two religious connections with that song."

"That's good," Frank said. "But he's back performing. He has released three albums since then and has gone on tour. He just calls himself 'Yusuf' now. He was inducted into the Rock Hall of Fame recently."

Kris said, "So that one song can reach a lot of people on various levels, rock fans, Christians, and Muslims."

"Cool." Mike stroked his beard. "That is some neat stuff."

"Let's try to think of some others that we can do that will reach people who don't understand what we're doing. And if you have any ideas for new songs, write them down. We need a lot of good material for this CD."

Twilight of the Gods

"Are we going to play today, or what?" Mike tilted his head. "What does everybody think?"

Sankar raised his hand. "I think we should listen to our CD *Twilight of the Gods* together and talk about it."

"What do you think?

"I think I'd like that," Carlos said. "We can get some new ideas maybe by listening to it."

"I'll put it in. Anybody want anything to drink? I've got soft drinks, beer, wine, water and snacks too."

"Yeah. Let's make this a listening party," Mike said. "I'll help you get stuff out, Kris, while everybody takes bathroom breaks or whatever."

They brought out the drinks, along with chips, a bowl of nuts, and some vegetables with dip. Kris put out cups, plates, and napkins. They lined up and filled their plates and got drinks.

"Great. are we all comfortable? Let's listen. We can talk about each song when they finish. Let's try to be critical. Pretend you don't know the song." Kris hit Play on the CD player, and they sat back. Some closed their eyes. Carlos was moving his hands in rhythm. Sankar's fingers moved with the sitar parts.

When the title cut "Twilight of the Gods" finished, Jimmy said, "That is such a radical, cool song,"

Mike responded, "I can't believe we did it. And I guess I can see why some people don't like it. It's not exactly traditional beliefs."

"I like the sitar parts," Sankar said, "Especially with the trumpet and the other instruments. Really creates a sense of East meets West."

They listened to the rest of the CD. Afterwards they agreed that they understood the music better with some distance from it.

"Now, let's get ready to do even better stuff for this new CD. Are we up for it?" Each musician smiled back.

"Let's make this next one a kick-ass CD," Mike said. "We can show that the first one is not just a flash in the pan."

"Great. See you guys next week. And let's be ready to play. Maybe we can have "Rose of Sharon" ready to work on, along with the Cat Stevens song.

Kris cleaned up after they left. Starr stayed after and helped. The trash disposed of and the food and drinks put away, he and Starr sat in the living room.

"What do you think of the new music?"

Starr smiled. "I like it. Just like Jimmy, though, I was surprised with the Song of Songs song."

"You need to go back and read it in the Bible."

Starr agreed, "I think Jimmy and I can read it together. "

How are you doing? I haven't talked to you in a while. You and Jimmy seem to be hitting it off."

"I'm doing well. Jimmy is a nice guy. It's funny that we knew each other in high school but didn't really get to know one another."

Kris said, "You grow up, and you mature. By the way, have you heard from your mom?"

I talked to Mom a couple days ago. She has finally recovered physically from being attacked. But emotionally she still seems a little rattled from it."

"How is your friend Jeffrey?"

"He's much better. He has managed to stay clean, though it's been a struggle. He joined a support group that has helped but you know what has helped him the most is listening to your CD."

"Really?" Kris was surprised.

"Yeah. He listens to it pretty much all the time. He may need a new CD. I think he'll wear it out. He loves the sound of the music, but the lyrics really get to him. He quotes the songs all the time."

"Really?"

Starr laughed. "Dad, I have to tell you. I'll be glad when you put out this new CD. I'm getting tired of the old one!"

Kris laughed loudly into the receiver.

"I know that's probably not a good thing to say, Dad, but it's true." I know every song by heart. But it really has helped him kick drugs. I didn't think anything would."

"He may be the first transformation from our music."

"Well, if you can reach some other people like you did him, you really can change the world."

"I hope so. Speaking of which, I need to call Sophia and update her. I know Peter and June will want to know what we're doing."

"I need to go. It's good to see you, Dad."

He called Sophia. She answered on the second ring.

"Hi, Kris. How are you? Any bombings lately?"

"It's been quiet since that night. I just wanted to let you know that we're starting work on the next album."

He told her about his ideas, about the Song of Songs connection and Cat Stevens.

"That sounds wonderful. I know that Peter will be interested. Would you like to meet with him to tell him yourself?"

"Sure. I haven't seen him in a while. How is he?"

"He's a little better. He listens to your CD, which seems to help. I'm going to call him right now. I'll call you right back."

She called back in five minutes.

"Can you meet for a drink tomorrow afternoon?"

"No problem."

"See you at Sam's at 4. Bring the 'Rose of Sharon' song. And can you bring a recording of the Cat Stevens song that Peter can listen to?"

"See you then."

Kris left for Sam's a little early the next afternoon. He had found a CD of Cat Stevens and dug out his portable CD player. The afternoon sun felt good on his face as he walked to the car. His face upward, he felt like an Egyptian worshipper of Aten, the sun god. He could understand why they worshipped the sun.

He walked into the bar. Sam stood wiping the bar as always.

"Hey, stranger. I haven't seen you in a while. You don't have security guards yet?"

Kris laughed. "I'm not that important yet."

"I saw that your CD is doing well. You are going to make some money off of it, I think."

"Maybe. We're starting to work on the next one."

"Let me buy you a drink. The usual?"

Sam poured a generous glass of Glenfiddich with two ice cubes, as Kris told him about the new music.

Kris had just finished the first drink when the door opened. Sophia entered first and held the door for Peter. Kris smiled and blinked twice.

In her mortal form, Sophia was stunning as always. She wore a beautiful gray tailored suit with a short jacket and a neat white blouse. Her skirt stopped just above the knee. When Kris blinked, her form as Athena stunned him. He had forgotten her divine Hellenic presence, and her gray eyes nearly floored him.

Peter wore an elegant suit, charcoal gray with pinstripes. Gold cuff links on French cuffs extended from the sleeves. A striped silk tie and matching kerchief completed the ensemble. Like Sophia, Peter's divine presence was literally awe-inspiring. His white toga blinded like a field of fresh snow in sunlight. He wore a regal laurel crown, an appropriate divine presence for the king of the gods. Kris felt a momentary impulse to kneel.

Kris blinked again and shook his head to clear his mind of the effect of their presence. Sophia sat on the seat next to him, and Peter sat next to her.

"Maureen isn't here?"

"No. She's still at work. Since our CD, they have had much new business from performers who hope to be 'The next big thing,' as they say."

"I hope so," Sophia said. "We need more good music in the world. This is just the beginning."

She ordered cabernet, and Peter ordered the same. Sam put their glasses on the bar.

"Drinks are on me. I'm honored to have celebrities here."

Sophia smiled at him. Kris saw Sam's response to her expression. He knew how Sam felt.

Peter raised his glass. "Kris, I am so glad that your music has been well received. We have all felt the response that it has created in people. Your lyrics for the songs you have written are inspiring."

"Thank you, Peter." Kris bowed slightly and raised his own glass.

Sophia said, "Kris, why don't you show Peter the 'Rose of Sharon' lyrics?"

Kris handed the song to Peter. As Peter read the lyrics, Kris watched for a reaction. He saw Peter smiling slightly toward the end.

"They are exceptional," Peter said. "I have read a little of the Bible, but that book stands out. I am surprised, frankly, that it is in there."

"I agree. When I read it before I started writing the song, I couldn't believe that it is in the Bible. It seems too passionate, too sensual, in a book that generally downplays that part of human life."

"Maybe people just need to be reminded of that part of their lives." Sophia raised an eyebrow as she smiled.

"I think that is what we want our music to do."

"I offer a toast to you, to the band and the music. May music be the spark that renews hope in human life." Peter raised his glass. They all touched glasses. Kris shivered as he sipped, a feeling of the moment, like a true communion, touched him.

"Kris, when do you think you will be ready to record the new CD?"

"I hope soon. We have some cover songs that we are working on, plus the ones that I'm writing. We have been rehearsing some of them. Sankar is composing the music for the 'Rose of Sharon.' It all seems to be moving fast."

"That is an excellent plan," Sophia said. "We want to take advantage of the publicity that we have had. Even the bombing has turned out to be positive for us."

"That's sad, but true. People do respond to violence, sometimes more than to any positive stimulus." Sophia shook her head and sipped her wine.

Sam had been standing to one side quietly. He cleared his throat.

"I hope you don't mind my interrupting. Did you see the little comment in the new *Rolling Stone Magazine*?"

Kris stared at him, puzzled. "What are you talking about?"

Sam smiled. "I just got my new copy this morning. Gotterdammerung got a brief mention."

"No kidding?!" Kris put down his empty glass.

"One of their writers noticed the CD listing in the Top One Hundred list. He read that earlier article. He used the term 'Ragna Rock.' Apparently, that term is making the rounds in music circles."

"Wow!" Kris shook his head. "I need to see that. Do you have it here?"

"I left it at home. I meant to bring it, but I was running late. You know how that goes."

"I can go get a copy. I need to let the other guys know. I know they'll want copies too."

"It's just a small paragraph, but I thought it was cool."

"Thanks, Sam, for telling us. Peter and I will let the others know as well." Sam grinned at Sophia's words, obviously smitten.

"We are going now. Peter needs to rest. Let us know when you are getting close to recording again. We anticipate the new songs."

"I'll keep you informed," Kris said.

Sophia took the last swallow of ruby liquid. "Long life."

"And to both of you. Be well."

Sophia followed Peter out the door. A shimmer of light surrounded them as they opened the door.

The other band members were excited about the magazine mention. Kris called Maureen and told her, and she said she would pass on the news to her boss. Starr actually screamed when Kris told her about the article.

"I can't wait to tell Jeffrey. He will be so excited. Your music has changed his life."

"It certainly has changed mine. I can't believe all of this has happened. It just seems like yesterday I was sitting in the library reading mythology and writing little poems about it. And now this."

"I know, Dad. I can't believe it either. My dad is going to be famous!" She grinned, pumping her fist in the air.

"I just hope the music does what we expect it to. Without that, the fame and the money are worthless."

Two days later the band met to rehearse. They were so excited about the Rolling Stone article that Kris had trouble getting them to focus.

"I know that it's big news. But we need to get this next CD out. Sankar, have you finished the music for 'Rose of Sharon'?"

Sankar's brown face smiled. "I think you will like it. I've worked out the melody, and I have some ideas for the other instrumental parts, but of course everyone will have their own ideas as well."

He sat on his cushion and picked up his large gleaming instrument. He tuned a couple of strings and then paused. He closed his eyes and played the opening bars. The music was slow and lilting. Then the pace increased, becoming more insistent in tempo as the volume increased. At the peak, he paused, then the volume and tempo decreased. The final note hung in the air and disappeared.

"That is beautiful, Sankar! How did you come up with that?"

"Actually, I read the book in the Bible. Then I read the lyrics a number of times and tried to imagine the lovers as they appear in the Bible and in the song."

"But there's something else about the music. Something that doesn't sound like either text."

Sankar smiled sheepishly and blushed. "I know. There was another inspiration."

"What was it?" Kris asked.

"I'd like to know that too," Mike said. "That music doesn't sound like anything out of the Bible."

"Actually, I got on the internet and researched pictures of a Hindu temple in India, the temple in Khajuraho. The statues depict the positions from the Kama Sutra."

Jimmy blushed. Starr grinned and flushed from her face down her throat.

Sankar continued. "It's not like anything you would see in a Christian church. But the images in Song of Songs are so sensual and even erotic that I thought there is a connection."

"I agree," Kris said. "I can't wait to play it and see how an audience responds."

"Let's start working on the instrumentals," Mike said. I can already hear some guitar riffs that would be great under the sitar."

Carlos grinned. "Wait till you hear the percussion. And Frank, I know your bass line is going to be incredible."

Sankar played the melody again, and they began to work on the song. It would be as great an opening number for the second CD as "Twilight of the Gods" was for the first. They began the creative process that would bring forth *A Joyful Noise* for the desperate world.

Chapter Twenty-Eight

The next couple of months were hectic for Kris and for the rest of the band. Once they had finished "Rose of Sharon," they started on the other songs that would comprise the CD. Kris spent a part of each day working on songs, smoothing out lyrics and trying to imagine the music. The other musicians focused on the music, trying to fulfill what Kris envisioned. Once somebody had an idea for a melodic line, the rest of them worked out their own instrumentals. The process was chaotic, stressful, and sometimes explosive as creative pressures led to conflicts. But out of that pressure-cooker environment the music was born. As all birth, all creation emerges from stress, from the explosive fusion of elements.

Despite the pressures that Kris faced as the catalyst for the artistic process, he had never felt better or more fulfilled. Maureen came over to the house occasionally in the evenings. She listened to Kris's excited monologues of the day's events. They sat on the sofa, wine glasses in hand, as he explained to her how each song progressed.

"You know the Cat Stevens' version of 'Morning Has Broken,' don't you?"

She answered, "I do. I always thought it was an unusual song for him. But then when he went through his conversion experience, I realized he was not just a singer. He has depth behind his music."

"Exactly. And that is what we're trying to get to. We want to turn the song inside out. To show that subtext. The song's Christian and Muslim, and everything else."

"If you can do that, I can imagine how people will respond."

Often when they had those conversations, they listened to the songs that the band was covering. Sometimes they listened to other music, especially Ravi Shankar, but also the Beatles, Moody Blues, and other performers whose music had a spiritual context.

Usually after dinner and a couple of glasses of wine, they retired. Kris was often tired but also keyed up from the day. One result of all of the creative activities of creating the new CD was passionate lovemaking. Maureen found Kris's energetic response to the music arousing. As she sat listening to his aesthetic soliloquies, she could feel the energy radiating from him, the heat warming her like an aura of arousal. As she responded to his artistic energy, he reciprocated. The result was fulfilling and exhausting sex. The blend of creation and procreative activities united them. Maureen felt like his muse.

The band had a gig scheduled in two weeks. Because of the success of their CD (and probably because of their notoriety as a result of the protests and the attempted bombing), they were booked into the largest venue in the city other than a stadium. Kris called the members to rehearse once more. They gathered on a Friday night, excited and ready to play the new songs.

"This will be important for us," Kris said. "We are introducing the songs for *Joyful Noise*, in addition to playing the songs from the first CD. After the attention, we have received from the media because of the music and all the other stuff, it's important that we make the right impression."

Mike asked, "Do you think those protesters will be there?"

"I just hope they keep it non-violent," Jimmy said. "They scare me."

Kris responded "Well, except for that one unbalanced guy at the recording studio, it hasn't been bad. and they have been some of our best publicity."

"I wish they would consider Gandhi for their inspiration," Sankar said.

"I don't think they want any inspiration beyond their own limited view of their own religious beliefs. It's our goal to change that. Now, are we ready to rehearse? I'm going to record the rehearsal so we can listen to it if we need to between now and the performance."

They all picked up their instruments. Sankar sat on his cushion and settled in with his sitar.

"I want to open with 'Rose of Sharon.' I'm really hoping that a song based on an Old Testament text will set the tone for the CD."

"This has been a real challenge," Pele said. "The horn parts are not what I'm used to. I try to think of what kind of wind instruments they would have had."

Kris reminded him, "Remember that the angel Gabriel plays a trumpet. Let that be your inspiration."

Pele grinned. "That works! I can hear that."

"Is everyone else ready? Sankar, the sitar is important in this song because it ties the two traditions together. We want an Eastern version of a Middle Eastern religion."

"I'll just keep those Kama Sutra images from the temple in mind."

Mike laughed. "I don't know that I can keep up with my chord progressions with those images running through my head."

"Just do your best. Ok, Sankar, let's start."

The low notes of the sitar began, the slow quiet notes rising from Sankar's fingers as they danced across the strings. Kris closed his eyes for the languorous opening bars, imagining the young woman in Solomon's love poem dancing for her beloved. Then Kris began to sing the lyrics he had written. The other instruments blended behind his voice, playing softly and slowly at first, then picking up the tempo. The song reached its peak, and Kris could imagine the two lovers intertwined as the music slowed to a gentle ending that faded with the last notes of the sitar.

The musicians stood for a moment. Frank said, "Man, that works, Kris."

The rest of the rehearsal included a mix of the old songs with the new pieces. The Cat Stevens' "Morning Has Broken" was easy to perform since they all knew his version. The Leonard Cohen song "Hallelujah" worked once they decided which version to use. They had listened to a dozen versions, from the original through versions by k.d. lang, Willie Nelson, and a number of other singers. They decided on an amalgam, beginning with a slow version that reflect the religious context of a hymn. They then sped it up in the middle, emphasizing the sensuality passion as David watched Bathsheba bathing. The tempo slowed again and became more devotional in tone.

They finished the "Hallelujah," then as the final notes dissipated, they stood in silence.

Jimmy said, "I think we are all ready. Now I just hope that the listening public is."

Kris called Maureen after everyone had left. "So how did rehearsal go?"

"Frankly, it was amazing. The music just seems to take control. The new CD is somewhat the same as the first, but there is a power under some of the songs that is hard to explain."

Kris called Sophia and updated her on the rehearsal. She was excited, and she promised to pass on the information to Peter and June.

"The effect of the music on them has been amazing. I'm sure you noticed how much stronger Peter seemed when you saw him the other day."

Kris acknowledged, "Actually, younger and healthier."

"The music and the positive energy it has started to create are having an impact. We were all starting to worry about him," Sophia said.

"I recorded our rehearsal," Kris responded. "We can videotape the show, and they can watch it at home."

"Great idea. I'll tell them. I'll talk to you before the show."

The day of the performance arrived. Kris had contacted everybody. Starr was bringing Jeffrey, and Maureen and her boss would arrive together. The band members decided to arrive quietly this time, without the limousines and the fanfare that had made them targets before. They wanted the focus to be on the music, not on them as people.

Kris drove to the venue early to be sure that the setup was good. Despite the fact that he arrived three hours before show time, the crowd was already building out front, and he saw people getting protest signs from their cars and vans. The protest would be larger.

Kris called Sophia when he got inside. "Sophia, I just wanted to let you know that the protestors are already here. You were probably right not to bring Peter and June."

Kris went to the stage. The instruments were already in place. Sankar's cushion was front and center, and his sitar rested on it. When the band members arrived, they would do a soundcheck and then be ready to go.

All of the band members arrived together. Carlos owned a big van that he used to move his drums to performances, so he had

174

room. They went to the stage and began the sound check. The process went smoothly, and they had an hour before they began.

Mike shook his head. "There are a lot more protestors this time, maybe twice as many. They seemed louder and more aggressive. I'm glad we didn't arrive in limos."

"They'll be able to hear the music outside. Maybe the music will quiet them."

"Music hath charms?" Jimmy asked.

"We hope that it doesn't just release the Beast," Mike said, frowning.

"Scary, isn't it? We forget some of the really terrifying stuff in the Bible."

"It's like the Hindu goddess Kali. It has two sides, creation and destruction," Kris said.

"That's the whole point of this."

They took their places on stage. The curtain opened and the concert started. "Rose of Sharon" was an immediate hit. As he stood at the front singing, Kris saw people swaying to the music, and by the end of the song, he saw two couples kissing. The passionate energy of the song worked.

The rest of the concert was a success. The audience obviously knew the songs from the first CD; when Kris announced the songs, people applauded. They played the older songs, mixed with material from *A Joyful Noise*. The new material was well received, and the covers of "Hallelujah" and "Morning Has Broken" received enthusiastic applause.

They closed with "Twilight of the Gods." As soon as Pele began the opening notes from Wagner on his trumpet, the crowd cheered. The entire audience stood and moved to the entire song. When the final notes faded, they cheered, applauded, and shouted for at least two minutes. The band's anthem had become a signature sound for the new musical genre, Ragna-rock.

After the audience dispersed, the band packed up their instruments.

"That was awesome, Kris," Mike said as he put his guitar in the case."

"Sure was," Jimmy responded. "I'm exhausted though. I feel like the Bob Seger song, 'Every ounce of energy you try to give away.'"

"You both are right. I don't think a musician can get a better response than we got tonight. But it is exhausting. When a crowd responds like that, I want to give even more."

"It should be good PR for the new CD," Sankar said. "I was thrilled that they responded to the music for the 'Rose of Sharon' song."

Jimmy and Starr walked out holding hands.

The rest of the band finished packing up and left. Kris kissed Maureen good bye as she left. Then he departed.

Kris turned on the news when he got home. The coverage of the protests showed a few people who were worked up over what they saw as blasphemy.

Some people we just are not going to reach. I guess they are too insecure about their own beliefs. Maybe people will respond to a Joyful Noise.

Kris shook his head as he turned off the television and headed for bed.

Chapter Twenty-Nine

The next morning Kris was drinking coffee and humming "Rose of Sharon." He put his cup down and went to the study to get the Bible and the lyrics of the song. He reread the Bible story.

My God. How did I not see this? It's perfect. This is a love song. Two people are singing in the text, not one. I need to rewrite this. But first I need to call Maureen.

She answered the phone. "Hi. Have you recovered from last night?"

"I'm already on my second cup of coffee, if that tells you anything."

"Not surprised. What's up."

"I have to ask you a question. Do you sing?"

Maureen paused. "Well, uh, yeah. I haven't in a while. I used to be in a band years ago. Why?"

"I was just reading 'Rose of Sharon' this morning and then the biblical text. The Song of Songs is a man and a woman singing to and about one another. The song should be a duet."

Maureen was quiet.

"And actually, thinking about this gave me another thought. Right now, we are a boy band of sorts. The harmonies will be more interesting with male and female voices. And the whole point of our music is to reach everybody. Do you think you could join us, sing the female parts?"

"Makes sense. Do I need to audition or something?"

"No. If you say you can sing, I believe you. Do you know our songs?"

"Of course. I have just about worn out my CD of "Twilight of the Gods. I sing the songs all the time. They run through my head constantly."

"Great. We can start working on the parts and the harmonies. I know the guys will love it."

"How about tonight?"

"Wonderful. I need to go start rewriting this song. See you tonight."

Before he started rewriting "Rose of Sharon," Kris called the other musicians to tell them about his idea. He knew they would agree, but he didn't want to just spring it on them. Better to let them start thinking about it. Most of them were not home, so he left messages for them. Then he went back to his now-cold coffee and the Old Testament.

Maureen arrived at six. The had a glass of wine and then started to work.

"What songs do you like the most? I want you to be comfortable with the songs you sing."

"I especially like 'Morning Has Broken.' I think it lends itself to a female voice. I also like 'Hallelujah.' I've heard a couple of women sing that, and I think the harmonies can be really interesting. Especially when David is watching Bathsheba."

"Those are a great start. Why don't I put in the CDs with those songs, and you can just sing along?"

Maureen grinned. Her creamy freckled skin turned a little rosy across her shoulders and neck. "Ok. I'm a little nervous, embarrassed. I haven't sung in front of anyone is awhile. What if you don't like it? I couldn't stand it if you didn't."

"I could not possibly be disappointed with you. You will be great, I know," Kris assured her. "Let's start with the Cat Stevens."

Kris put in the CD. As the music started, Maureen waited until after the first phrase was finished and then picked up, picking with the line "blackbird has spoken." Throughout the song she harmonized in some spots that she thought appropriate. Her range went from a surprisingly low register to a soprano range that surprised Kris.

"That was great, Maureen. I love it. You have a lovely voice with a remarkable range. Your harmonies were dead on, and you chose the right places to come in. I can't wait to hear what you do with 'Hallelujah.'"

"I'm ready," Maureen said enthusiastically.

"Before we do it, I want to show you a YouTube video." They went to the study, and he turned on the computer.

"What are we watching?" Maureen asked.

"This is Celine Dion singing with the Canadian Tenors. She only comes in at the end, but it's what I have in mind for you."

They watched the video.

"I think you have the range to do what she does, to lift your voice over the male lead, at least for the Hallelujah sections. You might sing the other parts in a lower register."

"I think I can do that!"

They put in a CD of the song, and Maureen did as Kris suggested.

When Maureen finished, Kris was wiping his eyes. He was quiet for a moment.

Kris breathed in and then exhaled. He shook his head. "I think that is one of the most moving renditions of that song I have heard. I've probably listened to a dozen versions, but this is exceptional! You are now a member of the band."

"Do you think the other guys will be ok with it?"

"Trust me. They will be as blown away as I am. I can't wait to do 'Rose of Sharon' with you as a duet! I think it's going to make people rethink that book of the Bible. I think the audience will love it. The passion in the text should come alive in the song."

Maureen smiled. "This is exciting. I can't wait. Meanwhile, let's have another glass of wine and listen to some of the songs. Who knows, the passion in the texts may come alive tonight."

She grinned at him, and he leaned over to kiss her. Her lips opened, and he felt her breath on his face.

"Solomon should have been so lucky," he whispered to her.

Kris finished rewriting "Rose of Sharon" the next day. As he wrote, hearing the new verses in his head, he thought of Maureen the night before. Her passion and her love filled him as he wrote the verses that she would sing in the song. The parts for the male singer expressed what he felt for her. She really was his muse.

He sent the other band members copies of the new song, and he also gave one to Maureen and watched her as she read it.

Robert C. Covel

Rose of Sharon

HIM: Oh, my love, she kisses me
           and her lips are honeyed, soft.
           Her breath like perfume, like sweet incense
           carries my heart aloft.

HER: My love stands strong, and he holds me close.
           I gaze in his loving eyes.
           I lie content in his loving arms,
           to his touch my passions rise.

BOTH: Our love fills our souls like the bees' honeycomb,
           The sweetness is food for our hearts.
           Our passion a garden of plenty,
           From which we will never depart.

HIM: Her breasts like nestling turtledoves,
           her belly like heaps of wheat,
           the orchards of her fertile love
           fill me, leave me complete.

HER: His arms entwine around me
           like tendrils of fruited vines.
           Kisses intoxicate, entrance
           As cups of crimson wine.

BOTH: Our love fills our souls like the bees' honeycomb.
           The sweetness is food for our hearts.
           Our passion a garden of plenty,
           from which we will never depart.

HIM/
HER: She is my rose of Sharon,
           (I am his Rose of Sharon)
           as pure as lilies' bloom.
           (he holds my perfect bloom)
           The bouquet of her perfect love
           (he calls forth my perfect love)
           a heavenly perfume.
           (Our heavenly perfume).

BOTH: Our love fills our souls like the bees' honeycomb,
           The sweetness is food for our hearts.
           Our passion a garden of plenty,
           From which we will never depart.
           Our passion a garden of plenty,
           From which we will never depart.

"I love it!" she whispered. "I can't wait to stand on stage and sing this to you in front of an audience. It will almost be like being an exhibitionist, singing these words in front of people. They don't hold much back."

They both laughed out loud, and Kris gave her a big passionate kiss. She responded and pressed herself to him.

The next rehearsal included Maureen as vocalist. Before they started, Kris asked what they thought of the new version of "Rose of Sharon."

Sankar responded. "I can't wait to hear your voice singing those words. I get a feeling that it will be like a biblical soundtrack for those Kama Sutra statues in the temple."

Pele said, "I think I want to do a flute part with it. There are some songs that have really good seductive flute solos. 'Fill the Wine' is one of them. The flute will emphasize the woman's part."

"That sounds promising. Do you think you can do that today?" Kris asked.

"Sure, Kris. I already have it in my head. I can improvise with the other parts. It'll work."

"Let's get to it. We'll start with some of the other songs to get Maureen into the music.

They sang a couple of the covers, including "Morning Has Broken," and the other band members complimented her voice and her harmonies.

Mike agreed. "You wouldn't know that you haven't been on stage in a while. You're a natural."

"Thanks, Mike. Now I'd like to try 'Rose of Sharon.' I think that may be the best song for me, especially because it has a part specifically for a woman."

Kris said, "On that last verse, I want to do it as a kind of round, where your line comes in on the end of mine each time. And then the last two lines we'll do in unison."

"Wonderful."

"Does everyone have the instrumental parts down? The music hasn't changed, it's just expanded to more verses. Pele, do you just want to do the flute parts when she sings?"

"That's excellent, Kris. I'll play when she sings, and at the end I'll play with the last refrain."

He stood facing Maureen. The music began, and they sang, transformed into the people in the song.

When the music faded with the last refrain, the flute notes holding, Kris and Maureen smiled.

"It really was like those temple carvings," Sankar said with a shy smile.

"Maybe we can reach some people we haven't reached before. We can show them that music is universal in all religions, among all people."

Jimmy played a chord on the keyboard, the opening of "Amazing Grace."

Kris shrugged and grinned. "I know that kind of sounded like a sermon. I think we're ready to record this CD. What do you think?"

"Absolutely! Let's do it. It's going to be a righteous work."

"A Joyful Noise, indeed," Kris said. "I'll get in touch with Pantheon and let them know we're ready. I'll let Sophia know, and she can pass the word to Peter and June too."

Chapter Thirty

In two weeks, they were in the studio to record *A Joyful Noise*. The marketing people at Pantheon had sent out notices to the radio stations about the upcoming release. As he was driving to the studio on the second day of recording, Kris heard "Twilight of the Gods" on the radio,

"Here's a song from a local band that has hit the big-time. Their first CD got a lot of attention. Now their new CD is scheduled for release soon. This is the title cut from the first CD."

Kris laughed and turned up the volume. He glanced to his left and saw a young girl in a red Mustang convertible with the top down. She had turned up her volume as well. She gave him a thumbs-up as the trumpet began, and they grinned at one another as the light changed to green.

Takes me back to my youth. Listening to a hot song and seeing a young girl with the same station. Of course, in my time it was probably the Beach Boys or maybe the Doors. Funny that the music is from my band. I hope the publicity makes the new CD sell. And that it will get people to be more tolerant.

The recording studio was a tight fit with all seven people in there at once with all of their instruments. Once Sankar got situated with his sitar, the rest of the musicians stood behind him at the microphones. Kris and Maureen stood on either side, gazing over Sankar as they sang.

As they were getting ready to record, Kris laughed. "We look like we're posing for a painting or a photograph for an album cover. It's like the cover of *Sergeant Pepper*."

Mike grinned wickedly. "Or the musicians' version of The Last Supper."

"That's a good way to see it. Maybe this should be our CD cover. Someone needs to get a picture of this!"

The recording technician obliged. He took several shots as people posed in various ways.

"Ok. Now let's play some music. We're doing 'Rose of Sharon' today."

Sankar played the seductive opening notes, and they began. Maureen gazed at Kris as he sang the opening verse, smiling. They played through the song the first time but decided that it was not tight enough.

"Kris, I think I came in about a half beat too late in that one part. Could we do it again?"

"Sure Mike. I think that with the duet, it's important that we be tight. We don't need the instruments getting in each other's way or drowning out the voices. We ready to do it again?"

They started again. The final stanza, with Kris and Maureen singing back and forth, worked beautifully. Maureen picked up each time just as Kris was finishing his line. The lines and their voices blended well, and the harmony underscored the lines' content.

The last note faded. "That might have been it," Kris said. "Let's hear that, if you don't mind."

The technician played back the take.

They all listened, eyes closed, as the music drifted around them. Kris opened his eyes. Maureen smiled and winked at him. He shivered.

Carlos said, "I don't think we are capable of doing any better, Kris." He was usually so quiet that they were surprised at his comment.

"I'd say that is the version we go with. I think we are well on our way to finishing this."

Over the next several days, they recorded the remaining songs for the CD. The marketing people at Pantheon stepped up their promotion, including releasing "Rose of Sharon" to the radio stations. The local stations picked it up first, and then some of the bigger stations began to play it. Kris began to hear the term Ragna Rock as they introduced the song. The CD was scheduled for release in a month, and Pantheon planned an even bigger release party than for the first CD.

Sophia called Kris a week after they finished the recording.

"Kris, I heard that the new CD is even more powerful than *Twilight*."

He agreed. "I think the religious elements come across more. Especially in the 'Rose of Sharon' song and the Cat Stevens song."

"The more positive response we get the better. We have already seen improvement. I can see Peter and June getting stronger by the day. They listen to your music, which helps. But I think the fact that other people are responding helps more."

"That's good," Kris said. "The new CD will be out at the end of the month. Pantheon has started advertising it, and pre-release orders online are going well."

"I know that Peter and June will be at the party. And probably everybody else."

"The protestors will be there too," Kris said, worried.

"Maybe if we can get them to listen to the music, it will help."

"I hope so, Sophia. It worries me."

"Me too, but the risk is necessary. I'll let everybody know to start making plans. This should be an Olympian event!"

Kris laughed. "I hope we can live up to that expectation."

The plans for the release party were completed, and Pantheon pulled out all the stops. They were planning a red-carpet event at a concert hall, the biggest indoor venue in the city, the Orpheus, a movie theater from the age of elegance.

Kris called the band members and Maureen to discuss their plans for that night. He invited everyone to the house to eat and talk about their plans. Everyone brought food and drinks. The kitchen was filled with the fragrance of food, everything from the curry dish that Sankar brought to the fried chicken bucket that Mike brought. They loaded their plates and sat in the living room.

After they settled, Kris announced. "This is going to be a great night, guys."

"I can't wait," Mike said. "I have dreamed of playing there. It's elegant."

"I know," Jimmy said. "I'd love to get to play on that huge organ. Big Mo, or something like that."

"We will never forget the night. Pantheon is doing it right. We will be taking limos there, of course, and there will be a red carpet. I expect the press will be there."

"I'm going to have a new dress," Maureen said, "if I'm going to have my picture in the paper."

"Are we dressing up?"

"I think we probably should, Frank. After all, everybody will be there. Who knows, we could be on the cover of the *Rolling Stone*!"

"Man, I'm going to have that Dr. Hook song in my head now."

"Sorry, Frank. But we can dream."

Carlos put down his empty beer bottle. "Are there going to be protestors there again?"

Kris shook his head. "Probably. I expect it will be bigger this time after all the publicity we've had. I know the police will be there, but we need to be ready."

"I just hope it doesn't get bad," Maureen said.

"I do too, babe." Kris said. But we just need to stay focused and not get too involved in it. Let's just enjoy it and not worry about any of the other stuff."

They finished eating and left.

Kris and Maureen cleaned up the kitchen. Kris hauled out the trash while Maureen washed the glasses and put them away. They then sat together on the sofa with a glass of wine. Kris held up his glass to Maureen and said, "To success tomorrow. And beyond." She touched her glass to his and sipped.

Chapter Thirty-One

The night of the release party, Kris and Maureen dressed early so they would be ready when everyone arrived. Kris wore a tuxedo with a shirt with a ruffled front. He put a foam green handkerchief in his jacket pocket to match Maureen's dress. Her dress, a flowing creation in silk, reached just above the knee, and the bodice revealed enough cleavage to be distracting. She emerged from the bedroom when she had finished dressing, and she swirled around to show her dress.

"Wow! You are stunning. I can't believe that I get to escort you down the red carpet. I will be the most envied man in town!"

Maureen smiled and winked.

"The limos will be here soon. I think that Peter and June will arrive a little earlier than we do. Sophia and Barney will be with them. And, of course, their security."

The black limousines pulled up in front of the house. The drivers emerged and stood by the open doors. Kris thought they looked like a bunch of high school kids headed to the prom. Excited and scared at the same time. He knew that he had never had a date like Maureen in high school.

As they approached the Orpheus, Kris saw the crowd when they were still two blocks away. "Maureen, can you believe this?"

"I knew there would be people, but this is amazing."

As the car eased through the throng, they saw people pointing in their direction. The driver moved slowly as police directed traffic, letting them through the intersection. A block from the theater, the protestors were evident. Not only were there more than last time, but they also seemed more organized. And more aggressive.

"That's good, Kris."

"I know. I just hope that Peter and June got inside without being attacked."

"The crowd probably didn't notice them. After all, it's the band that is the focus of the protest," Maureen assured him.

"True. We just need to get inside as quickly as possible. I hope we have enough security to get through the crowd without incident."

The three cars pulled up to the red carpet that led to the entrance of the Orpheus. The driver let Maureen out first, and then Kris. As he emerged, he heard the noise. The crowd cheered, but he also heard boos and chants of protest. The police had created a path for the band, but Kris felt the tension in the air.

The musicians glanced around as they walked toward Kris. Jimmy and Sankar were scared, and the others were excited and nervous. "Let's just try to get inside as quickly as we can. I don't want this to get bad."

Kris led the way, and Maureen followed, her hands on his shoulders. The rest of them followed, single-file. The crowd pressed forward as they walked, Kris saw police pushing the people back. The band pressed past reporters, who pushed microphones in their faces, but the noise of the crowd drowned out their questions. Kris felt like he was leading a charge through a hostile enemy. He could almost feel the emotions like waves of raw animal passion, the anger and hatred from the sign-carriers in the back. The happiness and love from the supporters in the front. All mixed together in a chaotic rainbow of emotions, an aura of reds, blues, greens in a swirl. And some darker shades, almost black.

Faces like masks from Greek and Roman drama. Or the faces I saw in a catalog representing the Seven Deadly Sins. I'm glad that the supporters are in front. At least I can hear people who like our music. The chants in the back are scary though. Glad we have the police here.

They weaved their way through the crowd to the door into the lobby.

"I didn't expect it to be that bad. Not exactly what you see on television for the Oscars or the Grammys," Maureen observed.

"Thank you for leading the way, Kris. If I hadn't had my hands on your shoulders, I think I would have just died of fear out there."

"Well, we're through that madness. Let's just focus on these people in here. They have paid to see us and hear us. We are here to play music. To change the world. So, let's smile and be who we are."

The crowd in the lobby saw them enter and moved toward them. At first their reaction was to cringe from the onslaught. But once they realized that the crowd was no threat, the members of the band relaxed into the adulation of their supporters. Kris put his arm around Maureen. They both smiled at the crowd. A number of people were in formal dress, generally the older couples, while the younger people tended more toward jeans and bright tops.

"Certainly an eclectic crowd, isn't it, Kris?"

He smiled at Maureen. "It is. That's good. We want our music to reach everybody. I think *Joyful Noise* will do that even more."

"I do too. I just wish it would change some minds of some of those people outside."

"Maybe it will. You want some champagne?"

"I don't think one glass of champagne will hurt. After the ordeal of running that gauntlet, I need something."

"I know. I was just thinking how good a scotch would taste. That will have to wait."

He took two flutes of champagne from the bar, and they walked around, mingling and exchanging pleasantries with people. Kris noticed the other band members had relaxed somewhat, Sankar and Jimmy still a little skittish, but he attributed that to their youth and culture shock.

A man in a tuxedo approached Kris a few minutes later. Kris recognized him as an employee with Pantheon.

"Mr. Singer, we need to get the band members on stage. We'll be starting in a little bit, and we want to be sure that the setup is acceptable and that the sound system is good."

"Thank you." Kris collected the other musicians, and they followed the Pantheon representative to the stage.

Their instruments were in place, and the microphones were as expected.

"Let's go back stage. We need to get focused before that huge curtain goes up."

They gathered just off stage and sat in a circle. A technician brought bottles of cold water for them.

This reminds me of *Stranger in a Strange Land*. Here we are, Water Brothers."

"I haven't thought of that book in years. Back in the late 60s it was a cult book. Jefferson Airplane had a song that referred to it."

"I guess that was before my time," Jimmy said.

"It was, but you should read it. The ideas in the book are a lot like our music."

They finished their water. A technician came back stage. "We're starting in about ten minutes. There will be some announcements. Then talking about your first CD and the new one. Then you will be introduced, and the curtain will go up."

"We are here to make a joyful noise tonight. Let's forget all that stuff outside. We are here to make music." Kris made eye contact with each one. They took their places on stage.

The announcer on the other side of the curtain began announcements about cell phones and the other routine information that precedes a performance. He then began to talk about their first CD. Kris could not hear every word. He heard "twilight of the gods" and "ragna rock." Then he heard "Joyful Noise, their new release."

Everyone was poised to play, standing like a wax display of a rock band.

"And now, playing from *Twilight of the Gods* and from their new CD *A Joyful Noise*, here they are. Gotterdammerung!"

The curtain rose, and the spotlight hit them as the applause and shouts from the crowd engulfed them.

Pele's trumpet raised its first clarion notes from Wagner, and they began their anthem to the Nordic gods. Sankar's sitar picked up the melody, and Kris and Maureen began singing. The crowd roared as the song began.

As Kris was singing, his eyes adjusted and then lifted up to the loge. In the front and center, he saw Peter and June. On either side were Barney and Sophia. Seated behind them were the two imposing guards.

They played two more songs from the first CD, and then Kris stepped forward to the front of the stage.

"Good evening. We are Gotterdammerung." The crowd cheered.

"We are so glad you like our first CD, and we hope you like the second one even more. As you probably know, the title comes from one of the Psalms: Make a joyful noise unto the lord."

The crowd cheered.

"We want our music to be a celebration of life, of love, and of belief. We want to reach out to everybody. People of all beliefs. We're going to play a couple of songs from *A Joyful Noise* now. This first song is based on the Song of Songs from the Old Testament. It's called 'Rose of Sharon.' We hope you like it."

He stepped back and turned toward Maureen. Pele opened with his flute, and then they began singing the duet.

As he and Maureen sang, Kris tuned out the crowd. Even on stage in front of a thousand people, the song had a kind of intimacy to it. He could see that Maureen felt the same passion.

When they reached the last verse, alternating lines, Kris heard the crowd noise begin to swell. As they sang the last note of the final refrain, the audience erupted in full voice. The feeling was passionate, almost erotic.

Carried on the waves from the audience, they played two more songs. The music and the emotions swirled around them, a lava lamp of colors, feelings, and sounds. The band members were smiling as they played, obviously feeling the moment. As they finished, the announcer returned to the stage.

"Ladies and gentlemen, let's hear another round of applause for Gotterdammerung."

Most of the audience was already standing, so a standing ovation was a given. The band members all waved and bowed to audience. Kris blinked twice. Peter and June, in their divine presence, glowed as they bowed to him. Sophia and Barney, in their identities as Athena and Dionysus, acknowledged him as well. Kris stood overwhelmed in the moment, perhaps the greatest moment of his life.

The curtain dropped, and everyone on stage was speechless. They put down their instruments and hugged one another, slapping backs and laughing. The Pantheon representative led them off stage and back to the lobby. Peter, June, Sophia, and Barney were waiting for them.

"Kris, that was a truly inspiring and inspired performance."

"Thank you, Sophia. The crowd response was overwhelming."

Peter stepped forward. "I want to thank all of you. Your music is making a difference. The world is a better place tonight for what you are doing." He shook Kris's hand and then went to each musician. Finally, he hugged Maureen.

June smiled. "We are honored by your performance tonight."

They bowed slightly.

The two bodyguards entered from the street.

"Pardon us. Your car is waiting outside."

Peter acknowledged the comment. He and June followed the two burly men. Sophia and Barney walked behind, and the band followed. Kris and Maureen followed behind the group.

Kris and Maureen had just emerged from the theater. As Peter and June walked toward the limousine, Kris saw someone walk toward the group, a man with long hair and a beard, wearing a t shirt. As the unkempt man saw Peter and June, he began to run toward them, one hand extended toward Peter.

"There is only one God!" He shouted. Then Kris heard a loud crack, the sound startling him as he searched for the source.

"Peter!!" June screamed.

Peter crumpled, his knees buckling as he fell to the pavement.

"He's been shot!"

The bodyguards pushed the crowd aside and knocked the gunman to the ground. They then turned to Peter on the pavement.

Sophia knelt beside him as June knelt on the other side, crying. Blood stained his white shirt. Beneath Peter's body, sprawled on the pavement, his flowing blood formed a puddle. Everyone else stood motionless, aghast. Kris blinked.

Lying on the ground before him was Jupiter, his toga stained a brilliant crimson. On either side knelt a goddess, with Hercules, Thor, and Dionysus behind. A horrible parody of a scene from mythology played out before his horrified eyes.

Hercules raised Jupiter's head and torso from the pavement as Juno, sitting back on her heels, reached to hold him, the white bosom of her toga stained by the blood. She bent over the face nestled against her.

Juno's voice wailed, "Oh, no. Oh no. This can't be."

She kissed his forehead. Jupiter blinked up at her.

Jupiter whispered, "My dear. It will be ok. You know it will."

Juno sobbed. "But I don't want it. I need you now."

Jupiter, the fallen god, murmured. "It will be fine. The Bifrost is coming. The Rainbow Bridge will carry me home." He gasped.

He lolled his head toward Kris. "Thank you. Your music. Keep playing, performing. Because of you—"

He sagged back into Juno's arms. As Kris watched, Jupiter faded, leaving a frail, mortal human form on the pavement. Peter's eyes stared upward, sightless, toward the night sky.

Kris blinked twice, and the scene became an ordinary crime scene. June held the still form, bending over him, her tears falling on Peter's face.

Sophia shook her head. "He's gone. For now."

Kris shook his head in disbelief at Sophia. "I can't believe this. After all of this, the talk of the music, of changing the world, of saving everything. And now he's dead. Now what? He's just gone?"

Sophia's gray eyes returned his gaze, her expression serious. "For now, Kris."

He stared in disbelief at the form on the pavement, silent.

Sirens surrounded them. Police and EMTs arrived. From that point on, the chaos of medical care, the arrest of the gunman, and the turmoil of the moment pushed everyone back. June refused to release her hold on the still, bloody form until the police and EMTs insisted. Peter was placed on a gurney and put into an ambulance, leaving a stunned group behind.

Chapter Thirty-Two

The limousines followed the ambulance to the hospital, arriving as the EMTs rushed the gurney through the doors to the Emergency room. As Kris emerged from the car, he saw the form on the stretcher, its face covered by the sheet. He led Maureen inside, as they followed June. She sobbed, holding onto the burly guards who kept her from collapsing.

The place erupted in noise and energy, doctors and nurses shouting orders as they pushed the gurney into an examination room. The guards led June to a chair, where she sat with her face in her hands.

An attendant came toward the group, clipboard in hand.

"Is anyone here a relative?" Sophia pointed to June. "His wife." The attendant asked June, "Can you give me his name?"

Sophia interjected herself. "Yes. His name is Peter."

"Last name?"

"Theophiles."

"Has he been a patient here before?"

"No."

"Does he have a family doctor?"

Sophia shook her head.

The attendant perused the rest of the chart a moment.

"I don't think the rest of these questions are relevant. Could his wife sign this form?"

Sophia handed it to June and whispered in her ear. She took the pen and scrawled a shaky signature on the form.

They sat quietly around June. They could hear the activity in the room where they had taken Peter, but from the tone and the lack of urgency in their voices, Kris knew that the medical team was going through the motions. The curtain pulled aside, and a young doctor in green scrubs emerged, removing latex gloves.

He stood before the group, uncertain whom to address.

Sophia approached him. Kris saw him falter a moment. He knew the effect of those gray eyes.

"Doctor, I am Sophia. This is his wife June."

The doctor cast a glance down at June she uncovered her face. Her mascara had run, and her expression of haggard grief reminded Kris of the heroine of a Greek tragedy.

"I'm Dr. Bohannon. Mrs. Theophiles. I am sorry. We could not revive your husband."

June stared up at the doctor, silent. Sophia touched her shoulder.

"Is there anyone who can make arrangements? The police will want an autopsy probably."

"If you don't mind, I'll make the arrangements," Sophia said. "I'd like to talk to the police. I don't see what good an autopsy will do. The cause of death is obvious, and they have the shooter."

The young doctor pointed to the uniformed officer who stood by the entrance. Sophia walked over and talked quietly. The officer glanced away, shaking his head. Sophia walked back to the group.

"They're not going to do an autopsy, June. You can see him before you leave." Sophia spoke to the doctor, and then June went into the trauma room, the guards on either side and Sophia behind her.

They were in the room for five minutes. Kris heard June sobbing. Her quiet voice was barely audible as the rest of the group sat, staring at one another.

They emerged from the trauma room.

Sophia walked to the group as June sat down again, still sobbing. "I'll make the arrangements. Then we need to arrange the memorial service. Of course, that will be a big event. We need to start letting the others know. It may take a week or so to make the arrangements and to get the guests here."

Kris walked over, Maureen's hand still in his. "What can we do, Sophia?"

"The service will be huge. You have never seen an event like this. All of you will be there, of course, and you will be expected to play as a part of the service. We have an amphitheater where events of this magnitude are held. One of our members has a ranch, and the amphitheater is there. "It's in Montana. You will be flown at no expense, of course. It will be a private jet. I'll send you the details as soon as I have them."

"Is there anything else we can do?"

"No. Just go home and get some rest." The two guards stepped forward. "Take her home. And stay with her."

They helped June to her feet, then supported her and guided her through the automatic doors to the limousine. After she left, the other band members left quietly.

"Kris, Maureen, I'll be in touch."

Kris and Maureen walked to the limousine. As they rode home, they held hands, mute. They went to bed quietly. Kris lay staring at the ceiling, the evening's events replaying in a loop in his restless mind.

Chapter Thirty-Three

Light through the window stabbed his eyes as he opened them. The only way Kris knew he had been asleep was that his eyes had been closed, but he certainly did not feel refreshed. Maureen still slept. As Kris eased from the bed, he heard her ask, "Was that a nightmare?"

"Sorry, but it was real. I can't believe it either. I'll get coffee." Kris staggered to the kitchen and made coffee. As it was finishing, he turned on the television. The shooting was the headline for the local news. He turned to a cable channel. While the announcers talked about a terrorist threat, details of Peter's shooting ran across the bottom of the screen. Kris turned back to local news and took Maureen her coffee.

She sat on the edge of the bed, head down, her red hair covering her face. "This is like the worst hangover, but we didn't even drink."

"I know. It's all over the news, of course."

"Not surprised."

"I'm going to take my coffee in there to see what they're saying. Take your time getting up."

She made a sound acknowledging his statement. He wandered to the living room as the announcer was returning to the story. "At the Orpheus last night, tragedy struck as a protestor shot and killed entrepreneur Peter Theophiles as he and his wife were leaving a release party for the band Gotterdammerung. Theophiles was shot once, and he died at the scene. We have a reporter at the police station getting information on the shooter. Stay tuned, and now the weather."

Kris turned off the television and drank his coffee. Maureen padded in and sat beside him on the sofa. She was wearing his unbuttoned pleated-front shirt from the night before, and her hair fell across her exposed breasts.

She sighed. "It's going to be a hell of a day."

"They just mentioned the band name. Not exactly the kind of publicity we wanted."

"I can't imagine how June feels this morning. Are you going to call Sophia later?"

"Yes. I'll let her get functional this morning. I'll bet she will be inundated with funeral arrangements and everything. She will need all the wisdom she has to get through this."

"I'm going to take a shower and see if I can do something with my hair." She kissed him on top of his head and dragged off to the bathroom.

Kris stared into his empty cup.

Unbelievable. Literally unbelievable. He's a god. But he's not immortal. What's the term for what happened? Oh, deicide. Killing god. Not a term that comes up in conversation. I don't think we used that in church.

He called Sophia at 9:00. She was already up and said she had been on the phone the last two hours.

"Hi, Kris. How are you and Maureen?"

"Frankly, awful. I keep expecting to wake up. I can't believe he just died."

"I know. I just talked to June. Her people are taking care of her, but she is devastated."

"Of course."

"I have been on the phone. So many people from everywhere saw the news this morning."

"Have the reporters contacted you yet?"

"I expect that at any moment. Mostly I have been reassuring people, and especially the Others. So many questions."

"To be expected. I sure have questions. and mostly the kind without any answers. The biggest one being 'Why?'"

"Sometimes things don't appear to have easy answers."

I know the guys in the band will have questions about what happened, what will happen next, the memorial service."

Sophia asked, "Have you heard from anyone?"

"I haven't. I expect the guys to call any moment. But most of them are not early risers, as I know you are probably aware."

"I'll call you back later today. Try not to feel too bad. You and Maureen need to take care of one another. The music is even more important now. Get some rest."

Maureen went home to get changed to go to work. She knew that there would be interest in the studio related to the recordings, and she needed to be there to answer the phones and handle the inevitable press calls.

Throughout the day, Kris talked to the other band members. Starr called him, distraught over the news. But along with all of the negative emotions from Peter's shooting, Kris also had a call from Pantheon. The news had resulted in increased sales of the new CD, along with a resurgence of interest in *Twilight of the Gods*. He felt guilty about the positive side to the tragedy of the death.

Kris watched the noon news to see if there were any updates on the shooting. The reporter had obtained a video clip of the event, apparently from the cell phone of a bystander. Fortunately, the images were not graphic, but they were sufficient to bring back the awful moment for Kris. He did see a brief shot of the shooter's face, not someone he recognized. The expression in his eyes disturbed Kris, the manic emotion of hatred, of visceral brutality. The reporter said that the person was to be arraigned later, and they would have an update on the case, on the charges the shooter would face. He turned off the television and went to the kitchen for a Coke.

On the front porch, he took the first swallow and closed his eyes, leaning back and raising his face to the sun.

This whole thing is insane. The purpose of our music is to inspire people, to bring back a sense of belief, of the possibilities of the universe. But instead it inspires this?

He opened his eyes and watched a robin listening intently and then pouncing on a worm. Overhead he saw a mockingbird warbling its complex song. In the distance two crows cawed at one another. Then a couple of other songs from birds he didn't know. He smiled and took another sip of his drink.

For the birds, it's easy. The birds get it. Music ties it all together for them. The harmony, the notes, the math of it all. And we are reminded all the time if we pay attention. The Bible and the Quran both talk about having ears but not hearing. Music ties all the religions together. We all want a joyful noise. We just need to hear it.

He finished the soft drink and stood.

"Mr. Robin, I hope you find a good lunch. The rest of you, thank you for the serenade."

He went in to prepare lunch and to make more phone calls. The next couple of weeks were going to be a rollercoaster of emotions as they prepared for the memorial service and as the CD sales marketing demanded his attention. Clouds and silver lining.

That evening he and Maureen turned on the news again to see if there were any more details. One story involved a group of ministers and members from churches. They were speaking out against the violence, the protestors, and the shooting in particular.

One minister wearing a Roman collar spoke for the group.

"We deplore this violence in the name of Christianity. We do not believe that Jesus would support these attacks."

"What is your attitude toward people who may have other beliefs than yours?" The reporter put the microphone back in front of the minister.

"Of course, we hold our faith very dearly. But we also understand that other belief systems feel the same way. We think there is room in the world for many religions and beliefs. We respect all beliefs, as we hope they will respect ours. And we deplore any violence in the name of any religion."

The reporter asked, "What do you think about this band's music, especially their new CD *Joyful Noise*?

The minister smiled. "Well, I'm not much for rock music. But that's just my musical taste. As for their message, they have a couple of songs that have a biblical connection. The song based on the Song of Songs, the Hallelujah song, and even the George Harrison song. I like the message for all of them. I think they may have something to teach us."

"And what do you think they teach?"

"That we can all learn from one another. That all religions, all belief systems have some common messages."

"Thank all of you for being here tonight. We hope your message spreads and stops the violence." The reporter smiled into the camera.

"There may be hope after all," Maureen said smiling.

Kris agreed, "It's amazing he actually did a little bit of a plug for the CD!"

The CD sales of *Joyful Noise* did take off. Pantheon's marketing division kept Kris apprised of the sales numbers. The news of the shooting continued as the police released details to the press, and as the news continued to cover the gory details, the sales continued. The song "Rose of Sharon" received increased radio play, and one morning Kris received the news that it was on the Billboard Top 100.

A couple of days later, Jimmy called Kris.

"Man, you won't believe what I just heard!"

"What? I hope it's nothing bad."

"Quite the opposite. There's a Christian station I listen to occasionally, WROK. They tend to play more progressive Christian music."

"Yeah. I've seen their bumper stickers."

"Well this morning they played 'Rose of Sharon.'"

"No kidding!"

After the segment on the news the other night with the minister talking about our music, the station has had requests for our music."

"Wow! Or as we would have said in the 60s, 'Far out!'"

"We might actually be reaching those people who were protesting against us."

Kris called the other band members to tell them about the Billboard listing and the Christian station, and then he called Maureen at work.

"I know, Kris. Everybody here is celebrating. Our little studio is on the map. Are you thrilled?"

On the other end of the line, Kris shrugged. "I am. But it also really bothers me. I don't know how much of the success of the CD is the music and how much is the notoriety because of Peter's murder."

"It does kind of cast a pall over the success of your music."

"It almost feels ghoulish to me. Peter was sacrificed so we could be successful. After all, the purpose was to save him and all of the Others. And we just got him killed."

"Try not to dwell too much on that. I know how you feel. But the music is successful. Sophia says that's the most important thing."

He sighed. "I know. I just feel bad. And guilty."

"I understand. Have you heard any more about the memorial service, speaking of which?"

"Sophia's supposed to give me the details today. I know we're flying to an airport close to the location and then driving from there. I just don't know the timeline."

"Ok," Maureen said. "Just let me know when you get the details. I have to plan. Packing is not easy for us girls, you know."

"I will, love. I'll call you as soon as I find out. Love you."

"Love you back."

Sophia called two hours later.

"Hi, Kris. I have the details for the memorial. As you can imagine, this has been an epic effort. I think the only thing I can compare it to is planning the funeral of a head of state."

"Well he was, uh, is important."

"More than almost anybody actually knows. You'll see when you get to the memorial."

"So, do you have the details?"

"Yes. The service is on June 21st."

Kris checked his calendar. "That's the first day of summer."

"That's intentional. For so many cultures and religions, that is an auspicious day. We want this to be a true celebration of life."

"Do you have the travel details?"

She dictated the specifics of the itinerary, and he wrote down flight details, car rental information, and times and places.

"Your tickets are already reserved. The same with the cars. And everything else. Oh, and let me ask you. How are you? I know this has been a real shock to you."

"I'm ok."

"The music is of supreme importance. Peter would tell you that if he could. We can talk more about it between now and the memorial. Pass on the information to the band members. We only have a couple of weeks to get ready. And you have a lot to do."

"I'll get started."

"Oh, and you need to be ready to play at the memorial. Music will be a huge part of it, of course, and your music in particular."

"I'll pass on that info to the guys. What should we be prepared to play?"

"The song 'Twilight of the Gods,' of course. And 'Rose of Sharon.' Maybe the George Harrison song 'My Sweet Lord.'"

"We'll be ready."

The next week and a half were chaotic and confusing. The band decided to rehearse once more for the memorial. In addition to the songs that Sophia had suggested, they chose "Hallelujah." Sophia told them that some other music would be performed, including music by a symphony. Kris relayed the details to the band members.

"How big is this memorial going to be?" Mike asked, his eyebrows raised.

"Probably bigger than any memorial you have even been a part of. I don't know how many people will be there, but it's being held in an amphitheater, apparently a big one."

"So, this is going to be like a stadium concert? Jimmy asked.

"Yes."

"Like a Super Bowl Halftime?"

"Could be, Frank. We need to be ready for whatever it is. We'll be ready," Kris reassured them.

Four days before the memorial, a moving truck arrived at Kris's house to pick up the band's instruments and other equipment. They helped load their instruments, making sure that they were protected for the trip.

"Our setup will be ready when we get there, and the sound system will be in place. A lot bigger one than we have ever used."

Mike laughed. "I never thought I'd be a member of a band that would have roadies!"

Kris agreed. All they had to do now was to pack and to get ready for the biggest event of their lives.

Chapter Thirty-Four

Maureen arrived early the morning they were to leave for the memorial. She had two large suitcases, a carry-on bag for the overhead, and a bag to put under the seat. Kris helped her put her suitcases in his car, which filled the trunk and over half of the back seat.

Kris said, "The guys will meet us at the airport. Sophia went on ahead. She'll probably meet us when we arrive in Montana. She has a lot to do."

Maureen said, "That's true. Are we ready to go?"

They arrived at the airfield where the small jet awaited, and the rest of the band members met them. Several were checking phone messages. Mike and Sankar had in earbuds and were sitting with eyes closed.

Kris said, "Sophia's supposed to be there when we get there. Cars will meet us and take us to the amphitheater. The luggage will be delivered to our rooms."

Mike shook his head. "I could get used to this."

"Couldn't we all?" Maureen said. "Like being rich."

They boarded the small jet and settled into their seats, buckled their seat belts, and eased back for the flight.

"Has anyone ever been to Montana?" Mike asked.

They all shook their heads.

"I know that they have a lot of people who are into militias. Or at least that's the impression I get from the news."

"I've heard that, Frank. I remember that the band The Mothers of Invention did a song 'Movin' to Montana' in the 60s."

The jet began to taxi away from the gate, and they sat back in their seats. Kris squeezed Maureen's hand as they moved down the runway and lifted off. "Here we go, babe. I think this will be amazing."

The flight only took a little over an hour, barely time to eat the bag of pretzels and to drink the small soft drink they were served.

They emerged from the jet and walked into the airport, a much smaller facility than the international airport they had just left.

Mike grinned. "Man, this is smaller than I expected. This is like a Mayberry RFD airport."

Jimmy asked, "A what?"

"Before your time, kid."

Kris heard a voice behind them. "So, you made it. How was your flight?" Sophia approached, serene as usual, wearing a gray business suit with a short jacket and a neat tight skirt. Her hair was in a bun.

"We had a good flight."

"Good, Kris. The cars are waiting. You don't need to worry about luggage."

"What's the plan immediately?" Maureen asked

Sophia answered, "I thought we'd go out to the amphitheater so you could get a sense of it in advance. It can be a little overwhelming at first."

Kris asked, "What do you mean by overwhelming?"

"The setting, the size of the place. It's usually more than people expect. The drive will take about an hour."

Sophia led them outside, where four limousines waited for them. As they walked toward the cars, Sophia said, "I arranged for some food and drinks in the cars. I know a bag of pretzels doesn't go far. You'll find some sandwiches, soft drinks, beer, and some other food that will hold you until you can get proper nourishment."

Pele exclaimed, "This is great. I feel important."

Sophia answered, "Pele, you are important. What you are doing is not just playing some music. Don't forget that. Sankar, if you get in the first car, I think you will find some Indian food that you will appreciate. It's vegetarian. And Kris, Starr, and Maureen, the same for you in the second car."

They entered the black cars and settled in for the ride.

As Kris expected, the food was stunningly good. They had vegetarian wraps with avocado, bean sprouts, and a peanut sauce. Kris, Starr, and Maureen enjoyed the food, including bags of chips and fresh fruit cut up in bowls. They drank Perrier.

"If the food in the other cars matches this, Kris, the guys are going to think they went to heaven," Maureen said.

"I have to say that Sophia and all the Others know how to eat. And I think that the reference to heaven may not be far from wrong."

They drank their bottles of sparkling water and surveyed the landscape that flowed by.

"Can you believe this, Kris? Man, those mountains!"

"Isn't it amazing, Dad?" Starr asked as she watched the scenery.

The verdant flat pastures that extended into the distance gave a new meaning to the term "green." Like a natural carpet, the lush grass flowed uninterrupted until it disappeared in the distance. And the majestic peaks of the Rocky Mountains stretched beyond, pointing up to a sky of deep blue.

"I wish I could paint," Maureen said. "This landscape is like some artist's ideal of a pastoral setting from some Arcadian poem."

Kris answered, "I had no idea that the land would be this monumental! I know now why people refer to Big Sky country. Living in this landscape has to affect how people see their lives."

An hour later, the cars turned off the highway, onto a smaller stretch of pavement that crossed the grasslands. A tall white iron fence extended off in the distance in both directions. A large ornate gate crossed the pavement. The gold gate was decorated with green grape vines, and figures of nymphs and fauns lounged among the vines, eating and drinking from chalices. The gate would not have been out of place on a Medici palace during the Renaissance.

Maureen pointed, "That gate, Kris! I can't imagine what this place is going to be if this is merely the entrance."

"The term 'Olympian' comes to mind. If we ever forget who and what these people are, this will remind us."

They passed through the gate. Kris saw a palatial house in the distance, not at all what he would think of as a ranch house, though the barn and other out buildings suggested that this was in fact a ranch.

Then the cars entered another smaller gate, and before them stood the amphitheater.

"My god, Kris!"

He only shook his head in wonder. Sophia was right. The view was overwhelming.

The scope of the structure reminded Kris of the Colosseum in Rome. The blinding white edifice, constructed of white marble, loomed over them as they approached. The cars stopped at an opening, and everyone emerged from the cars. The musicians all craned their heads upward, mouths open and eyes gaping. Only Sophia stood imperturbable.

"Wow, Kris," Mike finally said. "Did you believe that view as we were driving? And that gate. It's like something that Michelangelo designed! And now this."

Sophia's lips turned up in a slight smile. "It is impressive, I must say."

"Impressive suddenly sounds like massive understatement," Jimmy said, still staring upward.

"I've seen beautiful temples in India," Sankar said, "but compared to this, they're little huts."

Sophia agreed. "I want to take you inside to see the stage and to see where the audience will sit."

They walked through the cool tunnel. Kris could see carved figures on the walls, more images from various mythologies, some of which he did not recognize.

The emerged into the bright sunlight, temporarily blinded. They stood on the stage eyes turning upward at the seating area.

"This could be a football stadium!"

"I know, Kris." Sophia smiled.

"The stage itself dwarfs any idea I ever had of a stage. You could fit a thousand musicians on this without any crowding."

Mike's head rotated clockwise and then counterclockwise. "So, this is where we perform for the memorial?"

"It is," Sophia answered.

"How are acoustics?"

"We do have a sound system, probably the best in the world. But with the design of the building, the sound system is largely redundant. If you did a stage whisper, someone could probably hear it up there." Her finger pointed upward at a far corner of the seats."

"How many people do you expect?" Frank asked.

"I'm not sure. We expect the amphitheater to be at least half full, maybe twenty thousand?"

"Really?" Jimmy's voice quivered.

Sophia said, "You have no idea how important this event is."

"I hope we're up to it." Sankar responded.

Sophia assured him, "You will be. Actually, your music is the reason this is happening."

Kris asked, "You mean because Peter died at our concert?"

"No, not entirely," Sophia said. "Your music is having a profound impact on our lives. And because of that, an impact on the whole world."

Maureen agreed, "I'm starting to see that."

"We probably need to get you to the hotel. You have a big day tomorrow. You are going to need your rest, and I know you are probably tired."

They drove back to the hotel in a small town that was dwarfed by the buildings they had just seen. As they drove, Kris watched the majestic landscape drift by, holding Maureen's hand. She brushed her red hair from her face with the other hand. "Penny for your thoughts?"

Kris touched her cheek. "Just thinking about the memorial service. And about that place."

"Me too. It's all a little overwhelming."

"Maureen, I don't know exactly what to expect tomorrow. How will the people respond to our music? We have never played any venue even close to this size. I feel like we're going from Little League to the Majors overnight."

Maureen squeezed his hand. "I think we just need to trust Sophia. And most of all, we need to trust the music. When we get on stage, no matter how many people are out there, on stage it will just be us and the music."

Kris smiled and kissed her. "Thank you, darling. You're right, of course."

They all met in the hotel restaurant for dinner that night. Sophia had reserved a dining room for them. As they walked in, she told them to enjoy their meal.

"Your meals are included. Order what you want."

"Thank you, Sophia. That's generous."

"Not at all."

The servers brought wine for everyone and took their orders. When everyone had ordered, Kris turned to Sophia. "What are the plans for tomorrow?"

She sipped her wine and put down her glass. "We will be leaving here fairly early, probably about 9:00. You will have a chance to do a sound check and to get used to the size of the place. Then you'll have some free time before the actual memorial service begins. It will begin at noon. The whole thing will last several hours. There will be an actual service. And a lot of music. Of course, you will be a highlight of that part. And we will have a symphony and a choir for part of it. The symphony is the Euphonia Philharmonic, and the choir is the Concordia Discors Chorale. They'll be performing classical music."

Kris asked, "Do you know what the symphony is playing?"

"I know they are doing part of Mozart's *Requiem*. Also, Siegfried's Funeral March from *Gotterdammerung*."

Everyone laughed when Sophia mentioned the Wagner piece.

"That is too cool!" Mike remarked.

"They will probably close with Beethoven's Ninth Symphony, The Ode to Joy. When the ceremony and the music are done, we will release Peter's ashes. There will be music for that too, and there will probably be some chanting and other ceremonies from the participants in the crowd."

"Like what?" Kris asked.

"It's hard to tell, Kris. There will be people there from many cultures. And beliefs. It could get crazy. But nothing violent or scary. Other than that, it will be pretty open."

"Not exactly a church service, huh?"

Sophia shook her head. "Not any kind of church you have probably ever attended. Just remember that not every culture has the same reserved attitudes as western cultures."

Kris shrugged his shoulders. "So, this could be more like a rock festival?"

"Think Woodstock on steroids."

Sankar smiled. "This could end up being like that temple with the Kama Sutra carvings."

"Don't be surprised. For some cultures, a funeral is a celebration of life. Lots of eating and drinking and dancing. And other more sensual activities."

Maureen winked at Kris, "I guess we'll be onstage, so that won't affect us."

"Believe me," Sophia said as she drank her wine, "you will not be the same after tomorrow."

The food arrived, and from that point, most of the sounds at the table were of the famished people drinking and enjoying the meal. Kris thought of Da Vinci's *Last Supper*.

The death of a god as a sacrifice for others. And others eating and drinking. Maybe everything does connect.

After dessert and after-dinner drinks, everyone retired. As they left the dining room, Sophia turned to the group.

"Get some sleep. And I would recommend that you have a good breakfast tomorrow. You're going to need both. Sleep well."

When the elevator reached their floor, the band members streamed down the hall toward their rooms. Kris watched them disappear one by one, then he and Maureen walked into their room.

"I don't know about you Kris, but I'm exhausted."

Kris agreed. "It seems about three days ago that we left home. I'll set the alarm on my phone. But I'll probably wake up early."

"I think I'm going to take a shower." Maureen went to the bathroom, and Kris lay on the bed, listening to the water running. He could hear Maureen singing "Hallelujah."

A few minutes later she emerged, a towel wrapped around her.

"Like an Earth Goddess," Kris said, propped on one elbow.

"Thank you," she smiled. "What a lovely compliment."

"I know how David felt watching Bathsheba bathing on the roof."

"I'll think of that tomorrow when we're singing on stage."

"I'm going to take a quick shower too."

When he returned from the bathroom, Maureen was asleep. She had turned down the bed, and she lay on her side, her naked damp body uncovered. He gazed at her creamy skin and her vibrant red hair spread across the pillow, then Kris covered her and kissed her head. He lay down and was asleep in five minutes.

Chapter Thirty-Five

Kris woke from a dream of music and chanting voices. He opened his eyes, easing into consciousness as he became aware of where he was. He turned his head to see Maureen's face next to him. She had a slight smile, and he wondered if she was dreaming. He eased from the bed and padded to the bathroom, closing the door behind him so as not to disturb Maureen. He flushed the toilet, hoping that Maureen would not wake, but when he emerged, she was lying with her head propped on one hand.

Kris touched her face. "Good morning. Did you sleep well?"

"Yes, except for crazy dreams of gods and goddesses, dancing and singing."

"I had some pretty crazy dreams too."

"What time is it?"

"About five."

She smiled. "It's bound to be a big day. I can't imagine what it's going to be like."

He shook his head. "I don't know. I don't think we'll ever forget it."

They showered and dressed. Maureen did her hair and makeup quickly, and they went to the lobby for coffee and breakfast. As they were finishing their second cup of coffee, the other band members straggled in. Most of them sleepy and excited at the same time.

Mike sat down with his coffee, which he had loaded with cream and three sugars.

"Mike, you need a caffeine jolt this morning."

"Caffeine, sugar, whatever I can get." He sipped the steaming beverage.

"We probably all need to eat this morning," Kris said. "We don't know when we will eat again today, and we are going to need every ounce of energy we have."

"The breakfast selection was impressive. They loaded their plates with scrambled eggs and sausage, waffles, and fresh fruit. Sankar ate a plain toasted bagel and some of the fruit. He picked up a banana and an apple for later.

When they had eaten and had more coffee, they sat back.

"When are we leaving?"

"I think pretty soon, Carlos. We need to get there early to do a sound check and to check out the acoustics. The cars should be here soon."

As Kris was talking, Sophia entered. "Are we ready for the day?"

Mike sat mesmerized for an instant as Sophia appeared. She had that effect on people, particularly men. Kris thought of it as a terrifying beauty. No matter how often Kris saw her, he felt that charisma.

Sophia continued, "The cars will be here in five minutes. There will be fresh coffee and some pastries, in case you need more. You have evidently eaten well. Kris, I'm going to ride with you and Maureen, if you don't mind."

By the time they walked through the lobby the limousines had arrived, and the drivers were standing by the open doors. Everyone entered the cars, and they moved onto the highway toward the day's events.

Kris poured another cup of coffee for himself and Maureen.

"Would you like coffee, Sophia?"

"No thank you, Kris."

As they sipped from the porcelain cups, Sophia said, "Kris, this is going to be a most eventful day for everyone involved."

"I get that feeling."

"I have talked to the Others, and I am going to give the band members some of the elixir that I gave you the first night you met Peter and June."

"Ok," Kris said, putting his cup on the small table before him. He regarded Sophia, his eyebrows raised.

"I want them to experience the full effect of the day. The people in the crowd will represent every culture, every religion past and present. I think it's important for the other musicians to understand the significance of the day, of their music. It's time."

"They won't have any after-effects, will they?" He was especially concerned about Jimmy, the youngest.

"No. Other than the residual effects on their awareness of a larger reality."

"Will they have the ability to recall that vision as I do?"

"No. It will eventually fade, like your first experience did."
"What if they want to have the fulltime effect?"
"That will be possible. It will be up to them."
"I understand."
"I just wanted you and Maureen to know in advance."
"I appreciate your letting me know." He sipped his coffee. "I can only imagine how they will feel."
She smiled, her gray eyes serious.
As the cars arrived, the sun was already above the horizon. The sky was a deep cerulean blue, and fluffy clouds drifted overhead. The mountain peaks glistened in the distance.
They stopped in front of the amphitheater, the white marble shining like an image in a fairy tale. It seemed an edifice created by some powerful magic, placed here for a mythic king and his court. Kris regarded the walls, his head rotating to take in the beauty. The other band members did the same as they emerged from the cars.
"Are we ready to do the sound check and get ready?" Sophia led them to the stage. Their instruments were in place on one side of the stage.
"The other side of the huge stage was filled with chairs and music stands. Behind them were tympani and other percussion instruments. The setup was for at least seventy-five people.
Risers for the choir were set up next to the symphony.
They moved to their instruments, and the tech people appeared to turn on the equipment and to do the sound check. Sankar's cushion was in its accustomed place, but it was on a raised platform.
"Sankar, we want you to be more visible to the audience. After all, there will be thousands of people out there who will want to see your playing."
"Are those video screens back there?" Kris asked.
"They are. Because the place is so big, we want everyone to be able to see the proceedings. We are also recording the day's events. The audio and visual record is important."
By ten o'clock they were done with the rehearsal and soundcheck.

"I need for all of you to gather around me," Sophia's voice and her gaze held their attention.

"This day will be like nothing you have ever experienced or will likely ever experience again. Many of the people in the crowd today will not be what they appear to be. This will be the most unusual crowd that has ever appeared in one place."

The band members frowned, unsure.

"I am giving each of you a small vial of liquid to drink. It is not dangerous, not addictive, and it won't hurt you in any way."

Jimmy asked, concerned. "What is it then?"

"It will help you to see the people as they really are. Kris, do you want to tell them?"

"Guys, I have taken it. Believe me, it will change how you see. It will make today make sense on a whole new level for you."

"This sounds like something out of *Alice in Wonderland*," Frank said. "Is it like acid or magic mushrooms?"

"No, Frank. You have never had anything like this. Don't worry."

"I've just gotten clean, and I don't need to take anything that will change that."

"It will be ok, Frank. You can trust me."

She handed out small vials to each of them. Kris recognized the vials as similar to the one he had first received.

"The effects will last today. By the end of the day, they will have subsided."

They held the small jeweled bottles.

"You can drink. Be prepared for your vision to change. I will seem transformed to you."

Mike drank first, and the others followed. Jimmy drank last, l unsure.

They stood still, waiting. Then the elixir took effect.

"Sophia!" Frank and Carlos exclaimed at the same time.

"Oh my god!" Jimmy's eyes were as wide as possible.

"Now you understand why I wanted you to drink this elixir. You will see many people today as they really are."

They turned toward Pele, and they gasped again.

"Man, how did we not know who you are! No wonder you are so good on the flute and trumpet."

In his guise as Kokopelli, Pele smiled. "Now you know."

Sophia addressed the group, "You might want to sit backstage and rest a little now to recover. The crowd will be coming in soon."

They went back stage and sat in the chairs set out for them. Bottles of water awaited them.

Mike asked Kris, "So, you have known about all of this?"

"I did. Actually, Maureen and I are not entirely as you see us." Then he explained his own parentage and Maureen's background.

"What about Peter and June? Who are they?"

"Good question, Jimmy." He answered Jimmy's question.

"So, when Peter died, it was a really big deal?"

"Yes, Mike. That's why all of this is happening."

They all sat quietly. Kris saw each face as they comprehended the reality of their changed perceptions, their expressions like someone who had been blind and who was seeing for the first time.

Sophia came back stage.

"June has arrived. And she has the container with Peter's ashes. She wants to see you. She is in the front row. If you would follow me. And be prepared for her changed appearance."

Sophia led them down to where June sat. She sat on a throne under a pale blue silk canopy. As a normal human, her full-length white dress draped across one shoulder, leaving the other bare. She had a small coronet on her head. Then Kris blinked twice and saw her regal beauty. The other musicians stood agape, eyes and mouths wide open.

She smiled graciously at them. "Good morning. We appreciate what you have done for us. And for Peter." She reached her right hand to touch a gold, jewel-encrusted box on the table beside her.

"Because of what you have done, because of your music, there is hope. Peter died knowing that. I thank you."

Kris approached and knelt before her, his intuition telling him that it was appropriate.

She reached and touched the top of his bowed head. He felt the power in that touch.

Each of the others followed his example. Kris watched their reactions to her touch, as each responded to her divine power.

Afterward, they stood before her, heads bowed.

"May your music be worthy today. We rejoice in your harmony, and we thank you for the vital force you bring to us all. Long life to you all." She smiled at each one.

Sophia led them back to their places backstage.

"She wanted to thank you before anyone else arrived. The crowd will be entering now."

From where they sat, they could hear voices entering the amphitheater. The volume increased, and they heard a cacophony of voices talking, laughing, singing in many languages, some that they recognized and some in forgotten tongues that had not been spoken in normal discourse in millennia.

They sat and listened, heads tilted.

"I can't even imagine that crowd," Mike said.

"Believe me," Kris responded, "It will be like nothing any of us has ever seen. Especially since you drank the elixir."

Jimmy shook his head. "All those languages. I don't even recognize most of them. This must have been what it was like at the Tower of Babel."

"Good comparison."

Sophia came backstage, in her true appearance as Athena. Kris knew how the other musicians felt. He had become somewhat accustomed to her divine appearance, but it still startled him.

"Are you ready?"

They all looked like adolescent boys ogling the new girl in school, overwhelmed with simultaneous feelings of adoration and lust by her appearance.

"You go on in ten minutes. I know you are opening with 'Twilight of the Gods.' Be prepared for the audience reaction. It will be overwhelming. And their appearances will be unexpected. Just so you know. The important thing is to play the music."

She departed, and Kris spoke, "This is it, guys. This is why we are together. This is why we play. Today will be our Woodstock. Focus on the music. And remember who we are." He extended his right hand.

They all rested their hands on his.

"Who are we?"

"Gotterdammerung!"

"May the gods smile on what we do today!"

They heard the announcer's voice. As he said their band name, they walked out on stage to a roar of voices unlike anything they had ever experienced or even dreamed of. Kris walked to the front of the stage with Maureen. Sankar sat on his cushion, and the others took their places with their instruments. The roar of voices was nearly deafening.

Kris scanned out across the crowd and then back at Maureen. Both wide-eyed, they shrugged and grinned at one another. The other musicians stood paralyzed in amazement at what they saw before them.

While the sound was phenomenal to Kris, the view was overwhelming. Thousands of people filled the amphitheater, probably many more than Sophia had estimated. He blinked twice. As Kris turned from one part of the crowd to the next, he saw every imaginable attire, skin color, and type of humanity. The number of altered presences, the Others, was a true historical Pantheon. One group wore elaborate feather headdresses in many hues, with flowing robes to match.

He saw figures in Egyptian dress, as though they came from the walls of an ancient pyramid. Hindu raiment with flowing saris, Celtic outfits of many shades of green, Norse battle armor, African garments made from animal skins with elaborate shields and long spears. And many others. The overall visual impact stunned Kris and Maureen.

Kris could also smell a bouquet of fragrances, apparently from burning incense. He could see clouds of smoke rising from the crowd and drifting overhead toward the stage. Frankincense, myrrh, sandalwood, patchouli, and other sweet scents drifted and surrounded them, filling his nose and his mind with their fragrance.

This is a microcosm of human culture and history. And every possible religious system, from the very beginnings of human history. And the voices! How many languages are out there, how many languages that no one has spoken in millennia?

His mind whirled. June, Sophia, Barney, and many Others sat in their regal, divine presences. June held her right hand up, palm forward in a formal gesture. The band members all bowed.

Pele, in his guise as Kokopelli, raised his trumpet. When he played the opening notes of "Twilight of the Gods," the Wagnerian theme for the Ride of the Valkyrie, the crowd went wild.

Kris saw figures waving their hands, groups applauding and screaming. Those in Viking armor slammed their swords on their shields.

As the opening trumpet notes played, Sankar echoed the melody on the sitar, and those in saris and other Eastern dress began to dance to the rhythms. Kris and Maureen began to sing the band's anthem. The other instruments carried the song, and the intensity of the lyrics and the music flowed from the stage across the audience. At least thirty thousand people cheered, and danced, and sang, as the music flowed across the crowd, the headdresses and costumes moving like waves beneath the sound of the music, a divine wind inspiring them.

The notes swirled out to the crowd as the incense swirled back. They finished the song, Kris and Maureen's voices fading in the last lines of the lyrics, and as the notes died away, the volume from the crowd picked up. A multitude of voices, of languages from many cultures throughout history, shouted and sang back their approval.

Kris and Maureen bowed, and gestured to the other band members, who also bowed. Sankar held up a hand to gesture his gratitude as he sat on his cushion.

As the cheering subsided, they began "Rose of Sharon," Kris and Maureen singing back and forth to one another. They sang over Sankar, swaying to the music and smiling. Kris could feel the deep eroticism of the song ebbing and flowing as they sang.

In the crowd Kris saw more than a few men and women who had worn little clothing were nearly naked as they entwined around one another. Sankar's inspiration of the Kama Sutra temple obviously had the sensual effect he intended. They were performing the original Dance of Love. As Maureen and Kris sang the last stanza, singing back and forth, they saw the entire crowd singing, the men singing one part as the women sang back to them. They already knew the lyrics to the song.

The song's conclusion brought another onslaught of sound from the crowd, and as the band were taking their bows, Kris saw the Euphonia Philharmonic taking the stage. Then the members of the Concordia Discors Chorale took their place on the risers. The emcee came to the front of the stage and took the microphone.

"Let's hear it again for Gotterdammerung!"

Another round of applause and cheers erupted.

"They will return later as we continue our tribute for our dear brother, for Jupiter. And now, we hear our symphony orchestra as they play an excerpt from Mozart's *Requiem*."

The somber beauty of the symphony and the choir voices served as a powerful counterpoint to the band's music. From backstage, Kris could see people moving slowly, eyes closed and hands raised, to Mozart's magnificent musical edifice. June sat in her throne, her head bowed and her right hand on the gold cask on the table beside her. Sophia on her other side held her hand.

The musicians stood with heads bowed reverently before Mozart's music. Kris glanced at Maureen. She took his hand and squeezed.

"Awesome. Just awesome," she whispered. Maureen shivered as the music continued.

The final notes of the symphony and choir faded. Once again voices shouting phrases in many languages floated on the breeze.

The symphony and choir departed the stage, and other musicians played, one group after the other, some musical styles familiar to Kris and the others, while others were strange to his ears. Kris saw many types of percussion instruments, woodwinds and brass, string instruments, some that he recognized and some that he had never seen.

When each group took the stage, another segment of the crowd cheered, presumably because the music represented their culture.

This is a musical history of the human race. I had no idea that so many kinds of music, so many harmonies, so many voices and instruments existed. A universal harmony somehow ties them together.

As the last group left the stage with their instruments, the emcee once again stepped to the microphone.

"The music that we have heard has stirred our souls. It reminds us that across the millennia, from culture to culture, from religion to religion, we are all united."

Over the cheers from the crowd, the emcee continued, "We will have more music. But first, let us pay tribute to our beloved leader, our head, our divine father. Athena will lead us in our tribute."

She stepped onto the stage, her regal terrifying beauty flashing in the sun.

"Kris, would you and the members of your band come and stand behind me? Your music is an essential part of why we are here."

As the musicians walked out and stood behind Athena, the crowd cheered their approval.

Athena held up her flashing spear and shield to the crowd. "Please repeat after me, in whatever language you speak. All of our languages, like our music speak a universal harmony."

The crowd stood silent, expectant.

"Jupiter. Odin, Ra, Brahman! All Father of the Gods!"

The crowd responded, replying in many languages. Somehow, they understood Athena.

"We honor you as you go before us! May your path be glorious as you tread the Bifrost. May your entry to Asgard, to Heaven, to Valhalla, to Nirvana be celebrated across the Realms."

The crowd once again responded.

"We acknowledge the lessons of unity. We follow you in your many incarnations. We thus salute you."

Athena, hands now empty, held up her right hand, as the crowd followed. Kris saw the flash of rings, of bracelets, of weapons across the thousands of upraised hands.

Athena held up her index finger, and then all five fingers extended.

"The One and the Many!" The crowd answered.

She then held up her outspread fingers and then closed them in an extended fist.

"The Many and the One!" Once again, the crowd followed her words and her gestures.

She repeated the words and the gestures three times, and each time thousands of voices and hands followed.

"The One and the Many."

"The Many and the One!"

Athena continued, and each time the crowd responded, repeating the line, their voices reverberating.

"We honor you and follow you in life and in death."

"In life and death together, the Circle is complete."

"Our beginning is our ending, as our Cycle spins Eternal."

"We acknowledge you, All Father, as you leave us, to return."

"The Rainbow Bridge will descend once more, will bring you back to us."

With the last line, the crowd erupted, the decibels and the passion of their voices overwhelming. Kris and Maureen shook their heads, and the other musicians were stunned to silent awe.

Athena bowed and left the stage. The emcee stepped forward and gestured for Kris and the others to take their places again.

"We now ask that Gotterdammerung play "Hallelujah," Leonard Cohen's song, in tribute to our departed father and brother. The symphony and choir will perform with them, and then we will close with the Funeral March from Wagner's opera, appropriately named *Gotterdammerung.*

Kris and Maureen stepped forward to begin. As the band began to play "Hallelujah," the Euphonia Philharmonic picked up, playing under them. The Concordia Discors Chorale sang with Kris and Maureen, the male and the female voices lifted together in complex harmonies.

The crowd swayed with the music. Throughout the audience, Kris could see male and female figures entwined, celebrating the sensuality of the music, an explicit celebration of life and passion as they played and sang on stage.

As the song ended, the symphony began Wagner's music, a celebration of Siegfried's heroic life and death. The music began in somber tones with tympani and brass, the strings slow and heavy. As the music continued, the tone changed to more triumphant sounds, a celebration of Siegfried as an epic hero. As Kris listened, he was glad that they had chosen Gotterdammerung as the name for their band. The music had a power, a majesty, a gravitas that he liked.

The symphony played to the audience who stood or sat quietly, rapt in attention in honor of Jupiter, their fallen leader. When the music finished, returning to the somber themes from the beginning, a roar arose from the crowd, less exuberant than previously, but still powerful honoring the music and their fallen leader.

The emcee returned to the stage and thanked the band, the Philharmonic, and the Chorale for their performance.

After the applause had stopped, the emcee stepped to the microphone again.

He announced, "The afternoon will be a celebration of life and the values that make life worthwhile. Just after sunset we will conclude our ceremony with the release of Jupiter's ashes and a final firework display in his honor. Until then, please eat, drink, celebrate life, love, and the harmony of the universe in whatever ways you find most meaningful. Share food, share drink, share your lives together in a communion of oneness. The music will continue on stage as various groups perform. We honor your diversity."

Kris spoke, "We don't have to perform again until the fireworks begin, so I suppose we are free to join the crowd or to do whatever we like."

Mike smiled. "I think that I want to share in that communion. I saw some beautiful young women out there I think I would like to get to know. If you know what I mean."

Maureen laughed, her red hair bobbing around her face. "You go for it, Mike. And the rest of you, as the saying goes, 'Eat drink and be merry.' We are celebrating Peter, or Jupiter, and his life. And the joys that make human life meaningful."

They walked down the steps that led offstage and were lost in the crowd. Jimmy and Starr, their arms around each other's waist, disappeared into the crowd. Kris noticed a male figure standing next to a woman dressed as a milk maid. The man wore a flowing peach-colored top and white linen pants, a flute in his hand. He smiled at Kris.

Maureen touched Kris's shoulder. "What do you want to do, Kris?"

"I noticed a place backstage with blankets and pillows. I think I'd like to get some of the food they are passing around down there, and then lie down with you, share some food, and rest together."

"I think that sounds wonderful."

As they spoke, several young women in scant clothing brought trays of food and wine for them. Kris was surprised until he saw Sophia offstage.

The afternoon passed, a languorous day of beauty, peace, and sensuality. Kris and Maureen sat on the cushions sharing the fruit, spicy dishes of curry and sautéed vegetables with rice, and the sweet red wine.

Kris lay back, leaning on one elbow as he gazed at Maureen. She was eating red grapes, popping them in her mouth one at a time as she plucked them from the stems, her red hair framing her creamy white face and her green eyes sparkling as she smiled at him.

This must be Heaven, or the Garden of Eden, or some kind of multicultural Garden of Earthly Delights. Somehow this is what we wanted in the 60s at Woodstock, in San Francisco, and elsewhere. The Age of Aquarius.

The music continued on stage during the afternoon, as all of the groups that had played in the morning played again. Kris and Maureen listened, lying on the blankets. Lulled into serenity, they slept, entwined. They woke refreshed and happy. They ate the remaining food and drank from a pitcher of ice water that had been placed there. The band members appeared one by one, evidently fulfilled by their afternoon's activities.

Kris walked out onstage, the multitudes before him. Some were dancing and singing, others entwined in a more sensual dance. The sun had just slipped behind the mountain off to the west, the snow-covered peaks glistening like flashing semaphore messages.

Kris returned backstage. "The sun is just setting behind the mountains. I suppose it won't be long before we have the grand finale."

The Philharmonic returned to the stage with the Chorale. They tuned their instruments, and the conductor took the podium. The crowd had settled before them. After a moment of quiet, the conductor raised his baton and brought it down. The strings began their quiet introduction, then the horns answered them. The choir voices raised in celebration as Beethoven's anthem to Joy swirled from the stage out across the crowd.

Standing backstage and watching the audience reaction, Kris shivered as the exuberant notes touched him, filled him. He closed his eyes and let the music take him. It was as though he had never heard the piece. It felt as though he stood before the throne of the divine. at the front of the saw June, in her divine presence as Juno. Her hand rested on the golden box beside her, eyes were closed, head tilted back. Kris could see a tear coursing down her cheek. She felt the music too.

The symphony and the choir finished the segment from Beethoven's piece, and the audience cheered. When the applause died down, the band took their places on stage.

Juno stood, and Athena took the box containing the ashes. They walked to one side of the stage as the crowd parted. Hands reached out to touch the gleaming casket as they passed. An inflated balloon awaited, a small basket attached. As Juno reached it, she bent and kissed the top of the box. Kris could see her lips moving as she spoke her farewell.

Sophia took the box and placed it in the basket. She released the tether, and the balloon began its slow ascent. As it rose above the crowd, the box gleamed in the last flash of sunlight, answering the solar semaphore message that flashed from the distant mountain peaks.

They began "My Sweet Lord." Mike began with the guitar lead, and then Sankar picked up with the sitar part. Kris and Maureen sang, and the crowd swayed with the music, singing along. They flowed back and forth to the music's harmony, moving like a field of flowers, the multiple colors of the varieties of dress representing all of human culture swaying with the breeze. All eyes were raised, watching the balloon as it rose on the breeze, becoming smaller as it ascended. The last touch of sunlight flickered across the golden container, and the lid opened. The crowd cheered, singing "My sweet lord" over and over as the ashes drifted, shimmered like gold dust, and disappeared into the twilight air.

As the balloon disappeared in the distance, Kris heard a distant concussion, and then the first flash of fireworks. Again, a cheer erupted. For ten minutes, the fireworks filled the sky, reds, whites, purples, yellows and blues exploded, the colors intermingling in a constant spectrum of joy. There was a pause as the last colors faded and the crowd quieted. Then another concussion and a red flash, an arc across the darkening sky. Then, one by one another arc, and then another, all of the colors of the rainbow, then finally a streak of violet on the bottom.

"The Rainbow Bridge!" The crowd cheered as they recognized the symbol. June spoke into a microphone. "The Bifrost awaits, you All Father!" As the colors faded, the crowd became quiet. Eyes turned upward to the violet of the evening sky.

Kris saw Maureen's face, shaded in the dark, with a bittersweet smile. She whispered, "What a send-off. I had no idea what to expect."

Kris shook his head. "And now he's gone."

The crowd stood gazing upward into the indigo sky, quiet and contemplative as the first stars gleamed. The sky darkened. People began to disperse, gradually thinning and disappearing into the night. Sophia appeared on stage. "Your cars are waiting. We go back to the hotel tonight and leave in the morning. I know you must be overwhelmed, exhausted."

"Definitely overwhelmed," Mike said.

They followed Sophia to the limousines. Maureen and Kris entered their cars and settled in next to one another. They were asleep when the cars stopped in front of the hotel.

Chapter Thirty-Six

The next morning everyone met for breakfast. Kris drank his first cup of coffee, aware of the tired faces around him. Despite their apparent exhaustion, they were exhilarated.

"That was unbelievable. When I woke up this morning, I thought it was a dream."

"I know, Mike," Frank said. "I have played bass for many bands in many kinds of venues, but never anything like that."

"I won't ever be the same," Jimmy said. His shy smile and Starr's returning gaze revealed their joy.

"Kris, you know that liquid that Sophia gave us? That really was incredible. I admit that I have taken just about every drug there is. But nothing like that. I'm sorry the effect is gone. But I can still feel it."

"Mike, I know what you mean." Sankar agreed.

"I will never see the world the same way again. Just knowing that what we see is not all there is. After that, I don't need drugs. I think I'm officially clean for the rest of my life."

Sophia strolled in. "Good morning. I trust everyone slept well. Have you recovered?"

Mike said, "I don't think you ever recover from something like that."

"I know that June feels better this morning. She misses Peter, of course, but she doesn't feel desolate."

Kris said, "That was amazing. But I feel bad too. With all the peak experience and the celebration, Peter is still gone. Our music was supposed to make a difference. But he's dead."

Sophia stared directly at Kris, her gaze holding his eyes an instant.

"Kris, don't you understand? Your music did make a difference."

"But how?"

"He is only gone for the moment."

"What do you mean? That sounds like what they say at funerals."

"Don't you remember when I first talked to you about all of this, I explained how we are? Our bodies do die. They are imperfect. But our spirits, or whatever you want to call them, our real selves, don't die."

"So, you are immortal?" Sankar asked.

"Kind of, Sankar. Think of the avatars in Hindu mythology. We take on new forms as we pass from one body to another."

Kris asked, his eyes wide. "So, he really is not gone? At least not for good?"

She responded with a small smile.

"Nothing is ever gone forever."

They sat quietly, overwhelmed by Sophia's last statement.

Sophia broke the spell. "The cars will be here in a few minutes to take you to the airport. I'll be in touch when we get back. I know that Pantheon has big plans for you. They are talking about a concert tour. International."

"Really?" Kris asked.

"After yesterday, your music is spreading across the globe."

The limousines arrived, and they left for the airport. As they flew home, Kris noticed that everyone was unusually quiet, absorbing how their lives had changed in the last twenty-four hours.

The plane landed, and they retrieved their luggage. As they left, they shook hands and hugged.

Kris smiled. Then he held up his right hand, fingers extended. Then he closed them into a fist. "I'll be in touch in a couple of days. We'll need to get ready for this tour that Sophia mentioned."

They thanked Kris and left the airport. He and Maureen caught a cab and went back to his house. They were quiet on the way back, both lost in thought. They glanced at one another and smiled once, and Maureen squeezed his hand. By the time they got home, it was 4:00.

They walked into the house and dropped their suitcases by the door.

"I'm hungry."

"Me too. I'll get us something to eat. What would you like?"

He shrugged at her. "Whatever you want to fix. I'd be happy with just a sandwich and some chips or something like that."

"Let's eat on the screened-in porch."

"Sounds great. I'll go out and set the table."

He took napkins, plates, and glasses and put them on the glass table. From the screened-in porch over the back yard, Kris heard birds singing in the trees.

When Maureen brought their sandwiches and a bag of chips, she asked, "Do you want a beer?"

"That would be perfect."

She returned with two bottles, the amber glass glistening with drops of condensation.

"Let's sit on the glider instead of at the table."

"Good idea," Kris said, taking her hand.

As they sat eating, a breeze ruffled the leaves of the dogwood tree.

"The first full day of summer, and we are going to have a thunder storm."

The dark clouds moving overhead. Maureen said, "I love summer storms."

As she spoke, a rumble of thunder pealed in the distance.

Kris turned to Maureen. "We used to say it was Thor's hammer. Isn't it amazing that we know him!"

Maureen laughed. "Just incredible."

They sat watching the storm come in. The clouds drifted in and darkened, and the breeze picked up. A flicker of lightning among the clouds, then a louder rumble of thunder. The first large drops splattered as they hit the ground. The intensity increased, the rain pouring in sheets, blowing as the wind increased. Thunder boomed directly overhead, rattling their drinks on the table and startling them.

Maureen snuggled over. Kris put his arm around her, as they watched and listened to the storm. As the lightning flashed across the clouds, they tensed, waiting for the clap of thunder. Kris heard the water pouring through the downspouts. He glanced over the side to see a small river flowing from the gutter and down across the grass.

Earth, air, fire, and water. All the elements, the forces of nature.

After a few minutes, the rain subsided, from downpour to shower to mist. And then it stopped.

Kris took his last swallow of beer and watched the clouds. The dark thunder clouds lightened, became fluffier cumulus clouds. They dispersed, showing specks of blue behind. Then the late afternoon sun appeared.

"That was spectacular," Maureen said.

"It was that. The *sturm und drang*, the storm and stress."

Maureen smiled and snuggled closer.

They watched the clouds break up, drifting apart to reveal splotches of blue. The birds sang as they emerged from their shelters in the trees and bushes.

A robin chirped its cheerful notes, followed by a mockingbird, its complicated song sounding like half a dozen birds. Kris closed his eyes, listening to the squawk of blue jays and the distant caw of crows. He could hear squirrels in the pine tree as they chattered at one another, a cacophony of beautiful bird songs with the other chirps and squawks.

Maureen pointed. Kris opened his eyes. The afternoon sun touched the prism hanging at one end of the porch. On the wall opposite, tiny flashes of the rainbow spectrum danced, the colors blending as they whirled.

He smiled at Maureen and listened again to the birds as the swirling sounds resolved themselves into a complicated chord.

"Somewhere over the rainbow, complete with bluebirds."

"You're right, Maureen. After the chaos, the darkness, the storm, it's all harmony and rainbows."

"It is, Kris. It is."

Chapter Thirty-Seven

The next several weeks were a roller coaster for Kris and the other band members. Kris mourned the loss of Peter, and despite the attention that their music was receiving, the world felt a little darker to him.

A month after the memorial, Kris sat in Maureen's kitchen watching her prepare dinner. He had cut vegetables and chopped walnuts to put on the salad. The bowl of mixed greens sat on the counter. He sipped his wine.

"Do you feel like the world has changed after the memorial, Maureen?"

She put the vegetables in a Corning Ware dish and popped it in the oven.

"I do. All of the hoopla about the music is nice, but Peter's death is a cloud. I keep thinking about that thunderstorm when we sat and watched it, but it's like the clouds won't lift."

"I know. I need to call Sophia to ask how June is doing. But I put it off. I guess I don't want to know. I can't imagine the depth of her sadness."

"How do you recover from something like that?"

Kris shook his head and sipped the wine. "How long have they been together? When you are a god and goddess, how many millennia do you spend together? Normal humans count their lives in decades and losing a partner after forty or fifty years is devastating. What about after hundreds or thousands of years? I can't imagine."

"If the world feels darker to us, she must feel as though all of the light in the universe has gone out."

She walked over behind him and wrapped her arms around his shoulders. She kissed the top of his head. He turned his head toward her, and she bent to kiss him again, this time on the lips.

"I think I will call Sophia. She and June deserve that."

He poured himself and Maureen another glass of wine and called Sophia.

"Hello, Kris. I was just thinking of you. Is Maureen there too?"

"Hello, Sophia. Kris has the phone on speaker."

"Great. First of all, how are both of you coping with our loss of Peter?"

Kris said, "It has been hard. We were just talking about it. How is June?"

"She has really struggled. But she is recovering. She has a strong personality, and she has had a number of real tragedies in her life. She knows how to cope."

"But how does a woman handle that kind of loss? She has to be a lot stronger than I am."

"She's had a lot of practice, Maureen. That's part of being a god. Living a long time just gives you more challenges to cope with."

"I suppose so. How are you coping, Sophia?"

"I am coping. The attention that the band's music has received is keeping me busy. Kris, the band needs to do a tour. I know the fans are starting to ask when they are going to get to see you."

"I thought that might be the next big step. But I don't have any idea how that works. After all, this whole scene is new to me!"

Sophia laughed. "I suppose this feels odd after being a teacher."

"You got that right. Just coping with the daily attention around town takes some getting used to. Just yesterday, the young man at the grocery store who took my groceries to the car asked for an autograph. I laughed. I think he thought I was laughing at him. But I gave him an autograph."

"Get ready for more. The recording company is getting calls every day. *Rolling Stone* and *Billboard* want interviews. They had a call from a publication that covers the Christian music scene. That's why you need to go on tour. This is the time. Your star is rising."

"What do we need to do?"

"Keep practicing. Work on a playlist for the tour. The people at the recording company will set up the gigs and make all the arrangements."

Maureen asked, "When are we talking about doing this?"

"Soon. The arrangements are already in the works."

"Do I need to start packing yet?"

"I would certainly think about what you need to take with you. It won't be long before you will be on the road."

Kris called the other musicians to tell them the news. They agreed to meet on Friday to start talking about the playlist.

Kris suggested to each member, "Why don't we each make a list that we think would work, and then we can incorporate all of them? That way, we will all have some input."

That Friday night they all showed up with their lists.

"Kris, I can't believe we're going on tour!" Jimmy pushed his glasses up on his nose and grinned.

"It is amazing. I probably have bruises from pinching myself to make sure it's real."

. "I've been in music off and on for most of my life," Mike said, "but I never thought of myself as a real musician. But I sure do now. I have girls stopping me on the street. At one time, they would have crossed to the other side of the street when they saw me coming!"

They passed around their suggestions for playlists and discussed them. After they had agreed, Maureen said, "I'll type this list and send it to everybody."

Kris smiled. "And if anybody has any suggestions later, we can talk about it and rearrange. Thanks everybody for your input. This tour is going to be a dream come true."

Several days later, Sophia called. Kris had just poured a glass of wine as he sat in his study to consider the playlist again.

"Got a minute, Kris?"

"Hi, Sophia. Sure. How are the tour plans coming along?"

Sophia paused. "The plans are going well. As a matter of fact, we are working to move up the tour."

"Oh? Why is that?"

"Well, Pantheon Records got a call yesterday. The tour suddenly has become more important."

Kris could hear that her voice had changed. "Why more important? Who called?"

"The people who represent the Grammys. Gotterdammerung is being considered for a Grammy."

Kris stood staring at the phone. He drank his glass of wine in one gulp.

"Kris, are you there? Did you hear me?"

He paused for another moment. "Oh, uh, yeah, I think I heard you. Did you say Grammy?"

"I did. Actually, for more than one."

"Holy god."

"You might say that. Or goddess." He could hear her smiling.

"More than one? How? Which ones? I don't understand."

"*Joyful Noise* has had a lot of attention. The press has been all over it. Radio stations everywhere are playing it. It's selling like crazy. Didn't you know all of that?"

"I had, I guess. But I really haven't paid as much attention to it, especially after Peter's death."

"The CD is being considered for Best Alternative and for Best New Age recording. And Gotterdammerung is on the list for Best New Artist."

Kris forced himself to focus on Sophia's words. "Would you repeat that?"

She repeated, more slowly.

"Now you see why we need to get the band on the road. You need more hype, more play time, more press attention."

"That makes sense. When do we start the tour?"

"Not sure yet. But soon. I think you will kick it off locally. That way you will get a lot of press, a big crowd. Start the tour with a bang. And then it will be to as many major cities and major venues as possible."

"Ok. This is a lot to take in. I need to call everybody. Keep me informed."

Sophia hung up, and Kris called Maureen, Starr, and the band members.

Two weeks later, Gotterdammerung made the headline in the local paper: "Local Band nominated for Grammy Awards." Below the headline a color picture appeared, and Kris recognized the picture from when he and Maureen sang "Rose of Sharon" the first time. In the picture, he and Maureen stood with Sankar between them and the rest of the band on either side.

Kris read the article, including the details of the upcoming tour and the Grammy nominations. The article quoted Sophia and a representative from Pantheon Records, ending with a brief explanation of the possible nomination categories. Kris read the article twice and sat staring at the picture.

I can hear the music from that moment, feel the excitement from the crowd. I remember staring into Maureen's green eyes, singing not just with her but to her. And that moment has led to all of this.

The phone rang all morning. Kris talked to the band members, Maureen, and people from Pantheon. That afternoon a reporter from *Rolling Stone* called.

"Hello. This is Michael Moriarty from *Rolling Stone*. Is this Kris Singer?"

"Uh, yes. It is. Could I help you?"

"I think so. I need to do an interview with you about your band and the Grammy nominations. Do you think we could arrange a time to do that?"

"Absolutely!" Kris almost shouted into the receiver.

"I think that it would be convenient for both of us if we did the interview over the phone."

"I can do that. How do you want to do it?"

"Well, Mr. Singer. I could send you a list of some possible questions so you would have an idea of what to expect. And then we can go from there. We won't necessarily stay on script, but you'd have some sense of what I need to know."

"That works for me. I'm available at your convenience."

"If you'll give me your email address, I'll send the questions. Could we do the interview later today. I have a deadline coming up."

"Sure," Kris answered. He gave the reporter the email address.

"I'll send these questions right now. Can I call back at 3:00?"

"Great. Could I have Maureen O'Kelley here too? She's the female singer in the band."

"I think that would be good. We can include the feminist perspective on the music. The readers will love that."

The questions came through five minutes later. Kris called Maureen at work.

"Maureen, this is Kris."

"Hi, Hon. How has your day been?"

"Crazy. I've been on the phone all day. And I just got a call from *Rolling Stone*. They want to do an interview over the phone this afternoon. And they want to interview you."

"Oh my god. That's amazing. What time?"

"Three o'clock."

"I'll tell Mr. Burdett I need to leave early. I know he won't mind for this! I'll be there by 2:30."

Kris glanced at the questions. They were generally what he expected: how the band started, how they found inspiration for their songs, what the band name meant, and how they felt about being nominated and going on tour.

Maureen arrived on the dot of 2:20.

Kris kissed her as she walked in.

"Do you think we might have a glass of wine?" Maureen asked. "I'm a little nervous about doing this. It still feels surreal."

"I think one afternoon glass of wine won't turn us into out-of-control rock stars!"

She laughed and took the glass of chilled Chardonnay.

As they sipped their wine, Maureen read over the questions.

"What do you think he will ask me? There aren't any questions here specifically related to being the only woman in the band."

"He mentioned the feminist perspective. I'm sure you can handle anything he could possibly ask. You're not really shy after all."

She hit him on the shoulder. "It's probably a good thing I'm not."

The phone rang at 3:00. "Mr. Singer. Are you ready to do the interview?"

"We are. I've got the phone on speaker, and Maureen O'Kelley is here."

"Great. Why don't you just tell me about the band, how it began, your inspirations, and the band name? Then we'll see where we go from there."

"Sounds good."

"Ms. O'Kelley. Please feel free to add anything you want."

"Ok." Maureen smiled at Kris as he began.

Kris followed the lead of the questions.

"Ms. O'Kelley. How does it feel to be a part of this band?"

Maureen responded in an animated voice, "It has been an amazing experience. I work for the recording studio that did the demo for the song 'Twilight of the Gods.' That is how I met them."

"So, when did you start singing with them?"

"Actually, it was when they were getting ready to do 'Rose of Sharon.' Kris decided it should be a duet. So, he asked me."

"I have to say it was a good decision. I love that song. I have listened to both CDs, and that one really touches me. It works."

"I agree." Maureen said.

"I do too," Kris interjected. "I had already written it and then went back and reread 'Song of Songs' in the Bible. Then I knew the song had to be a love duet."

"The passion comes across."

"Thank you." Kris and Maureen both said.

The reporter laughed. "I wouldn't be surprised if some of the listeners use that song to inspire some of their own amorous activities!"

Maureen felt herself blush. "So, the passion comes across?"

"It does. Now tell me, Ms. O'Kelley, what does the band's music say to women about their place in the world?"

"I think it shows that men and women have equal importance, in relationships, in the world overall. The Yin and the Yang have to work together to create totality. Gods and goddesses are both important in the world."

"Hmm. I didn't think of it on that kind of metaphysical level. Our readers are going to love that."

The interview took a half hour. At the end, Mr. Moriarty said, "I'll be back in touch with you, Mr. Singer. Ms. O'Kelley, thank you for being a part of the interview. Our female readers are going to love your comments."

They were quiet a moment. Finally, Maureen spoke. "The *Rolling Stone*! Can you believe it?" She shouted, waving her hands in the air.

Kris grinned and shook his head. "I think I'm willing to risk being a dissolute rock star. I need a drink!"

Two days later, Michael Moriarty called back. "Mr. Singer. Your interview is going to be in the next issue. They're putting a rush on it. With your tour about to start and the Grammy Awards being announced, the publishers want to get the issue on the stands."

"That is amazing!" Kris exhaled and inhaled slowly.

"One more thing. When can we get a photograph of your band? We need it soon."

"As soon as you want. Just let me know. Tell me where and when," Kris promised eagerly.

"We can have a photographer there tomorrow. How about in the recording studio where you did your demo?"

"We'll be there."

"Oh, and dress up a little. At least how you want the readers to think of you."

"Ok," Kris agreed. He knew how beautiful Maureen would be. A knockout!

"After all, this is going to be the cover photo of the issue."

Kris held on to the kitchen counter and forced himself to breathe slowly.

"Thank you, Mr. Moriarty, thank you."

. *On the cover of the Rolling Stone! And we joked about that. Nothing could top this.*

Chapter Thirty-Eight

The sun rose bright, and the air was crisp. Kris sat on the screened in porch and drank his coffee. Despite not sleeping well, he felt as good as he ever had. He listened to the music from the birds, the notes passing back and forth from tree to tree. The leaves had started to turn, and he saw touches of orange and yellow as the sun dappled them. The phone rang.

"Good morning. Did you sleep well?"

"Hi, Maureen. Not really. But I feel amazing. How about you?"

"I feel like the first morning of creation. Like the song says, 'Morning has broken, like the first morning.' I'm so excited about today."

"Me too. I need to go get dressed. What are you wearing?"

Maureen paused. "I have a new dress, a lovely pastel green. I think you'll like it. It's sexy without being too much. And I'm doing a braid in my hair with a forest green ribbon."

Kris exhaled into the phone. "I can't wait to see it. I'm going to wear my dragon shirt. I think it is sufficiently exotic without being over the top."

"I think that's a good choice."

"See you in a little bit. I can't wait to see what the others wear. We'll be great together. On the cover of the *Rolling Stone*!" He sang the last line, imitating the song.

Maureen laughed and hung up.

When Kris arrived at the studio two hours later, the other band members had not yet arrived. Maureen sat at her desk. When she stood, Kris whistled.

"Wow. Just wow!"

She twirled to show off the dress. The color complemented her red hair and creamy complexion. The pleated skirt fit across her hips, and the bodice showed just a hint of décolleté. The ribbon braided into her wavy hair highlighted the color.

"You like?"

"This may be the number one *Rolling Stone* cover of all time! Talk about a Celtic goddess!"

Twilight of the Gods

Maureen smiled, her blush making her even more desirable to Kris.

The other band members arrived soon after. Mike wore neat blue jeans and a button down blue shirt with a leather vest. Sankar's outfit reminded Kris of images he had seen of Krishna. His shirt, a bright orange, flowed across loose gold silk pants. He wore sandals with colored beads imbedded in the straps. Kris could imagine him surrounded by sensual milkmaids.

The other members were better dressed than Kris had ever seen them. Pele's outfit, leather buckskin with a necklace of feathers and a bear claw, emphasized his native American features. Jimmy walked in with Starr, who held his hand and smiled up at him. He wore a rose-pink shirt with black dress slacks and loafers. Kris thought that Starr had probably chosen the shirt for him.

Maureen said to the group as they stood waiting, "I have to say that you clean up well. These may be the clothes you need to wear when we go on tour." They grinned at her compliment. Kris noted the admiring glances in her direction.

The photographer arrived with Sophia. As usual, her clothes were businesslike, a gray and black pants suit with vest and A-line slacks. Her conservative appearance did not mute the power of those gray eyes.

"Are we ready to get the picture for the cover?"

They moved toward the recording studio. John Burdett had emptied the studio so they would have room to pose for the photo. Sankar had brought his sitar, and Mike and Frank had their guitars. Pele held his flute.

After setting up his equipment, the photographer arranged the musicians. Sankar's elaborate cushion lay on the floor.

The photographer pointed at them as he arranged the shot. "I want you to sit here with your sitar, and you two (pointing to Kris and Maureen) on either side. Then I want a guitarist on either side. The flute player on one end and the young man with the glasses on the other end. A nice balanced composition."

They moved into position, glancing at one another, suddenly a little nervous. When they had created a tight enough shot, the photographer stood behind the camera.

"Remember. This is for *Rolling Stone*. Everyone say 'Grammy'!"

The lights flashed as the photographer took several shots. "I think we have it. Do you want to see them?"

They crowded around the camera, excited as children getting their school pictures.

"Wow! That's amazing. We clean up good!"

"We do, Mike. Wait till you see it on the actual magazine!"

Jimmy pushed his glasses up his nose. "I can't wait. My parents will freak out." He glanced at Starr, who smiled up at him.

The photographer packed his gear and left, and the band members laughed and talked excitedly about the *Rolling Stone* cover, as well as the Grammy nomination. Kris watched them, the transformation in their appearances and attitudes never more evident.

As they stood in the lobby, a black limousine stopped in front.

"Everybody. I have one more surprise for you," Sophia announced.

"June wants to see everyone at this moment. She knows what all of this has meant to you. She wants to share your celebration and your music."

The driver opened the rear door of the limousine on the driver's side, and a man emerged. He was tall, and his dark hair showed a touch of gray at the temples. He was attired in a dark suit with a white shirt and gold cuff links. His dark eyes and aquiline nose reminded Kris of a bird of prey. As he walked to the passenger side, his erect posture emphasized his regal bearing. Kris inspected him, puzzled. Somehow, he knew the man, though he did not think they had ever met.

The man opened the rear passenger side door and extended his hand to help June step from the car. She wore a tailored suit the color of the summer sky. Her golden hair gleamed in the sun, and the tiara on top of her coiffure added an additional sparkle. She smiled up at the man who still held her hand, her face serene. She was evidently twenty years younger than the last time Kris had seen her at the memorial. The man smiled at her and then acknowledged at the group.

That is an elegant suit. And those shoes are beautiful. I can't imagine what his clothes cost. Probably made by an Italian tailor. He is so familiar somehow.

Sophia gestured toward the man. "Everyone. This is a friend of June's. His name is Pietro Deodada. He is from Rome. You will probably be seeing a good bit of him, and I know you will get to know him. Especially you, Kris." She smiled and winked.

Kris turned to the man, his smile and tilted head again seeming familiar. Then Kris focused on the golden fountain pen that the man had removed from his shirt pocket. Kris blinked twice.

"Oh! Wow! How? What the . . .?" Kris stood open mouthed.

Before Kris stood the regal figure of Jupiter, his white toga and gold crown gleaming in the sunlight. June, in her form as Juno, gazed up at him smiling.

"Hello, Kris. It's good to see you again. And the rest of you as well."

Only Pele recognized Pietro in his divine form. The other band members frowned in puzzlement.

Mike spoke, "I'm sorry, sir. Have we met? Somehow, I feel as though I should know you, but at the same time you aren't familiar."

Sophia interrupted. "I know that most of you don't have the ability to see in the way that Kris and Pele do. You do know this man, if not in exactly this physical form. This is Peter."

Expressions changed from confused to stunned.

Jimmy pushed his glasses up his nose. "So, you really are Peter? But how?"

The man smiled, his expression beneficent.

"It is because of your music. When I was shot, my spirit was freed. But because your music gave me renewed strength, I was able to return, to be reincarnated, if you will."

"So, all of that stuff about our music wasn't just hype?" Mike asked, skeptical.

"No, Mike," Sophia reassured him. "It's quite true." The skepticism gradually melted into awe.

"The idea of an avatar is central to Hinduism," Sankar asserted, "but I never really thought that it was anything but a myth. So, this is real?"

Sophia, Pietro, and June assented to his comment.

Pietro turned to Kris. "Thank you for the revival you and the music have started. Our faith in you has been justified. I have heard from Sophia that your band is going to be on the cover of a magazine."

"It's true! I thought it was too good to be true. And we have been nominated for two Grammy Awards. All of that has felt unbelievable. But now I'll believe anything can happen."

Sophia stepped forward, "And now you are ready to really see the reality, Kris. Not just what is true, but what is True. Be prepared and watch. And the rest of you will see this too. You are all ready."

Kris stood, expectant. The others watched, unsure of what they were about to experience.

As Kris regarded Pietro, he once more became Jupiter. A light glowed around him, a pulsating halo.

"Wow!" The entire group gasped in unison.

The light pulsated faster and then began to change colors, a rainbow of colors as the hues flowed into one another. Then Jupiter's face and form began to change. First Kris saw three faces that he recognized at Brahma, Vishnu, and Shiva from Hinduism. Then those faces shifted into the Father, Son, and Holy Spirit. And then the three faces coalesced into Odin. Then into Ra. As the face shifted, the prismatic halo continued to pulse and shift.

"Oh, my God. They are all—one!" Kris shook his head

The faces continued to shift, becoming deities from many religions. Around Juno the same halo of light shifted colors as she shifted into the Mother Goddess, into Freya, into Parvati, Lakshmi, and Sarawati (the three mother goddesses in Hinduism).

Sophia had transfigured into Athena. She then continued shifting forms, becoming a Viking helmed figure that Kris recognized as a Valkyrie. She continued to shift into the forms of warrior goddesses from other cultures, the armor and the weapons changing as the faces altered.

The faces of the three deities continued to shift and change, from one god to another, from one goddess to another, as their garments and accoutrements changed. Kris and the others stood mesmerized, transfixed by the revelation. Gradually the light faded; Pietro, June, and Sophia stood before them in their human forms.

Kris smiled at Maureen, then at the others, who stood with their eyes and mouths wide open.

"So, the Truth is--." Kris fumbled for words.

Sophia acquiesced, "You know now."

"The chant at the memorial service. I get it! Now it makes sense!"

"Which chant, Kris?" Mike asked.

"The One and the Many. The Many and the One. All of the gods, the goddesses, all the religions. They're all one."

"Yes, Kris. Now you see. Now you understand. And your music--blending the styles, the religious texts, the cultural influences--shows that to your listeners."

"Everything that's happened makes sense, it all falls into place." Pietro's dark eyes shifted their raptor gaze to each, one by one, as they stood transfixed.

Pietro continued. "The names Gotterdammerung and Twilight of the Gods take on a new meaning. Every ending is a beginning of a new age of creation. The music shows it all, the harmony of morning song and evening song, the cycle of endings and beginnings."

Kris raised his right hand, index finger up. He extended all five fingers and then clenched them together in a triumphant fist.

THE END
AND THE BEGINNING

Reading List
and
Glossary of Mythological Names and Terms

The study of mythology, fairy tales, and archetypes provides a daunting task. Like the Tao in the *Tao te Ching*, the further you go, the deeper it gets. The reader wishing more information on this material will find a number of books and other sources useful. This list of books is not meant to be exhaustive, but it will provide some direction. The books are easily available in a library or online. Many other sources are easily acquired online. The only limitation is the reader's curiosity. The list of names and terms will give the reader a brief explanation of the names and terms without being overwhelming.

Suggested Books

Bettelheim, Bruno, *The Uses of Enchantment*.

Bulfinch, Thomas. *Bulfinch's Mythology*.

Campbell, Joseph. *The Hero with a Thousand Faces*.

Frazer, Sir James George. *The Golden Bough*.

Hamilton, Edith. *Mythology*.

Jung, Carl. Collected Works.

Glossary

Asgard—In Norse mythology the city of the gods, the citadel of Odin, Freya, Thor, and the other Norse gods. It is accessible by the Bifrost. Among the mansions in Asgard is Valhalla, the reward for warriors who die valiantly.

Astarte—Also Ishtar, from Bronze Age Middle Eastern religions, the goddess of fertility and sexuality.

Aten—In Egyptian mythology, this term was originally used to designate the disk of the sun. As such, it is associated with Ra, the sun god.

Athena--In Greek mythology, the goddess of wisdom and warfare. She is often depicted wearing a helmet and carrying a spear and a shield. The owl is sacred to her. She is known as Minerva in Roman mythology.

Avatar—In Hinduism this is an incarnation of a god. The most famous avatars are the ten forms of Vishnu. One of the avatars of Vishnu is Krishna.

Bacchus—In Roman mythology he is the god of wine. He is known as Dionysus in Greek mythology.

Bifrost—The Rainbow Bridge is the path of access to Midgard in Norse mythology.

Brahma—In Hinduism, he is the Creator, one of the three gods of the Triad (trinity), along with Vishnu (the Preserver) and Siva (the Destroyer).

Freya—In Norse mythology she is the wife of Odin, the father of the gods. She is the goddess of youth, love, and beauty. She is associated with Juno and Hera in Roman and Greek mythologies respectively.

Frost Giants—In Norse mythology, these residents of Jotunheim are the enemies of Asgard. Odin and Thor battle them.

Gopis—In Hinduism, these women are the milkmaids, including Radha, who dance with Krishna.

Gotterdammerung—Translated as The Twilight of the Gods, this term is also used for the Ragnarok from Norse mythology. The German composer Richard Wagner used this term for the last opera of his four-part Ring Cycle.

Heka, in Egyptian mythology, he is the god of magic and medicine.

Hercules—In Roman mythology, the half-human son of Jupiter and a mortal woman. He is known for performing the twelve labors, as well as for other great deeds.

Jotunheim—In Norse mythology, this is one of the Nine Realms. It is the home of the Frost Giants.

Juno—In Roman mythology, the wife of Jupiter, the protectress of marriage and women. In Greek mythology she is Hera, the wife of Zeus.

Jupiter—In Roman mythology, he is the king of the gods. His wife is Juno. In Greek mythology, he is Zeus, the husband of Hera. He is depicted as carrying a thunderbolt. The eagle is sacred to him.

Kokapelli--In Native American mythology, he is a fertility god. He is depicted playing a flute.

Krishna—Krishna is one of the avatars of Vishnu. He is a god of love and tenderness. Many of the major Hindu texts feature him, including the Mahabarata and the Bhagavad Gita. One of the popular stories about Krishna is his playing the flute and dancing with Radha and the other milkmaids.

Lakshimi—In Hinduism, she is the goddess of wealth and beauty.

Midgard—In Norse mythology, this is one of the Nine Realms, the one occupied by humans. The term Middle Earth (in Tolkien's writing) is associated with this realm. Midgard is joined to Asgard by the Bifrost (the Rainbow Bridge).

Midgard Serpent—In Norse mythology, this great serpent surrounds the Earth, its tail in its mouth. When it releases its tail, the Ragnarok will begin. Thor is the serpent's arch-enemy. Their battle is a significant event in the Ragnarok.

Nifelheim—In Norse mythology, this is one of the Nine Realms. A place of fire and ice, it is asspciated with creation. It is also associated with the afterlife of those who did not die a heroic death.

Odin—In Norse mythology, he is the king of the gods, the husband of Freya and the father of Thor. He is the god of wisdom, poetry, and war. He is also called the All-Father. He has a significant role in the Ragnarok.

Parvati—In Hindu mythology, she is the goddess of fertility, love, and devotion. She is the wife of Shiva.

Twilight of the Gods

Ra—In Egyptian mythology, this is the god of the Sun. The term Aten is associated with Ra.

Radha—In Hinduism, she is one of the milkmaids who dances with Krishna.

Ragnarok—In Norse mythology, this term signifies the destruction of the universe. The term Gotterdammerung (Twilight of the Gods) is associated with this event.

Sarawati—In Hindu mythology, she is the goddess of knowledge, music, arts, and wisdom. She forms the trinity of mother goddesses with Lakshmi and Parvati.

Shiva—In Hindu mythology he is the god of destruction. He is one of the members of the Triad, along with Brahma and Vishnu.

Thor—In Norse mythology, he is the son of Odin. He is the god of thunder and carries a great hammer, a weapon that only he can wield. He is an important figure in the events of the Ragnarok, the destruction of the present universe.

Valhalla—In Norse mythology, this is a mansion in Asgard where the souls of valiant warriors reside after death.

Valkyrie—In Norse mythology, they are the warrior women, the daughters of Odin, who retrieve the souls of valiant warriors to carry them to Valhalla to reward them for their heroic deeds.

Vishnu—In Hindu mythology, he is the preserver, one of the three gods of the Triad, along with Brahma and Shiva. One of his ten avatars is Krishna.

Yggdrasil—In Norse Mythology, this is the tree of the world. Its roots and branches unify the Nine realms of the universe. The tree will be the seed of new life following Ragnarok.

Praise for the Poetry

String Theory

It is exactly the ability of good poetry to stick with me and grow in my mind that made me want to bring it into my life, again. I'm grateful that I have String Theory to reinvigorate my love of poetry. The book is meditative and reflective, and like all really good poetry, the best examples from its pages have a way of making me feel connected with life and with humanity, again.
--Jeff Suwak, author of *Beyond the Tempest Gate*

The poems comprising "String Theory," are meditations on the universe, from the physical to the metaphysical, from the cosmic to the comic. They are about the interconnectedness of everything, and about the relationship between perception and reality in human life. Both stylistically and substantively, Dr. Covel's poetry, and the way in which I think it should be approached, reminds me of the poetry of William Butler Yeats and my undergraduate days at The University of Georgia. I feel that Dr. Covel's poetry, like that of Yeats, is best appreciated during or after some serious deep thinking and research (or at least with a dictionary and/or iPad at your side) in order to be read successfully and fully. Both use metaphors and references that can be missed or misunderstood from just a superficial reading. And this style of poetry is not your grandmother's nursery rhymes!
--Anita Buice, "Covel Connects with 'String Theory'," *Times-Georgian* newspaper.

Wind Song

WIND SONG is erudite, cerebral, yet amazingly accessible. It is thought-provoking as well as entertaining. The language is beautiful, overflowing with appropriate comparisons, images, and sensory details. Make sure to read the poems aloud to hear the music. Five stars plus.
--Dr. Eleanor Hoomes, Educator and poet, author of *Bread and Roses, Too*

Reading Robert Covel's poetry is a double treat. In "Wind Song," the poet's second collection of his works, calm and reassurance dominate his observations and lyrical lines even as you embark on a great journey of imagistic pleasure and intellectual incitement.
--Chuck Wanager, author of *Jackson Flats*, *Sixteen Windows*, *Play Sgt. Pepper One More Time*, and *Taking Our Love Offline*

Wind Song creates an exquisite poetic universe imbued with beauty, energy, and blissful epiphanies. *Wind Song* celebrates life, elevates the spirit, and enlightens the mind of the reader. And Robert Covel, the poet, does it with an art overflowing with grace and subtle humor.
--Dr. Cecilia Lee, Poet and Professor Emerita of Spanish and Literature

Acknowledgements

To paraphrase an opt-repeated African proverb, it takes a village to write a novel. This book began as a project for the National Novel Writing Month (Na-No-Wri-Mo) in November 2016. From that beginning, it has had many astute creative and careful minds that have shaped it and nurtured it.

Val Mathews, founder and editor-in-chief of the Exit 271 studio, is an editor extraordinaire. After transforming some of my poetry for publication, she provided keen insights into my plot and characters, helping to shape my direction. Like Ezra Pound, she is il miglior fabbro.

Penny Gardin Lewis, a writer and artist herself, read an early draft and made many suggestions, especially asking where some of the song lyrics were. Those songs might not have been included without her inquiry.

The Carrollton Writers Guild has encouraged me and given useful advice on the writing and on the structure of the book to make it a more effective story. I owe particular thanks to Stephanie Baldi and Frank Rogers, both excellent novelists themselves, as they have read, critiqued, and provided keen insights as I wrestled to create a novel.

Dr. Eleanor Woolf Hoomes is an educator, master gardener, and poet. She read and proofed an early draft of the novel, and her many suggestions on the food in the novel provided a list of recipes and culinary treats that transformed the sensual aspects of dining in the book. Her suggestions were so extensive that perhaps I should provide a cookbook as a companion volume. Nectar and Ambrosia: Olympian Cuisine?

Bruce Bobick an internationally known artist and the retired chair of the Art Department at the University of West Georgia, created the painting for my cover. I am grateful for his visionary aesthetic sense that translated my characters and themes into the image graces my book. I hope that the book is worthy of the cover.

Claudia Kennedy is a novelist, a colleague, and a longtime valued friend. Her dedication to this book, reading through more than one draft and offering encouragement, suggestions, and insights have proved her a true friend, the exemplary of Cicero's De Amicitia.

My wife Deloris Covel read my manuscript, offered many suggestions, and encouraged me to continue. She put up with my disappearing into the study to write. Her contributions to my work and to my life extend far beyond the boundaries of this novel. Her price is far above rubies.

Every artist should have such a village of readers, critics, and supporters. Artistic endeavors do not exist in a vacuum, and writers depend on the readers in the world to keep viable and thriving the Never Never land of imagination. To these readers here listed, and to the rest of the village of readers who read this book, I am grateful.

Made in the USA
Lexington, KY
21 August 2018